ALSO BY KATEE ROBERT

Court of the Vampire Queen

Dark Olympus
Stone Heart (prequel novella)
Neon Gods
Electric Idol
Wicked Beauty
Radiant Sin
Cruel Seduction

Midnight Ruin

KATEE ROBERT

sourcebooks
casablanca

Published by Sourcebooks Casablanca, an imprint of Sourcebooks
P.O. Box 4410, Naperville, Illinois 60567-4410
(630) 961-3900
sourcebooks.com

Cataloging-in-Publication Data is on file with the Library of Congress.

Printed and bound in the United Kingdom.
CPI 10 9 8 7 6

To Anaïs Mitchell.

*The seeds of this version of Orpheus and Eurydice
were sown with the soundtrack of Hadestown.
Thank you for all the inspiration!*

Midnight Ruin is an occasionally dark and very spicy book that contains violence, murder, blood, guns, pregnancy (not the heroine), and abortion (off-page, not the heroine).

THE RULING FAMILIES OF
Olympus

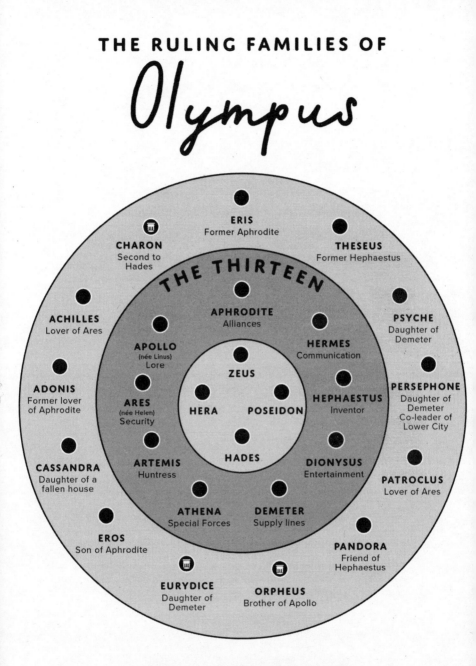

THE THIRTEEN

ERIS
Former Aphrodite

CHARON
Second to
Hades

THESEUS
Former Hephaestus

ACHILLES
Lover of Ares

APHRODITE
Alliances

PSYCHE
Daughter of
Demeter

APOLLO
(née Linus)
Lore

HERMES
Communication

ADONIS
Former lover
of Aphrodite

ZEUS

ARES
(née Helen)
Security

HEPHAESTUS
Inventor

PERSEPHONE
Daughter of
Demeter
Co-leader of
Lower City

HERA

POSEIDON

CASSANDRA
Daughter of a
fallen house

ARTEMIS
Huntress

HADES

DIONYSUS
Entertainment

PATROCLUS
Lover of Ares

ATHENA
Special Forces

DEMETER
Supply lines

EROS
Son of Aphrodite

PANDORA
Friend of
Hephaestus

EURYDICE
Daughter of
Demeter

ORPHEUS
Brother of Apollo

THE INNER CIRCLE
HADES: LEADER OF LOWER CITY
HERA: (NÉE CALLISTO) SPOUSE OF RULING ZEUS, PROTECTOR OF WOMEN
POSEIDON: LEADER OF PORT TO OUTSIDE WORLD, IMPORT/EXPORT
ZEUS: (NÉE PERSEUS) LEADER OF UPPER CITY AND THE THIRTEEN

MUSEWATCH

Previously in Olympus...

OLYMPUS'S SWEETHEART GONE WILD!

Persephone Dimitriou shocks everyone by fleeing an engagement with Zeus to end up in Hades's bed!

ZEUS FALLS TO HIS DEATH!

Perseus Kasios will now take up the title of Zeus. Can he possibly fill his father's shoes?

APHRODITE ON THE OUTS

After a livestream in which she threatened Psyche Dimitriou for marrying her son Eros, Aphrodite is exiled by the Thirteen. She chooses Eris Kasios to be successor to her title.

ARES IS DEAD!

A tournament will be held to choose the next Ares...
and Helen Kasios is the prize.

...LONG LIVE ARES

In a stunning turn of events, Helen Kasios has chosen
to compete for her own hand...and she won! We now
have three Kasios siblings among the Thirteen.

NEW BLOOD IN TOWN!

After losing out on the Ares title, Minos Vitalis and
his household have gained Olympus citizenship...
and are celebrating with a house party for the ages.
We have the guest list, and you'll never guess who's
invited!

APOLLO FINDS LOVE AT LAST?

After being ostracized by Olympus for most of her
adult life, Cassandra Gataki has snagged one of
the Thirteen as her very own! She and Apollo were
looking very cozy together at the Dryad.

MURDER FAVORS THE BOLD

Tragedy strikes! Hephaestus was killed by Theseus
Vitalis, triggering a little-known law that places
Theseus as the new Hephaestus. The possibilities
are...intriguing.

HEPHAESTUS AND APHRODITE ARE OUT!

Our new Hephaestus and Aphrodite have stepped down unexpectedly! But can a leopard really change its spots? We don't expect Eris Kasios and Theseus Vitalis to fully turn their backs on Olympus politics... even for the love of Pandora and Adonis.

1

EURYDICE

THE MUSIC IS A DEEP, THROBBING BEAT THAT SEEMS TO soak into every molecule of the room, inspiring the occupants to sin. Or if not inspiring, then at least smoothing away any lingering worries about clinging to the perception of purity that the upper city values so highly.

We're not in the upper city now.

I glance at my phone for the fifth time in ten minutes and curse under my breath when the text I'm waiting for finally comes through.

Ariadne: My dad put us on lockdown. I'm sorry, but I can't come tonight.

I've spent three weeks and tried half a dozen failed attempts to get Ariadne into Hades's kink club. Lying through my teeth about how no one will know who she is. Feeling guilty for coaxing her into what is essentially a trap when she shows all evidence of being a lovely person. That guilt has faded thanks to the events of the last month.

People are dying and the fault lies with the Vitalis family. With *Ariadne's* family. Her father might be the one pulling the strings, but the little hints Ariadne gave Apollo at that house party six weeks ago weren't enough. She knew this was coming and she didn't warn us.

That makes her the enemy.

An enemy who's not walking into my trap tonight. I sigh. Not that this is much of a *trap* exactly. It's more that I've been tasked with attempting to coax her over to our side. If that's not possible, then I suspect someone will just flat out kidnap her, but I'm the carrot in this situation.

Not that anyone knows it.

I look around, my guilt flaring for a completely different reason. I've been in my brother-in-law's sex club quite a few times in the last couple months. I have no doubts that Hades is aware of it, though I'm careful to only show up when I know he and Persephone won't be presiding over the activities.

This is the first time I've come alone.

It feels weird not to have Charon as my ever-present shadow. He wouldn't have approved of tonight's attendance, so I snuck out without telling anyone where I was going. The club manager, Hypnos, has seen me around enough now that the bouncers didn't stop me when I walked through the door. Zir doesn't know my arrangement with Charon, which works well enough for me. Charon initially allowed me access to the club, with one caveat: I'm only allowed to watch. I suspect that rule originates from my sister and brother-in-law, but Charon is the one enforcing it.

But Charon isn't here right now.

The room is a true den of iniquity, all artfully designed to seduce the senses. The lights are always low when the club is open, but a cleverly hidden waterway around the edge of the room throws dizzying reflections onto the ceiling, giving the impression of us being underground. I've seen the furniture arranged in a dozen different ways, but tonight it's the traditional layout, with couches and chairs and cushions situated to allow plenty of space for conversation and, well, fucking.

I inhale the scent of sex and smooth my hands down my tight minidress. My body thrums in response. It's been...so long. There's joy to be had in watching though, and I've learned a lot about the shape of desire and kink in general in the last nine months. But it's all in theory. I haven't participated. Truthfully, I haven't wanted to. For a long time, I was focused on putting one foot in front of the other and not letting the pain of Orpheus's betrayal break me.

But now?

I look around the room. I have a free night and no supervision. Maybe it's time to turn some of my fantasies into reality. To stop *thinking* about healing and attempt that first step.

"I've seen you around, always watching, never participating."

I jolt and turn to find a man has taken up a spot against the wall next to me. He's a very attractive South Asian man who's about my height with a slim build and smiling eyes. He also looks incredibly familiar, and not just because I'm sure I've seen him a few times during my visits here.

He holds out a hand. "Thanatos."

Recognition clicks as I slip my hand into his. "You're Hypnos's brother." Now that I say it, I see the similarities between him and zir. Same medium-brown skin tone, thick dark hair, and refined features. They also both have incredibly sensual lips. Not that I've noticed. Except I have.

"Guilty as charged." Instead of shaking my hand, he raises it to press a light kiss to my knuckles. It should be cheesy, but his dark eyes invite me to indulge him.

"It's nice to meet you." I find myself smiling as heat stirs to life low in my stomach. It's been so long since I've even *wanted* to indulge… No, that's a lie. But it's been a very long time since I've encountered someone who was safe to indulge with. Someone I could spend a fun night with and not worry about shattering a relationship I value in the process.

Thanatos lifts his head but doesn't release my hand. He holds me in a light grip I could break at any moment, heat licking into his dark eyes. "It strikes me that you haven't had a proper introduction to the delights of the club."

He's flirting with me. I don't know why that surprises me so much. I suppose I've become so used to blending into the background that I expect it to be the default. *It certainly is with Charon.* The man treats me kindly, but it's clear he's never felt the same flicker of desire that plagues me in his presence. *Not just desire. You care about him. If you weren't so broken, you'd let yourself love him.*

It might have been nine months since Orpheus took part in the events that led to the night that's caused scars on my soul, but I'm nowhere near ready enough to jump into a relationship again. Even if Charon was interested, which he's never given any indication that he is. But if he *was*, it wouldn't be casual. He doesn't do casual any more than I do.

Thanatos isn't asking for my heart. He's not asking for anything at all right now. I take a slow breath, inhaling the evocative scent of his cologne. He's still holding my hand. I find myself smiling. "By all means. Introduce me."

His grin is bright and charming. "It would be my pleasure."

I ignore the guilt that clings to me as he leads me to an empty couch near the wall farthest from the door. I'm not certain if it's intentional or not, but I appreciate the sliver of privacy the location offers. There's an unspoken rule that what goes on here isn't shared outside these walls unless my sister and her husband wish it to be so, but that doesn't mean I want to risk the gossip getting back to *them*.

They wouldn't understand. Oh, maybe Hades would, but Persephone? Never. To her, I'm her baby sister to be protected at all costs. She never stops to think that maybe the blanket of protection she and our other sisters provide is suffocating me slowly. If she knew I was here alone, she would sweep in with all the rage of a vengeful goddess to strike down anyone who dared look at me.

And should they *touch* me?

Unthinkable.

Except Thanatos is touching me now. He sits close enough that we're pressed together and turns over my hand to trace the fine veins of my wrist with the tips of his fingers. "You've been here many times in the last few months."

I lift my brows. "Have you been watching me?"

He shrugs, completely unselfconscious. "Everyone watches you,

Eurydice, and not just because you're beautiful." His fingers trail up to the inside of my elbow. "You're absolutely captivating."

I'm aware that he's trying to seduce me. He might not be the one I want if I'm being truly honest with myself, but what's the harm in allowing myself to be seduced? He has kind eyes. Maybe what I need to get over Orpheus once and for all isn't a great love to sweep away everything that came before. Maybe what I need is a string of kind lovers who don't stir my heart but are more than capable of stirring my body.

Thanatos certainly is doing a good job of it. His touch isn't anything that would be inappropriate in another public setting, but I find myself holding my breath as he continues to trace light patterns over my skin, each sending a zing of desire through me.

I relax slowly against the back of the couch and look up at him. "You're quite captivating yourself."

His smile takes on a self-deprecating tone. "I'm not too shabby." His fingers trail slightly up my bicep, the backs of his knuckles brushing against my breast. He holds my gaze. "May I?"

I can't quite catch my breath. I don't know what he's asking, but I want it all the same. "Yes."

Thanatos leans in, closing the last little bit of distance between us, and kisses me. It's a good kiss. It's light and intentional, a test and a seduction, all wrapped into one. It makes me shift in my seat, but my heart stays unfeeling in my chest.

Perfect.

At least until Thanatos leans back and I realize we're no longer alone. A familiar shadow has fallen over us, blocking out the low light of the rest of the club. A shadow belonging to… My heart gives a horrible thump in my chest.

Charon.

Thanatos goes still in response to my tension. He turns to follow my gaze and seems to stop breathing. "Charon."

"Thanatos. You're overstepping." His voice is calm. It's always calm. I once overheard Hades speaking with my sister, expressing concern that Charon had lost his customary humor in the last year. Persephone responded that he'd grown up a lot because of the events that continue to destabilize Olympus. I think they're both wrong. He's still got humor, but it's become a dry thing that flies right over my head at times.

He doesn't look like he's laughing now.

In fact, he looks almost murderous.

Thanatos shifts away from me. "I'm sorry. I didn't realize she was yours."

"She's not." He doesn't move, doesn't take his gaze from the other man. "But she's not for the taking."

"My mistake." Thanatos starts to stand. "It won't happen again."

I don't make the decision to move. My hand seems to lash out all on its own and wrap around Thanatos's wrist. "No." He pauses, standing over me, but it's not him I'm looking at. I hold Charon's gaze. "I'm the only one who decides who's going to be *taking* me."

Thanatos catches my hand again and raises it to his lips. "That may be true everywhere else, but this is Hades's club, and Charon is an extension of his will here. Sorry, love." A brush of his lips to my skin, and then he's gone, striding to the bar without looking back.

Actual anger licks up my spine. I turn to glare at Charon, who hasn't moved. "What are you doing here?"

"I could ask you the same thing." He sounds perfectly mild, but something dangerous flickers in his blue eyes. He sinks onto the empty seat across from me, his large body filling it. "We had an agreement. You only come here with me, and you only watch, never participate."

He's right, but I don't care. "Am I a child who needs a babysitter?" I certainly feel like it most of the time. It was already bad before the situation with Orpheus, and my family has gotten so much worse since. But Charon isn't my family. I might have allowed his babysitting because *he* allowed me a degree of freedom, but...

"I don't need your permission to take a lover." I don't know where the words come from, but once I voice them, it's impossible to stop. "If I wanted to fuck every single person in this room, then that's exactly what I'd do."

He lifts his brows. "Is that what you want to do?"

The question is so mild, it threatens to take the wind right out of my sails. I fist my hands at my sides. *No, of course not. I'm interested in exploring kink, but that doesn't mean I want to throw myself off the deep end just to prove a point.* And yet when I speak, it's not to back down. "And if it is?"

Charon sits back slowly. It draws my attention to the way his suit jacket clings to his broad shoulders and how the shirt beneath leaves little to the imagination. He has the kind of body built for sin, and I'd be lying if I said I haven't thought about what he might look like without his customary armor on. Not that I'll ever admit as much. I jerk my gaze back to his face.

Anyone else might smirk to have caught me checking them out. Charon just searches my expression with that same calmness in place. For the first time, it makes me want to do something to shatter it. He's always so damned contained. I used to find that a comfort, but lately it's become an itch I can't scratch.

He's my friend. My *best* friend. He also inspires some of the filthiest fantasies I've ever allowed myself to indulge in. But when he looks at me, there's nothing but gentleness in his blue eyes.

I need to let it go. I know what happens when I fall for someone who doesn't feel the same way—or the same strength of attraction. I end up discarded and broken. I refuse to go through that again, to bash myself against the wall that is someone else's reluctance.

No, that's not fair. I can't blame him for this when I'm the one who's walking around with half a heart. Charon deserves to be with someone who can be with him fully. Even if he wanted me, all I can offer him is sex that will end in heartbreak and disaster for both of us. I need to stop this and stop it now. "Charon—"

Charon shakes his head, cutting me off. "That's not what you want."

"Don't tell me what I want." I don't know what's wrong with me. I never talk to anyone like this—especially him. I'm the sweet one. The delicate one. The one who will shatter at a harsh word. I shove to my feet, fighting not to teeter in my heels. They're higher than I normally wear; I dressed up for Ariadne. I'm glad she didn't come now though, because having to explain *that* to Charon would be a special kind of nightmare.

Gods, I'm doing it again. Bending to him when I should be standing strong on my own. Fury at myself as much as him has me snapping words I would never otherwise speak. "Unless you plan on fucking me, get out of my way."

I make it a grand total of four steps before a hand presses to my stomach, stopping me easily and pinning me against a hard body at my back. *Charon's* body. In my heels, we're the same height, so he has no problem speaking directly into my ear. "Fine, Eurydice. You want to have this conversation? Then we'll have it. Right here. Right now."

CHARON

I SHOULD STOP. IT WAS NEVER SUPPOSED TO GET THIS FAR.
My feelings for this woman have been complicated since the first
time I saw her, left sobbing and bloody on the wrong side of the
River Styx, a lure Hades couldn't resist. She was the weapon the
last Zeus used, to start what could have become a war that claimed
the people I care most about in this world. For that reason alone, I
should have hated her.

Growing up in the lower city, you learn quickly that people
from the upper city aren't to be trusted. Their values are not our
values, and the entire history of Olympus is proof that when push
comes to shove, those in the lower city are the first to be offered up
as collateral damage. At first glance, she was exactly like the rest of
them, dressed to the nines and playing games that would get other
people killed.

But all it took was one conversation for me to make my peace
with the fact that no one could hate Eurydice. It's not just that she's
beautiful, though she is. She's tall and lean to the point of being

delicate, with long wavy dark hair, big dark eyes, and smooth light-brown skin. But it's more than that. Her beauty goes soul deep. I didn't intend to set myself up as her personal protector, as her confidant, as her...friend. It just happened. I value her friendship.

How I'm touching her right now is not friendly in the least.

Even as I tell myself to let her go, to step back and put the careful distance between us that I always maintain, I...don't. I can't when her words are ricocheting around inside my skull.

Unless you plan on fucking me, get out of my way.

I haven't stopped to think from the moment I got the text from Hypnos informing me that Eurydice had arrived at the club without me—a clear violation of our agreement. Even as I came down here, taking the route through the big house owned by Hades and Persephone, I had half convinced myself that she just wandered in out of curiosity. She's a curious woman, and if she's been more tentative expressing it in the past, it was a good thing that she was taking this step on her own without me as her security blanket. Even if I *like* being that security blanket.

Then I saw her with Thanatos.

Saw him kiss her. Saw him stroke her breast with the backs of his fingers. Saw the intention written in every line of their bodies.

That was my cue to turn around and leave. I might have become Eurydice's unofficial protector, but she's an adult, and like she said, she's more than capable of choosing her own bedmates. When it comes to that sort of thing, Thanatos isn't a bad candidate. He's kind and thoughtful, and he loves to spoil his partners. He wouldn't hurt her or scare her. He's a solid choice to rebound from that mess with Orpheus.

I know that. But it was like some demon took over my body.

I didn't make a choice to interrupt them. Just like I didn't make a choice to pin her against my chest like this. It just...happened.

Now is the time to retreat, to make our individual excuses and let this moment, pregnant with the possibility of changing things between us forever, go.

I don't.

Instead, I wait for her answer.

Eurydice is so tense, she's practically a statue in my arms. Just when reason has kicked in enough to tell me to release her, she relaxes against me. It feels so good to have her in my arms, to be holding her, that my brain actually shorts out. I can't move. I can barely breathe. I want this and I don't, and my shit is so twisted up that I don't know what I'm doing.

"We can't do this." Her voice is barely loud enough to be heard above the music, but I'm so attuned to her right now, I'd bet she could whisper and I'd still pick up the words.

She's right. It's a mistake. I care about this woman too much to fuck this up, and releasing the permanent choke hold I keep on my desire *will* ruin things. She's stronger than anyone gives her credit for, but that doesn't mean I won't crush her by accident. I've been very careful to keep myself leashed.

Until now.

"That's your choice." I barely speak loud enough to be heard over the throbbing music. "It's always been your choice."

She shudders out a breath. "I care about you, Charon. I don't want things to change, but just because we are...friends...doesn't mean you get to tell me what to do. Even if we were more, you still don't get to make those choices for me."

I know she's right, but that doesn't stop me going tense at her words. It doesn't stop my response from ripping free. "If we were more, you wouldn't be trying to ride someone else's cock without talking to me first."

She turns, and I loosen my hold on her just enough to allow it. I don't release her though. I don't think I'm capable of it right now.

Eurydice stares into my eyes. Her brows draw together. "That seems to imply you wouldn't mind me fucking other people as long as we discussed it first."

I've had plenty of nontraditional relationships in the past. I figure as long as everyone is on the same page and consenting, that's all that matters. That looks a little different with each relationship. With her?

I cup her hips. Part of me can barely believe I'm touching her like this. Talking about this. "Getting ahead of yourself. You haven't fucked me yet, and you're already talking about fucking others."

Her gaze drops to my lips. "You've become one of my best friends, and I won't pretend that I don't want you. But...that's all I can offer you. Sex. I don't have it in me to give anything else."

Gods, she has no idea how much I want her in my bed. If I cared about her any less, I wouldn't hesitate. That's the problem though. I'm trapped between what I want and what she needs. "I care about you too much. It would never just be sex with us."

"I know." She smiles, and the misery in the expression breaks my fucking heart. I need to release her right now, but I can't quite make myself break this moment. Not when it's looking like it will be both first and last. She presses her hands to my chest. "I care about you too. But..."

I don't want to say his fucking name, don't want to bring another person into this conversation, but the truth is that the shadow of *him* follows her around like some damned curse. "Orpheus."

She nods, her dark eyes sad. "Orpheus. I know it's pathetic and cliché, but the way things ended has prevented any kind of closure. I don't particularly want to go to the upper city and force a conversation, because I don't think that's fair either, but my heart is more than bruised, Charon. You deserve someone whole and healthy."

I can't decide if I'm proud of her or want to put her over my knee. "You want a clear explanation of intentions? Very well." I slide my hands down to cup her ass and pull her even tighter against me. "I've done right by you, Eurydice. I've given you space to figure your shit out and start to heal. I haven't pressured you, and I've done my damnedest to keep my attraction to you hidden."

She blinks. "But?"

"But you threw this gauntlet at my feet, and now *you* have a choice. You don't get to decide what I deserve. I'm the only one who can do that. I'm not expecting you to be without scars, baby. No one is. But I'm offering you all of me. Heart. Body. Soul. You said you care about me. Let's give this a shot." I shouldn't have let the pet name slip, but I'm laying it all out on the table right now. No reason to hold back.

She tenses. "Charon, that's too much. That's not fair. You're asking for everything."

"It's doesn't have to be everything." It kills me to say it. I never thought she'd give me any indication that she might want me as much as I want her. Now, she's done it and we're teetering on the edge of ruin. Fuck that. If I have to smother every bit of my attraction to her in order to keep her in my life, I'll do it. I take a deep breath and tell myself to let her go. I can't quite make my hands obey. "If you don't want me like that, then this won't happen again. I'll go back to being your safe friend."

"My safe friend," she echoes. "Just like that. You'll stand back and let me fuck other people."

It'll kill me to do it. "If that's what it takes." I realize I still have my hands full of her ass, but I can't quite make myself let go. This might be the last chance I get to touch her like this. "Take the leap with me, baby. We can figure things out on our way down. We already have a strong-as-shit foundation of caring and mutual respect. I love you." I'm making a mistake. This is too much, too fast.

But I still don't take the words back.

Eurydice opens her mouth but pauses. She takes a deep breath and releases my neck. It requires everything I have to let go of her. The small step she takes away from me feels like a part of my body being shredded.

I know what she's going to say before she shakes her head slowly. "I'm sorry, Charon. I can't."

Loss threatens to take me out at the knees, but I somehow manage to stay standing. "I understand."

"No, I don't think you do. I love you too." She lifts her hands like she'll touch me again but stops before she makes contact. "But I *can't* be with you like you need—like you deserve. I'm not capable of it."

I don't want to get what she's saying. It would be so much simpler if I didn't. But I know this woman. After a year, I won't pretend she doesn't have the capacity to surprise me—tonight is more than proof of that—but I understand her. There's only one thing that would put that look on her face. Or, more accurately, one person. I curse. "Orpheus. Still."

Her eyes shine in the low light of the club. "I'm sorry," she says again. "I know it's been long enough to be pathetic, but things still feel...unresolved. It's not fair to move on to something serious with you with that still hanging over my head. If I still haven't shaken it after nine months, I don't know if I ever will."

I don't ask her what she needs for closure with her ex. I don't ask her how long she needs. I don't ask anything at all.

I've loved Eurydice for a long time now. I can admit that to myself even if I can't speak it aloud to anyone else. I've waited this long. If I have to wait forever, then that's what I'll do. "Okay."

She looks absolutely sick. "If I could just talk to him—"

"No." I don't mean to bark the word, but I also don't take it back. "You are not crossing the River Styx. No one in the lower city is. Directive from Hades and Persephone."

Her nostrils flare. "My sister and brother-in-law do not rule *me*."

"You're in the lower city, so that's exactly what they do." She still looks stubborn, so I allow myself to lean in and speak directly into her ear. I don't touch her again, no matter how much I want to. "You know what's going on over there. It's not safe."

It hasn't been for weeks, ever since the citizens of Olympus learned of the little-known clause that says assassinating one of the Thirteen—the ruling body of Olympus—is a way to jump the line of succession.

Normally, those positions change once every few decades when the current person in power retires or dies. Nine times out of ten, their successor is pulled from one of the legacy families. Zeus, Poseidon, and Hades pass to their eldest child. Those in power stay in power and the rest of the city has no chance to change that.

Until now.

The chaos is only growing with each assassination attempt. There have been dozens in the last month, and their frequency only seems to be increasing. That's a problem in and of itself, because instability in the city grows in direct proportion. People don't care that they aren't following the proper protocol to actually take the title of the person they've killed. It's chaos.

Earlier today, someone sank a knife into Poseidon. He survived, but at the same time, someone broke into Triton's house and murdered him. He doesn't even hold a title. He might be nearly as rich as the members of the Thirteen, but that's only because he's Poseidon's cousin and his bloodline allows him to ferry people back and forth across the boundary that surrounds the city. There was no gain to be had from his death. That didn't stop someone from killing him in cold blood.

If family members aren't safe, then Eurydice is in danger on multiple fronts.

Her mother is Demeter. Her eldest sister is Hera. Her other sister Persephone is married to Hades...

It's entirely possible that some fool with more rage and ambition than sense will try to hurt her if she ventures into the upper city. At least our citizens in the lower city haven't lost their damn minds. She's safe here. "If you need to talk to him, he can come to the lower city."

"Yeah, right. As if that would ever happen." She turns and walks away.

I watch her go like the fool I am. I can't take the feeling that I'm about to ruin things between us forever. If she needs to see Orpheus to get closure, then I'll make that happen for her. Even if she still has feelings for Orpheus after all this time, even if seeing him again will surely reignite those feelings. Unfortunately, it's clear that she can't move on without seeing him, so that's a risk we're all going to have to take together.

I just hope it's not a mistake.

ORPHEUS

THE THING NO ONE EVER TELLS YOU ABOUT PAYING penance...

It's impossible to do if those you hurt won't talk to you.

"Let it go, Orpheus." My brother sounds as exhausted as he looks. There are circles beneath his eyes, courtesy of too many sleepless nights trying to hold Olympus together. It's not working. All anyone's talking about these days are the power shifts and the attacks on the Thirteen. I'm not as plugged in as I used to be, but even I can't miss how bad things have gotten. A lot of people think it started with the stranger from outside the city, Minos, becoming a citizen, or even with Helen Kasios winning the Ares title, but it's not the truth.

Olympus has been bad for a really long time. I just never bothered to notice until it affected me. Another sin to lay at my feet. I'm trying to do better, but when everyone I've ever surrounded myself with values the same shit I used to, it's hard to get perspective.

Everyone except my brother. He might be Apollo, one of the Thirteen, but he's not like the rest. He's a genuinely good person.

Concern lances through me. "Are you okay? Has anyone—"

"No." He shakes his head sharply. "I've taken Ares upon her offer of added security, and her people have more than lived up to their reputation."

That hasn't stopped our mother from worrying, but then one of her favorite hobbies these days is to worry about her boys. It doesn't matter that we're both adults. We'll always be her boys. It doesn't help that I've given her plenty to worry about over the last year. It's a fucked-up journey to go from being convinced I'm immortal and untouchable and as close to a god as walks the earth, to...

Whatever this torment is.

All the things that used to bring me joy make me want to throw something. I haven't painted in nearly a year. The company of others grates on my nerves. Not that anyone is seeking my company these days. Once you stop being the life of the party, you find out who your real friends are. I have none.

But my brother doesn't want to hear about my petty problems. I drag in a breath and try to set it aside. "Have you made any progress?"

"Orpheus, asking about someone other than himself? Will wonders never cease?" My brother's girlfriend walks into the room. Cassandra is a plus-sized white woman with red hair that draws the eye. I hadn't realized my brother had a thing for her when I hit on her all those months ago. I wish I could say it would have made a difference, but I was in a dark place at the time. I'd like to think I wouldn't have done it though.

"Cassandra." There isn't much censor in Apollo's voice. He knows my selfishness better than anyone. If it wasn't for him stepping in and giving me a much-needed reality check, I don't know where I'd be now.

"I only speak the truth." She bends down to give him a kiss on his cheek and shoots me a look. "You look like shit."

"Cassandra." Apollo's tone still isn't sharp, but it's not happy. "Please."

"Sorry." She doesn't even try to sound like she means it, and against all reason it makes me like her better. This is a woman who always says what she means, and fuck anyone who expects anything else. I admire that about her. I wish I cared less. Something else I'm working on.

"Things are as bad as they seem on the news." Apollo drags a hand over his face. "It doesn't matter what angle we try to take—this situation is out of control and only getting worse. They haven't managed to assassinate one of the Thirteen, but it's only a matter of time."

Worry slithers through me. My brother has always seemed so untouchable, but the reality is that he's only human like the rest of us. He could *die*. "Maybe you should step down. If we lost you—"

"Olympus needs me." He says the words with the air of someone who's repeated them often. "And besides, even stepping down now wouldn't help. The public isn't paying attention to details. They're just as likely to attempt to kill me regardless of whether I still hold the title. Triton wasn't one of the Thirteen, and that didn't save him."

"I saw the news." I should probably feel something about his death—it's tragic in the way that all violent deaths are, but Triton was a bastard and a half. I feel bad for his daughters though. "Are the girls okay?"

"Poseidon sent his people to secure the house and keep them safe."

I swallow the impulse to ask him again to step down. He won't do it, and we'll just end up fighting. He's probably right anyway, but the thought of losing him makes me sick to my stomach. My brother and I haven't always seen eye to eye; truth be told, growing up, we fought more than we spoke. That doesn't change the fact that I love him. He's family.

I shouldn't have brought my problems to him. Not when he's dealing with so much shit right now. I clear my throat. "There's a way out. You'll find it. You're too damned smart not to."

"Maybe."

"You will," Cassandra says from where she's pouring a large glass of wine in the kitchen. She eyes me. "But that means he doesn't have time for your...whatever is happening right now. Let the grown-ups deal with grown-up things."

Cassandra is as mean as a snake. Everyone in Olympus lies as easily as they breathe, but she's turned the truth into a weapon to be wielded, and she does it with a viciousness that awes me. The only person who seems exempt from her cutting remarks is my brother. They're two of the most practical people I know, and when they look at each other, they go all soft and sweet.

I'm jealous, if I'm going to be honest. I had a chance at happiness, and I fucked it all up. That doesn't stop me from glaring at her. "I'm twenty-six. I'm not a child."

"Then stop acting like one."

I open my mouth to snap back, but...she's right. I shouldn't have come here asking Apollo for favors again. He has enough on his plate. Old habits die hard. I push to my feet. "Sorry to bother you."

My brother sighs. "Orpheus, I know you want to make things right, but I meant what I said a few weeks ago. Sometimes making things right looks like letting things go. I delivered your message to Eurydice. If she hasn't reached out by now, she's likely decided not to."

He's right. I know he's right. But the thought of letting Eurydice go...

It's what I should do. I *know* it's what I should do. I wronged her by more than simply breaking her heart. I put her in literal danger without realizing it. If I hadn't been so focused on myself and my own ambitions and, fuck, my pretentious *art*, I would have realized exactly how fucked up it was that the last Zeus—a known killer— asked me to arrange for my girlfriend, the daughter of his enemy, to be in a certain place at a certain time.

Unforgivable.

I feel like I'm half a man lately. I realize that isn't Eurydice's problem, but...

Damn it, I'm doing it again.

I shake my head sharply. "Sorry. You're both right. I shouldn't have asked again." I promised Apollo that I'd do better, and I've been working on it, but I'm starting to lose hope that I'll actually become the man he wants me to be.

When he first cut me off, I was furious with him. I was a righteous and entitled little shit who I want to reach back through time and punch in the face. Since then, I've gotten a job that isn't selling my art—mostly because I'm not capable of *making* art right now— and moved into a small, more affordable place. No matter what else I fucked up, I had managed to save up quite the little nest egg, so I don't technically need to work to live for a bit. I still prefer to.

It keeps me busy.

"Orpheus." Apollo meets my gaze directly. "Be careful going home tonight. The streets aren't as safe as they used to be."

"I will." I nod to Cassandra. "Have a good rest of your night."

Cassandra sighs. "You don't have to run off. You can stay for dinner if you'd like."

As much as part of me would love to do exactly that, staying means witnessing something that I'm starting to believe I'll never have. My brother deserves to be happy, and I'm genuinely glad he found that with Cassandra. It doesn't change the fact that being in their presence actively hurts. Maybe at some point in the future, I'll be able to watch Apollo be in love without feeling like I'm choking on jealousy.

Maybe.

"I'm good. Thanks though." I leave before they can offer again. It's especially jarring that it's *Cassandra* doing it. She doesn't like me, but she pities me. That's how pathetic I am these days.

I take the elevator down and hurry through the lobby to step out onto the street. The first bite of winter is in the air. It will be some time before it fully sinks its claws into Olympus, but it's coming. I'm not overly superstitious, but considering how the last year has gone, I can't help a shiver of foreboding.

The city has changed.

Evidence of it is there in the way the few people out on the street hurry past with their heads down. Apollo lives in the center of the upper city, and up until a month ago, it had a rich nightlife. Now, businesses are closing not too long after nightfall. There isn't a citywide curfew, but there might as well be.

The threat of violence hangs heavy.

I duck my head and pick up my pace. There's no one around to have their eyes on me, but I feel watched nonetheless. Hunted. I'm not even one of the Thirteen. No one benefits from killing me in a ritualistic assassination. Then again, no one benefitted from killing Triton either, and that didn't save him.

Despite my unease, I make it back to my apartment without issue. That doesn't stop me from throwing the deadbolt as soon as I'm through the door. I also can't quite stop myself from doing a quick circuit of the small space.

It doesn't take long. I downgraded from a large penthouse suite to a studio apartment. I look behind the couch and check the bathroom, finding nothing. Of course I find nothing. I can't help feeling like a fool for even considering someone might be lying in wait, but that feeling of being watched is still riding me hard.

I scrub the back of my neck. "What the fuck?"

A knock on my door makes me curse and flinch. I stare at the door for a long moment, half-sure I imagined it. There's no reason for anyone to be visiting me right now. I lost pretty much every "friend" I had when Apollo cut me off and I stopped being the life of the party.

The knock comes again, a quiet, forceful sound that makes my skin prickle. The foreboding that rode me so hard on my way here comes back with interest. I really, truly do not want to open that door. It doesn't matter. They obviously aren't going away until I answer. I walk to the door, take a fortifying breath, and open it.

Only to freeze. "What are *you* doing here?"

Charon Ariti stands there, his shoulders taking up the narrow hallway, his expression carefully blank. We've never met in an official capacity, but one of the side effects of Hades coming to light—and marrying society darling Persephone—was that MuseWatch turned their hungry gaze on those around him. They ran articles on all of his subordinates they could divine, and Charon was top of the list.

He's a big white man with a handsome face that feels kind of timeless, like he might be found in the back alleys of the lower city, or perhaps bashing his shield into some guy's face back in the Middle Ages. Dude has *soldier* basically tattooed on his forehead.

I step back instinctively, and he moves into my apartment without hesitation. He takes in the place with an unreadable look and waits for me to close the door.

I don't move. "If you're here to beat the shit out of me, just know I'm partial to my good looks and I'll fold immediately."

Charon exhales harshly. "If I was going to beat the shit out of you, I would have done it back in December."

Back when Eurydice was hurt because of my selfishness.

I shut the door. "I deserve it."

"I'm aware." He looks around the room again. "Seems you're paying penance all the same."

What's that supposed to mean? I laugh without any humor. "Yes, absolutely. Living in a nice apartment with a steady job is penance. Sure."

He seems to be studying the paintings I've stacked haphazardly against the wall. I can't bear to throw them away, but treating them with care feels like...too much. "So. She's haunting you the same way you're haunting her."

Haunted. Yes, that's exactly how I feel. My sins dog my steps, a shadow I can never escape. Guilt is a nettle cloak I can't shrug out of. I've convinced myself that talking to Eurydice, *apologizing* to her, will be enough to bury my demons, but the longer this goes on, the less sure I am. "It doesn't really matter who's haunting who. If you haven't come to beat the shit out of me…why *are* you here?"

Charon turns back to face me, his blue eyes cold. "I meant what I said about you haunting her. She can't move on until she makes peace with you."

"Move on?" I stare. Why the fuck does he care if she…? Oh. *Oh.* Pain lashes me, hot and furious. I want to be jealous, to be angry, but all I get is a crushing force that makes me weave on my feet. "She wants to move on with *you.*"

"If you really want what's best for her, that wouldn't bother you." He holds my gaze. "You held her carelessly and shattered her. I won't make the same mistake."

I want to rail at him. To tell him to fuck right off and never return. I don't move, don't speak. He's not saying anything I haven't thought myself. Oh, I never imagined Eurydice moving on with someone like him, but eventually she had to move on, and it was never going to be with me. I had my chance with her, had the opportunity to treat her the way she deserved, and I fucked it up.

I take a breath that feels like knives in my lungs. "Let me apologize. I know it doesn't mean much, but maybe it will put things to rest once and for all."

"It's not safe for her in the upper city. Find your way to the lower city and make it right. You owe her that much." He turns toward the door.

My shock shatters. "Wait. There's a barrier between the upper city and lower city. How am I supposed to get through it?"

"I'm sure you'll figure it out." He leaves my apartment, closing the door softly behind him.

I stare for a long moment and curse. "What the *fuck* was that?"

EURYDICE

I'VE GOTTEN VERY GOOD AT DODGING MY SISTER AND brother-in-law. It's easier with her these days because she's massively pregnant with twins, so I hear her coming well before she has a chance to catch me slipping out the front door.

I'm not trying to be sneaky exactly. This is the lower city; there are few places I can go that Hades won't find out about. Or more accurately, that Charon won't find out about.

But he's off on some errand tonight, and so I'm taking advantage of his absence. Again. I have no doubt I'll face his disapproval when he finally tracks me down, and I'm not quite ready to face him after what happened last night...

We both said things we can't take back. No matter what he offered, there's no returning to the safe friendship where we both pretend there's nothing deeper. I've ruined it.

No. I'm not thinking about that. I need to focus. Ariadne texted me earlier that she could get out tonight, so we're meeting on the bridge. Not the Juniper Bridge. I still avoid that one, even three-quarters of a year later. It's not quite superstition that something bad will happen if I revisit the place where everything changed, but it's not *not* superstition. If I take the long way around to the Cypress Bridge every time I need to cross the river, well, that's my burden to bear.

Mine and Charon's, since he's usually driving me.

I promised Charon I wouldn't go to the upper city, but Ariadne has an open invitation to the lower city, courtesy of Hades. He hasn't explicitly said that he's aware of the task Aphrodite gave me—or I suppose she's Eris again, since she relinquished the title—but nothing happens in the lower city that he's not aware of. Eris promised me that Ariadne had an invite, and I don't see why that would have been revoked. Getting her to flip on her father is still the goal.

I'm not a complete fool though. I know better than to go out alone without letting someone know where I am. Since there's no way I'd clue in any of my sisters, I text Eris.

> **Me**: Headed to meeting with Ariadne. Plan on talking and maybe having a drink in the lower city.

She doesn't make me wait long for a response.

> **Eris**: I think my invite to the lower city is still good too. Want me to head your way?

I almost say yes. Eris is more than a little terrifying, but that's a benefit in this city and probably in this situation. She'll come in all sharp smiles and double-edged words, and I won't have to do anything but sit there and look pretty.

Which is exactly why I can't say yes.

If I really want to stand on my own, I have to *stand on my own.*

> **Me**: I've got it covered. I'll text you after I'm done talking with her.
>
> **Eris**: If that's what you want. Drop your location when you pick a place.

I frown at my phone. Really, that's too much. What's she going to do if I don't text in a reasonable amount of time? Ride to the rescue? Call in my *sister* to ride to the rescue? The thought makes me grit my teeth. When I was first approached by Eris at that ill-fated house party, I thought finally someone was seeing me for my potential instead of as the broken-winged bird to be hidden away from the world. And at first that was even true. Not so much now.

> **Me**: I said I've got it covered. Just wanted to keep you in the loop.
>
> **Eris**: Fine, fine. I hear you loud and clear.
>
> **Eris**: Be careful.

I flip my hood up and stride down the street toward the bridge. It's a good twenty-minute walk, and the night is plenty cold, but it feels good to be out on my own. Like maybe I'm really as capable as I've been pretending to be. It's not so late that people have all gone home, and I nod to those I see as I walk. Reports will get back to

Charon—to Hades—within the hour, but I hope they both see the value in what I'm doing and don't charge in to rescue me.

I'm the only one who can do this.

Ariadne Vitalis is a weapon in the making, and we need one now more than ever. Honestly, it might be too late. When Minos's foster son, Theseus, killed the last Hephaestus and took his place, it created ripples that are in danger of becoming a tsunami of terror and violence. I don't know what possessed the founders of Olympus to slip an assassination clause into the near-forgotten laws but…

No, that's a lie. I know *exactly* what possessed them. The founders were most likely carbon copies of the people who now hold the titles of the Thirteen, the ruling body of Olympus. Power-hungry and politically vicious. But there are rules, and that means that each of the Thirteen comes about their title in a different way…and then they keep it until they die or retire. Most of them don't bother retiring. They cling to that power until it's wrenched from their hands by Death themself.

Now we're left to deal with the mess their ambition created.

I have mixed feelings about Olympus. I always have. My sisters think I see the city with rose-tinted glasses, but the truth is that I am all too aware of the dangers lurking in the shadows. Maybe that wasn't always the case, but it is now. No matter what I think of the Thirteen, who use and discard people to further their goals—yes, even my mother is guilty of it—I will always have empathy for the rest of the people. They didn't choose to be born into Olympus any more than I did, and we're all just trying to survive the waves caused by those more powerful than us.

There's no telling if Ariadne has information we can use to

protect the people of this city, but I have to try. I'm no tactician, but even I can see this is only the first wave. They're softening the city up for the next blow, and that might be the one that breaks us. If I can do anything to hold the danger off, I'll lie and more to ensure the innocents who never asked for this are kept safe.

Or as safe as they ever are.

Fog curls in as I reach the bridge. Both remaining bridges that span the River Styx feel otherworldly, but Cypress Bridge is on another level entirely. The stone columns are wider around than most people and soar upward to create an arch. I know both upper city and lower city reside in the same realm, but it's hard to remember that when entering these arches feels like leaving the world behind. Especially tonight, when the fog hides the other bank from me.

Fear licks up my spine, whispering that this isn't safe. With the fog so dense, anyone could be waiting for me on that bridge. It could be another ambush, and this time there's no Hades and Persephone to save me.

No. Damn it, *no*.

I am not defenseless. Not anymore. I hitch my purse higher on my shoulder and slip my hand inside to touch the gun nestled there. Charon's been taking me to the private shooting range Hades owns, and while he didn't *technically* give me permission to borrow this one, it's just a little insurance. I'm sure I won't have to use it, but I have it if I need it.

One last jagged breath, and then I plunge through the arches and onto the bridge. I have a standing invitation to the lower city, so the boundary is barely noticeable as I stride down the bridge.

She's beat me to the middle of the bridge, and she huddles

against the stone railing, her arms wrapped around herself. She's a pretty, plus-sized woman with medium-brown skin, sweet dark eyes, and wavy black hair. She may take after her father, Minos, but only in coloring. He's handsome in a way that looks like he was hacked out of a mountain. She's much softer.

Ariadne looks up as I approach. She's easily six inches shorter than me, just a few inches over five feet. "I don't have as much time as I thought. I'm sorry."

"But you came all this way." It's almost as if her father knows she's not fully on his side. He's come up with reason after reason to keep her close since the house party where Theseus killed the last Hephaestus.

"Only because I have a warning for you. It's important, Eurydice." She shrugs, her expression pinched. "You heard about Triton?"

I nod. "He was killed in a fight when they tried to get to Poseidon."

Ariadne shakes her head. "No, he wasn't. His attacker was after *him*."

She looks out over the river, except it isn't visible through the fog. I can still hear the rush of water over rocks far below, but it echoes strangely. I press my lips together and debate whether to press her on this. Ultimately, that's why I'm here. "How can you be sure?"

"Because. That's why I couldn't get out last night." She turns those big dark eyes on me. "My father held a meeting with some person I've never seen before, and then they left. Less than an hour later, Triton was announced dead and *they* were photographed fleeing the scene. He wasn't killed by an Olympus citizen who doesn't understand the rules. He was assassinated by someone who answers to my father." She hiccups, a little sound that's almost a sob.

"Triton is one of the few who can ferry people through the barrier," I say slowly. Anyone from Poseidon's bloodline can, but that bloodline has gotten sparse in recent generations. Triton has a number of daughters, but he keeps—kept—them under lock and key. None of them worked for Poseidon. At this point, I think Poseidon's down to a few distant cousins. He has no siblings or children of his own.

If the other cousins are killed, I don't know who inherits the title once he's gone. I don't know if *anyone* can inherit the title. It passes down from parent to child, or in rare cases, to the closest in the bloodline. If there's no one left...does the title of Poseidon die?

I shudder. "The barrier is failing."

"That's what I hear." She tucks her hair behind her ear, but the wind immediately whips it free. "I don't know why they're targeting his family, but..." She stops short. "I really shouldn't be saying any of this. I shouldn't have come at all."

From my interactions with Minos, I've found him to be a misogynistic pig. He covers it well enough with charm, but it couldn't be clearer in how he treats his children. Ariadne because she's a woman. Icarus because he doesn't fit in with what Minos has arbitrarily decided a man should be.

I place my hand gently on her shoulder. I have to play this slow. Soft. "I know it's not easy for you in that household."

Her lower lip quivers. "It doesn't matter. I can't leave."

I'm going to lose her if I'm not careful. It's not even her father

I'm worried about now, though I'm plenty worried about him. I've seen the way the Minotaur watches Ariadne when he thinks no one is looking. There's a feverish quality to his gaze that raises every hair on my body. It reeks of obsession. She seems to be entirely unaware of it though. Or maybe not, because I doubt Minos is the one who's put the hunted look in her dark eyes.

I have to get her on my side. No matter what it takes. "Ariadne." I sink a bit of strength into her name. "People are dying. I know you're in an impossible situation, but surely you can see that you have information that will save lives."

She still won't meet my gaze. "Is that the only reason you invited me out last night?"

Yes. It's nothing personal. I like her a lot. She's sweet and nerdy and a little awkward, but she's got a good heart. I'm not sure how it's survived her family, but it's there shining beneath all the bullshit her father spews at her. But I wouldn't be pushing her so hard if she wasn't a Vitalis. I take a deep breath and tell the truth. "I like you, so I won't lie to you. If I met you under other circumstances, I would want to be friends. But you gave Apollo a hint that you possessed some really important information. I'm the only one you seem willing to talk to, so I'm the one making the overture."

She nods as if it's nothing more than she expected, but her shoulders dip a little bit. "Right. That's what I thought."

"We'll protect you." I reach out tentatively and place my hand on her shoulder. "We'll get you out and we'll keep you safe." I don't imagine that her father—or the Minotaur—will take kindly to us spiriting her away, but if Eris can see the value Ariadne brings, then surely the rest of the Thirteen can too. We have to get her out. We *have* to.

"That's what Apollo said." She tries for a smile but doesn't quite pull it off. Ariadne finally looks at me. "I have to think about it."

Frustration blooms, but I do my best to keep it off my face. This was never going to be an easy win. She's lived her entire life under her father's control, and even if people are dying because of his actions, it's hard to break that yoke. Understanding that doesn't stop me from wanting to shake her until she sees reason. "I'll be here when you're ready."

Ariadne nods. She looks frailer than she did at the house party. The last month hasn't been easy for her, but I swallow down my sympathy. She has information that might save lives, and she's not sharing. "If you know something…"

"I know a lot of things. I don't know what's important and what's not." She shakes her head. "Just be careful, okay? I don't think the lower city is going to be any safer than the upper city going forward. I have to go before they realize I snuck out."

Before I can come up with a response to that, she turns and darts away. The fog swallows her up before she's more than a couple yards away, and I shiver. I don't know if I made progress or not, but it was worth the risk. I turn back for my side of the river, mulling over her words. Do I tell Charon about the warning concerning the lower city? It's very vague, and I'll probably have to explain *why* I chose to meet Ariadne alone instead of bringing someone for protection, but surely the information is worth the uncomfortableness of talking with him so soon after last night?

I don't have an answer by the time I reach the arches leading to the lower city. Which is a damn shame, because they're not empty any longer. A familiar shape separates himself from the shadow of the one nearest me, arms crossed and blue eyes furious.

"Where the fuck were you?" Charon grits out.

Oh shit. I'm in trouble.

CHARON

I DO NOT, AS A GENERAL RULE, LOSE MY TEMPER. A YEAR ago, that might have been different, but I've seen too much shit since then to allow my emotions to get the best of me. That doesn't stop my fear and anger from damn near swallowing me whole at the sight of Eurydice walking toward the lower city across the Cypress Bridge.

I fight to keep it under wraps, but it slips through my fingers like the fog that blankets the ground around us. She nearly misses a step when she notices me, but I can see the exact moment when she decides to power through this on bravado alone.

She lifts her chin in a move I've seen Persephone do a hundred times and marches right up to me. "What are you doing here?"

"No."

That trips her up. She blinks those big eyes at me. "What do you mean 'no'?"

"No, you don't get to go on the offensive, when you're clearly in the wrong." Some of my anger seeps into my voice, and I can't stop myself from continuing. "You know it's dangerous to be out by yourself, let alone to be on this bridge. *Over* this bridge. You, of everyone, know it's dangerous. Why the fuck are you out here without an escort?"

"Zeus is dead."

"Zeus is alive and living in Dodona Tower."

She thins her lips. "He's not the same and you know it."

Yeah, I guess I do. I'll never be a fan of Zeus, regardless of who holds the title, but even I can't deny that this one is miles better than the last. I won't allow her to distract me with semantics though. "And you know damn well that he's not even the biggest threat out there right now. *Everyone* is a threat."

A year ago, she would have burst into tears at my harsh tone. Six months ago, she would have flinched and apologized immediately. Tonight, she doesn't do either. She steps closer and pokes me in the chest. "I am not a child."

"You keep saying that, and then you act like a foolish teenager."

She pokes me again. "No, fuck that. I will suffer the overprotectiveness from my family and Hades. Not from you. You took me to Minos's party. You trusted me to hold my own there."

Yeah, I did, and I regret the fuck out of it. I thought it was a safe enough adventure for her to experience, to tag along on my fact-finding mission. Her delight at accepting the invitation was worth the ass reaming I got from Hades and Persephone over it. Or so I thought.

Then people ended up in the hospital, and Hephaestus ended up dead.

"I regret that."

Her shoulders fall a half inch and then hike back up. "No. You don't get to do that. You are the only person who's looked at me and seen someone beyond a victim in waiting. You don't get to take that back. It's cruel."

She's right, but that doesn't change the fact that she's trying to distract me. I hate that it's working. The last thing I want is to hurt this woman. I've been twisting myself up in knots to ensure I don't make her uncomfortable. So, yeah, I might regret the danger she was in at the house party, but I don't regret how she came alive there in a way I'd never seen.

None of that matters in this moment though. Not when she's being reckless and trying to cover it up. "Where were you?"

"Where were *you*?" She's still in my space, her spiced perfume taunting me as much as the warmth coming off her body. "I texted you earlier and you didn't answer."

Guilt flares, threatening to hijack my anger. Going behind her back to talk to her ex without her explicitly asking me to was a shitty move, even if I did it with the best of intentions. Mostly. There may have been part of me that wanted to get a look at the man, to search for a hint of what it is about him that holds Eurydice captive, even a year and a fucked-up betrayal later.

He's attractive enough, even more attractive than his brother Apollo. Their father is Swedish and their mother is Korean, and while they both have her coloring, Orpheus favors her more clearly than Apollo. He's almost pretty, but the year of suffering has sharpened that beauty into something else entirely. His black hair was always longish, but now it reaches his shoulders in a careless fall of silk. The biggest change is in his dark eyes. He still has enough charisma that I was caught off guard, but the loss there called to something I refuse to look too deeply at.

I know what he lost.

I refuse to make the same mistakes he did.

"I had some things to take care of."

She searches my face for a long moment. "Uh-huh. Well, I also had some things to take care of."

"Eurydice," I bite out.

"Charon." She mimics my tone. "You don't get to keep secrets and then expect me to spill all mine."

My hands move on instinct, catching her hips. She's wearing a coat, but it's too thin; I can feel her body clearly beneath the fabric. "It's not the same."

"Okay." She flattens her hand against my chest. We've fallen into a bit of a comfortable friendship over time, but there's a new intention in the way we touch each other after last night. I know I should hold off, should put some distance between us, but with the Cypress Bridge looming over us, I can't quite make myself release her.

"You're right. I don't regret taking you to Minos's party. Because you held up your end of the promise and listened to me when I gave you an order. You knew it was dangerous, and you trusted me to protect you—just like I trusted you to not do anything reckless that would get you hurt." I lean down a little without fully meaning to. "Whatever you did tonight? It was reckless. I ought to put you over my knee and paddle your ass."

She smirks, and it's a bolt of sheer lust to my system. Eurydice doesn't fear me in the least, and I want to inhale her fledgling brattiness straight into my lungs. She shifts her hand, pricking my chest with her long nails. "You're all bark and no bite."

I don't mean to draw her closer, to back us toward the large pillar at the entrance of this side of the bridge. There's not much light to begin with, but here in its shadow, everything feels softer. Dreamlike. "I am trying to give you what you need."

"What about what *you* need?"

I know what she said last night. That I deserve more than a woman hung up on another man. Maybe she's right. I don't give a fuck. "Why don't you let me be the one to make that decision?"

"I don't want to hurt you," she whispers.

As if being so close to her isn't a glorious agony already. I don't say it. My desires are not her responsibility. But last night changed things, whether she wants to admit it or not. She wants me too. She *loves* me, and not only as a friend. "Life is full of hurt, baby. I meant what I said. I won't pressure you, and I won't throw this shit in your face." I should stop there. But she's close and touching me, and I can't let this moment slip past without telling her the full truth. "I know you have unresolved shit. I know your heart still hurts for him. But I'm not so selfish as to need your whole heart, Eurydice. Any pain that comes from being with you is far outweighed by the joy of having you in my life."

"You really mean that."

It's not a question, but it demands an answer all the same. "I do."

"And if I said yes? That I would give this a shot?"

My heart is pounding so hard, I'm surprised she can't feel it. Maybe she can. "I'd like to say I'd take you home and romance you slow and sweet."

"I don't want slow and sweet, Charon. I don't know if I ever did." She drags her hand lightly down my chest to my stomach. She's moving slowly, giving me plenty of time to stop her. Gods help me, but I don't. Not even when she cups my cock through my slacks. Eurydice squeezes me lightly. "What if I want fast and hard and...now?"

I have kept myself on a tight leash, and she's doing her damnedest to pick it apart, thread by thread. "I am trying to do right by you."

She leans back against the pillar. I can't see her expression clearly, but I know her well enough now to know she's got a challenge in her eyes. It's a flicker I've seen more and more often in the last few weeks. I shouldn't enjoy it as much as I do; when she's challenging me, she's not doing what I say, which means she might be acting out and putting herself in danger.

She's not in danger right now.

I'm standing between her and anyone that might be out on the street. I can't claim to know every bit of her, not when she's showing me glimpses of pieces I've never seen before. But I know *my* intentions.

"I am heartily tired of people thinking they know what's best for me." She rubs her thumb back and forth against the underside my cock where it flares. "Why don't you start worrying about *you*? What do you want, Charon? Right here? Right now?"

I want to marry you.

I won't say it. I might be all in for this woman, but she's not quite there yet for me. How can she be? Part of her still belongs to someone else. I've laid the groundwork for Orpheus to give those pieces of her back, but who knows if he'll take me up on it? Who knows if we even need him to anymore?

"Charon?"

There are a thousand ways this could go wrong. I meant what I said before about wanting to romance her soft and slow. But I'm not a fool. I know how to divorce what I think she should have from what she actually wants. "Is that what you want? Right here, right now?"

"And if it is?" There it is again, that brattiness that I want to wrap up and bolster for the rest of my fucking life.

I shift closer, pressing my cock more firmly against her palm. "Prove it."

"Prove it?" She leans closer until her breath ghosts against the front of my throat. "Like this?" Eurydice hesitates, but I don't have a chance to tell her to keep going. She undoes the front of my pants with quick fingers and delves her hand inside. "Or like this?"

The shock of skin against skin snaps what's left of my leash. I wrap my hand around her wrist, pinning her to me. "You know how this works. Give me a safe word, baby." Technically, this is a conversation we should have had well before it got to the point of her hand in my pants, but I might die if she stops touching me now.

"*Lyre*."

I don't ask why, but part of me can't help wondering if the word has something to do with Orpheus. I push the thought away. "Good girl. Now, you have a choice."

"Mmm." She ignores my hand around her wrist and strokes me slowly, exploring the length of my cock. "What choice?" Her voice has gone low and sweet, but a thread of the earlier sauciness remains.

"You're going to let go of my cock and walk with me to my car."
Her grip tightens. "Or?"

"Or I'm going to fuck you right here in public where anyone walking past can see us claiming each other." My brakes are gone. There are a thousand reasons not to do this right here, right now, but I can't think of a single one. Not with her little gasp of surprise ghosting against my throat. "Decide, Eurydice."

She makes me wait, the little brat. She strokes my cock another time, two, and I let her. I might be hanging on by a thread, but I won't toss her over my shoulder and haul her cute little ass to my car. She has a choice. It's a narrow choice, but it's still a choice.

For the second time this week, I have absolutely no idea what she's going to do.

"Quite the decision." She inhales deeply and drags her nose over my throat. "It's cold out here. Take me to your car." Eurydice kisses my neck. "Anyone walking by can see still us...claiming... each other." Her hand tightens around my cock. "But at least we'll be warm."

My brain barely has time to comprehend her words before my body moves. I dip down and toss her over my shoulder. My car is just around the corner, so I pause to tuck my cock back into my pants before I stalk down the sidewalk to it.

I half expect Eurydice to squirm or holler, but she's relaxed and loose over my shoulder. I'm nearly to the car when she tugs up the hem of my shirt and plays her fingers across the small of my back. "Hurry up."

I hurry the fuck up.

No point in bothering with the front seat. We both know where this is going, and it's not me taking her back to the house. I yank open the back door and spill her down across the seat. She grins at me and grabs the front of my pants. "*Hurry up.*"

I follow her into the back seat and drag the door closed behind us. The sedan isn't the largest, and I curse as we try to untangle our limbs. Or I try to untangle and Eurydice works on getting my pants off.

"This isn't how it's supposed to be," I mutter as I jerk her pants over her hips and down her legs. She has to fold her knees nearly to her chest, and I curse again when I reach her boots. I can't yank them off without hurting her, so I force myself to slow down and untie them. "Supposed to be private. Just us."

"You've thought about it?" She wrestles her arms out of her coat and pulls her shirt over her head.

One boot, two boots, then I'm finally able to free her legs. I end up kneeling on the floorboard between her thighs.

Thought about it? I've craved her like a fire in my blood, but it's more than that. I want to fuck her, to hear her little sounds of pleasure, to know exactly what gets her off the hardest. No shit I want that. But I want everything else too. The mornings and the late nights and the bitchy days and the happy ones. "Haven't you?"

"Yes." She hooks my neck and then her mouth is on mine. Kissing me with the same desperation surging in my blood. I knew she was right here with me, but this is just further confirmation. This is happening. We're in this together.

I've imagined kissing Eurydice more times than I can count. Soft and sweet. Hard and frenetic. Everywhere in between. Reality is so different, it's barely comprehensible. She's warm and soft in my arms, and she teases my mouth open and takes what she wants. She tastes like peppermint, and it drives me wild.

She works my slacks down my hips and pulls me tight against her. I freeze at the feeling of her pussy against my length. She's wet and so hot, she practically scorches me.

Slow down. Slow the fuck down.

I break the kiss and press my forehead to hers. I'm breathing as if I've run a great distance. "Not supposed to be like this."

"You keep saying that." Her nails dig into my ass and she rolls her hips, rubbing herself up and down my length. We're pressed too tightly together for her to get me inside her, and I'm both grateful and furious about it. "Tell me how it's supposed to be, Charon."

"Supposed to be slow." I hardly sound like myself. "Wine you. Dine you. Seduce you properly." I press my forehead harder against hers, until it almost hurts. Too rough, but if I don't do something to ground myself, I'm going to be inside her. "Tease you until you're begging for it. Not in the back seat of my fucking car where anyone can see you taking my cock like a good girl."

"Charon." Eurydice licks my throat. "Maybe I want them to see." She's writhing against me almost desperately. "If you don't fuck me *right now*, I think I might die. We've waited so long. You can seduce me properly later. *Please.*"

I should deny her, but I'm already shifting back so she can grip my cock and guide me to her entrance. The feeling of being dragged through her wetness muddies my mind, but I still have the presence to grit out. "Condom."

"I'm on birth control." She rubs the head of my cock against her clit. The lone streetlight outside paints her small breasts in vivid detail, but leaves everything else in shadow. Her breath hitches. "If you want a condom, we can use one, but we don't need to."

I haven't been with anyone in the last year, and neither has she. I don't know if I'm supposed to know she got tested the month after all that shit went down with Orpheus, but I overheard Persephone and Hades talking. She'd been furious her sister even had to worry about that on top of everything else, but it'd come back negative.

I don't think Orpheus cheated on her, but it's not my place to say as much. Not then, and sure as fuck not now.

I want to do this with her without a single thing between us. Maybe it's sentimental, especially when there *is* something—some*one*—between us currently, but the desire remains. "Are you sure?" I manage.

In response, she lifts her hips and slides the head of my cock into her. I curse, long and hard, and fight against every instinct demanding I drive into her, claim this thing between us once and for all.

Slow isn't something I'm capable of right now, but I need this to be just as good for her as it is for me. "Touch yourself. Show me what you like."

Eurydice doesn't hesitate. She gives my cock one last stroke and moves her hand up to her clit. I curse again, hating the shadows hiding everything but the motion of her fingers from me. Next time. Next time I will spread her out on my bed and look my fill.

Right now, I'll have to go by touch alone.

I cover her hand with mine, letting her motions teach me exactly what she likes. She moans and rolls her hips, but I have just enough room to edge back so I don't sink deeper. Even the head of my cock inside her is sweet agony. I won't hold it together if I go deeper. "Not yet."

"*Please.*"

"Make yourself come, baby." I can't stop myself from cupping her breast with my free hand. "Come for me and then you can have every inch of this cock." She sobs out a breath and picks up her pace. I shake my head. "No, don't rush it." I knock her hand away and take its place. She's slippery beneath my thumb. Warm and wet and just for me. I mimic the motions she was doing on her own, vertical strokes that tease her eager little clit.

"*Charon.*" She starts to shake, pressing her head against the seat hard as she tries to arch harder into my touch. "Don't stop. I'm so close."

I can't see her face clearly, but I can read all the signs. I shift my touch on her breast and pinch her nipple lightly. She jolts and arches even harder into my hand. "You like that."

"More!"

I give her more. A little taste of pain to heighten her pleasure. It's a delicate balance that we can explore more fully later. Right now, I just need her to come more than I need the next beat of my heart.

She grabs my forearms, holding me in place as her body goes tense and she cries out. There. *That's* what I will spend the rest of my life chasing. I surge forward, sinking into her to the hilt and taking her mouth again. She clamps around me, so wet and tight that I nearly blow on the spot. I try to slow down, to pace myself, but she wraps her legs around my waist and then her nails find my ass again, digging in just enough to have pain sparking.

I thrust deeper. "Oh *fuck*." It's too late. My orgasm hits me before I can stop it. I'm helpless to do anything but keep mindlessly thrusting, trying to get deeper. "Fuck, fuck, *fuck*."

I collapse against her. Eurydice shivers a little, each move sends sparks of pleasure so acute that it's nearly pain through me. I can't believe that shit just happened. Any of it. I gather her close and kiss her temple. I'm not twenty anymore—it takes me a little longer to recover—but my cock threatens to twitch back to life. Fuck, but that was barely enough to take the edge off. "Sorry."

"Don't apologize." She gives another of those delicious shivers again. "I like that I affect you like that."

I like it too. But that doesn't mean I want to make a habit of it. My cock gives another twitch and I can't help but thrust again. She tightens her legs around my waist. I close my eyes, letting myself sink into the feel of her, of this really happening. "Again?"

"It feels good." She rolls her hips. "I...don't want to stop." She kisses my throat, my jaw, the corner of my mouth. "Keep fucking me, Charon. Until we can't fuck anymore."

I don't tell her it will take a lifetime before I'm satisfied with fucking her. Instead, I lean back just enough to tear off my shirt. I want to be skin-to-skin with her. I *need* it. Eurydice helps me get the shirt down my arms and then her fingers are in my hair and her mouth is on mine.

This time. This time, I'll take her slow. It's not a bed, but we have nowhere to be and no one to interrupt us. I couldn't stop if I wanted to.

ORPHEUS

6

I DON'T EVEN TRY TO SLEEP AFTER CHARON LEAVES. HIS words keep rattling around in my head, but the thing that has me pacing around my apartment, unable to stay still, is the realization that things really are over with Eurydice. They must be if she's moving on with *him*.

I don't fault her for that. I don't even try.

We were never going to get back together. I don't deserve that, even if in my heart of hearts, I desperately want a second chance. That old saying about you not knowing what you've got until it's gone is far too accurate. The problem is that once you've done something to lose that priceless person, you don't deserve them back.

But if she's not able to move on…

"No." I shake my head, hard. "We're not going down that road." I'm barely holding on as it is. Hope will destroy me utterly. All this time, I've said I just want to be able to apologize. Get closure. All that shit. Hoping that Eurydice will do anything but spit in my face is a fool's dream.

I turn for my door, barely pausing to grab my jacket. Maybe I am a fool. It's the only explanation I have for finding myself, less than an hour later, standing at the Cypress Bridge.

I've never been to the lower city. Initially that was because *no one* in the upper city crossed the River Styx. Then, when Hades went public, I sure as fuck wasn't going to get an invite. In my time spent drinking alone in bars over the last couple months, I've heard people brag about trying to cross the bridge without an invitation. Apparently it's painful enough that all of them were driven back to the upper city, telling tales comparing just how far they made it before the sensation was too much.

I don't like pain. I never have. It's sure as fuck not something I seek out in my life, though I've had plenty dogging my heels since I fucked things up with Eurydice.

Penance.

This is just one component of it. She was hurt that night. Because of my actions. Because of the choices I made. Because I valued my ambition more than I valued the woman I loved.

I deserve a little pain. More than a little.

I take a deep breath and start across the bridge. The fog makes it feel otherworldly. Dangerous. Downright malicious, even.

Eurydice is on the other side of this bridge, and if I have to go through torment to reach her to make things right, it's nothing less than she experienced. I can do this. I *have* to do this. Neither of us will ever get the closure we need if I don't.

At first I think it's nerves causing my skin to prickle. But with each step I take, the prickling gets stronger. First irritating. Then painful, as if I left acetone on my broken skin. No, not acetone.

Fucking *acid*. I flinch and duck my head, but it makes no difference. The sensation follows me, digging in to my skin regardless of how I hold my body.

I'm not even halfway.

"It doesn't matter. I can do this" I pick up my pace, or I try. The soles of my feet ache as if I'm walking on knives. Sharp, stabbing motions pierce my soles, the feeling so real, I actually turn back to see if I've left bloody footprints in my wake. There's nothing but fog and concrete, and if that's not a metaphor I refuse to examine, I don't know what is. The upper city bank is no longer visible behind me.

The temptation rises to give up. Pain sears me and I know if I just turn around, just let my cowardice guide me, the pain will relent.

Instead, I turn back toward the lower city. For *her*. Putting *her* needs first for once.

I grit my teeth and keep going, staggering step after step. My world narrows down to putting one foot in front of the other. The knives beneath my soles turn into a fiery furnace that feels like it's melting flesh from bone. The burning of my skin morphs into a thousand pinpricks of agony, as if I'm being swarmed by a cloud of invisible insects.

For her. You're doing this for her, you pathetic monster. What are a few moments of pain compared to what she's suffered as a result of your actions? You say you care about her, that you want her to be happy and free? Prove it.

The voice in my head almost sounds like Charon, but it drives me harder, faster forward. I could weep with relief when I see the other arch if I had the strength for it. I don't. Instead, I just keep working my way, one shambling step after another, toward it.

Just when I think I can't handle it anymore, that the pain will actually kill me, or at least send me to my knees to suffer until someone comes along to put me out of my misery, I step through the arch.

Everything stops.

The sudden lack of torment hurts almost as much as the pain itself. I stagger forward. "Fuck. Oh fuck." Every breath is sweet bliss. I carefully shake out my arms and legs, testing to see if I'm really okay. Again, I look behind me, certain I left a bloody path along the stones of the bridge. Again, I see nothing.

I seem none the worse for wear, but that doesn't stop a shudder from working through my body. I don't understand how the boundaries work—not the one around Olympus, and not the one between the upper city and lower city. I don't know if I believe in magic, but it's hard to argue with it when I'm still feeling the phantom bites on my skin. I shudder again and rub my arms, willing away the memory of what I just experienced.

There's nothing to do but look around. I didn't have much of a plan when I set out from my apartment earlier, and now I realize how foolhardy it was to come down here.

I don't even have my phone. I'm lucky I remembered to grab my keys and lock my door behind me.

It's the middle of the night. It's not as if I can just ask around until someone tells me where to find Eurydice. Besides, I already know where to find her. Hades and Persephone's house. She's been mostly living with them for the last year.

Hades isn't Zeus, who marks his presence in his territory with a giant-ass skyscraper that can be seen from every corner of the city. Even so, surely it won't be that hard to find his home. I don't relish facing down him and his wife...mostly his wife...but it's a necessary step to get the closure both Eurydice and I need.

For me to apologize. To verbalize all the ways I've failed her and acknowledge that I can never properly make it right. To give her the closure she needs to be able to finally move on and be happy.

With Charon.

I pick a direction at random and start walking. Maybe I'll just wander around until businesses start opening up and go from there. If I see someone before then, I'll ask them. As far as plans go, it leaves a lot to be desired, but it's the best I have.

I almost don't pay attention to the parked car as I approach. It's a black sedan that looks identical to the ones the Thirteen and legacy families use to travel around, which means it's nondescript but high-end. That gives me pause enough to slow down. I see the fogged windows and grimace. "Not my business," I mutter and start to pick up my pace.

Then I hear the moan.

I would know that moan in my sleep. High and breathy and with just a hint of desperation that says she's close to coming. *Eurydice.*

Impossible.

Even as I think it, I approach the car. This is a mistake. *I'm* mistaken, and I'm about to make an ass out of myself playing Peeping Tom. But I don't stop. Not until I'm right next to the car.

The lone streetlight overhead gives off barely enough light to see through the fogged windows to the bodies moving within. Even with the slight distortion, I recognize them. Eurydice is on Charon's lap, her back to his chest, riding him with her legs spread wide. He kisses her neck and has one hand cupping her pussy, stroking her clit in the exact motion that will get her off, while the other plays with her tits.

He's got a big cock. It's a strange thing to notice, but even from here, I can see the way he spreads her. It makes my stomach flip and my skin go tight. Jealousy. Anger. Even desire. It's all there, but I can barely feel those emotions.

Not when the pit of loss opens beneath me, sucking them down, sweeping away everything. I really am a fool. I hadn't realized I'd started to hope, even as I told myself not to.

That hope is gone now.

Eurydice comes, making that sound I know so damn well. Charon grabs her hips, holding her firm as he drives up into her, chasing his own orgasm. I need to stop watching. They haven't noticed I'm here, too wrapped up in each other to realize they're no longer alone. But I don't move away.

Apparently she didn't need me to make the journey here, after all. She's moved on with him on her own strength, and even as it feels like someone is dicing my heart to pieces, I experience...relief. My shitty actions didn't ruin her chance at happiness. How arrogant that I thought they could in the first place.

I'm still standing there, staring like a fool, when Eurydice looks up and screams. Things happen quickly after that. A blink and the car door flies open. Another blink and a naked Charon has me pinned to the car with a gun pressed under my chin.

We really are nearly the same height.

The thought is so absurd, I almost laugh.

Charon's eyes go wide. "Orpheus?"

"You're still hard." I don't know why I say it. It doesn't matter that I can feel his cock pressed against me. It's the *gun* I should be more worried about. It's like the events of the last hour or so have broken me, taking what little self-preservation I still had.

"*Orpheus?*"

"Get back in the car," Charon barks.

Eurydice ignores him. She climbs out of the car barefoot without any pants on. She's stopped to shrug into his shirt, but that's it. She pushes her hair back from her face, a frown pulling her brows together. "What are you doing here?"

"*Eurydice.*"

I ignore the warning in his voice and answer. "I came to apologize." Each word causes the gun to dig into my jaw. Maybe he really will kill me. The threat of death should worry me, but it's as if my brain broke. Shock, maybe, though I thought shock only came from traumatic events.

This fits the bill.

"Charon," she snaps, tone harder than I've ever heard her speak. "You are *not* going to murder my ex-boyfriend. Put the gun away."

He hesitates long enough that I think he might shoot me and be done with it, but he finally shoves away from me with a curse. Honestly, it's not better. Because now I can see him...can see *them*. I don't miss the fact that Charon steps between me and Eurydice. He seems completely unbothered that he's naked standing on the street, but then why would he be? Hades rules the lower city, and Charon is his right-hand man. There isn't a single person on this side of the River Styx who would touch him.

I shouldn't look. Not at her and not him, but apparently I'm a glutton for misery. When I came across the river, looking to make things right, somehow I never expected to find this.

Charon is perfectly made. As good as he looked earlier this evening, he looks even better stark naked standing barefoot on the street. The streetlight catches the sweat glistening on his muscles, and the wetness coating his cock. I can't help staring. "You didn't use a condom."

"Why you—"

Eurydice catches Charon's arm, wrapping her hands around his bulging bicep. "Charon, we can't do this here."

"It won't take me long, baby. I'll take care of this, and then we can go back to my place." He doesn't sound like the man I met earlier tonight. Gone is the thin veneer of control, replaced by a barely contained rage. I knew he was capable of violence; he wouldn't have lasted long in his current position if that wasn't the case. Hades might have the public perception of being a benevolent leader, but this is Olympus. No one in power keeps their hands clean, which means no one who serves them does either.

"*Charon.*"

This is it. This is where he kills me. Again, some part of me, buried deep inside, is screaming that I am far too calm about this. I don't want to die, but I've spent the last nine months in misery, moving through my days in a strange sort of half life. I can't stand the thought of one more day of it. I don't like pain, no, but maybe it will clarify things.

At this point, it's the only thing I haven't tried.

But Charon doesn't raise the gun. He doesn't pull the trigger.

Instead, he allows Eurydice to urge him back several steps. She turns him to face her and shoots me an unreadable look, and then pulls him closer to speak in low voices.

Even though it hurts, I can't stop watching them. The way she touches him so casually. The way his hand comes to rest on the small of her back, even as his gaze tracks the area around us, searching for threats. He appears to be giving her his full attention, but I don't think anybody could get the drop on him right now.

And he's still fucking naked.

His back is just as impressive as his front, firm muscles with a delicious amount of softness, a thick ass, and equally thick thighs balancing him out perfectly. If I had any desire to paint these days... and maybe really did have a death wish...I might ask him to pose for me.

If we were different people, he might say yes.

If we were different people, I might try to use that opportunity to seduce him. He's not pretty, but he's damned magnetic.

I shake my head. I can't help but laugh a little at the absurdity of where my thoughts have gone. I've always had terrible taste in men and only slightly better taste in everyone else. Eurydice was the exception to that rule, and look how that turned out.

"Orpheus."

I blink. Eurydice has been saying my name for some time now, I think. At least her tone has an awful lot of exasperation that says this is the case. "What?"

It's not Eurydice who answers me. "Get in the fucking car." Charon doesn't wait for me to answer. He just grabs the back of my neck and hauls me where he wants me to go. Eurydice barely gets the back door open in time for him to shove me inside. It's a testament to his control that he doesn't bash my head on the side of the car in the process.

His clothes are scattered on the floor of the back seat—both of their clothes. The whole space smells like sex. There's a goddamn wet spot under my hand. Clearly, they had been at it for some time before I happened across them. I hate that...but there's some part of me that can't get the image of them fucking out of my mind. It's a curse of being an artist, but I have an exceptionally good memory. All I have to do is close my eyes, and I can see his big hands on her body and his even bigger cock spreading her pussy wide. I'm only human; I can't help that *my* cock hardens in response.

Eurydice takes the front passenger seat, and Charon slides behind the wheel.

Still. Fucking. Naked.

Neither of them speaks as he puts the car in gear and pulls away from the curb. At this point, I have nothing useful to say. I can't even guarantee what will come out of my mouth if I start talking. I came here to apologize, but I really don't need to be taken to a secondary location for that to happen.

But if that's what Eurydice wants, then that's what I will do. I owe her.

I expect them to take me to wherever Hades and Persephone reside, but I highly doubt that those two live in the neat little town house Charon finally stops in front of. There are no lights on in any of the buildings nearby, but he snaps his fingers at me. "Give me my pants."

The absurdity of the situation draws a slightly hysterical chuckle for my lips. "Yeah. Of course." It takes me a second to figure out which pair of pants is his, and then I hand them over.

Within a few minutes, the three of us are walking up the path to the front door. Charon unlocks it and stands aside so we can precede him into the town house. I don't know what I expected to find inside, but once Eurydice flips on the light with the familiarity of someone who's been here before, it reveals a surprisingly charming home.

Dark tile floors are softened by a thick rug that pulls the whole living room together. Dark leather couches, sturdy end tables that look like they're made out of driftwood, and a large fireplace round out the room. A huge TV hangs over the fireplace, and I recognize several different game consoles on the mantel, but I didn't expect the art that hangs on the wall.

Without thinking, I drift toward the pair of paintings. They *are* paintings—not prints. If I had stopped to think on what kind of art a man like Charon might have in his house, my first thought would've been that he wouldn't have art at all. My second thought would be that if he *did* have art, it would be some kind of cheesy hypermasculine nonsense. Not this.

They're landscapes.

The artist obviously intended them to be a matching set. While they are positioned differently, they both show the same gorgeous, moody forest. The longer I stare, the more details I pick up. The mushrooms growing out of the side of a tree trunk. The flowers tucked in the shadow of a boulder. A bird sitting protectively in its nest.

I could stare at these paintings for hours.

Unfortunately, that's not what I'm here for. I may have forgotten for a moment, but then Charon breaks the silence. "I'll ask you again, Orpheus. What the fuck are you doing here?"

"You invited me." I speak absently, a good portion of my attention still on the painting in front of me.

"I sure as fuck didn't."

"Charon?" The tone in Eurydice's voice brings us both up short. She looks back and forth between us, an expression flaring in her dark eyes that I've never seen before. Fury. "What is he talking about? *You* invited him here?"

7

EURYDICE

IT ONLY TAKES ONE LOOK AT CHARON'S FACE TO KNOW the truth. "You *did* invite him here." I can't help the betrayal that seeps into my tone. We may have talked about this last night, and I may have admitted that I have some unresolved baggage when it comes to Orpheus, but for Charon to go over my head and invite him to the lower city…

He had no right to do that.

He had *no right*.

Orpheus turns to face us. I still haven't quite processed that he's here, let alone that he looks so different. His hair has grown out a lot in the last year, now hanging to his shoulders. He's not dressed in his usual perfect style, his simple T-shirt and faded jeans the kind of thing he never would have been caught dead wearing in public. He also seems…tired. Worn down. I can't quite put my finger on why, but it's there all the same.

He caught me having sex with Charon.

I flush and then mentally curse myself for flushing. I have nothing to apologize for, but it doesn't change the fact that it's beyond an embarrassing situation to be caught by your ex-boyfriend having sex with... I'm not even sure what Charon is to me at this point. We haven't talked about labels. Does agreeing to give this a shot mean we're dating? Are we friends with benefits? The latter doesn't feel right, but I'm still aching from the feel of his cock and his hands on my body. I haven't had a chance to deal with any of it.

First Orpheus. Then Charon.

Except it's not that easy. Charon is the reason Orpheus is here, and he doesn't look the least apologetic about it.

I rub my face. I'm sticky and achy and mostly naked. This is not the way I want to have whatever conversation this is, but asking Charon to go get my clothes out of his car will leave me alone with Orpheus, and... Actually, that's a good idea. "I would like my clothes."

Charon narrows his eyes. "You're trying to get rid of me."

My patience is nonexistent right now. I glare. "Or quite possibly, I don't want to have a serious conversation with my ex while wearing your shirt with you dripping down my thighs."

Orpheus clears his throat and turns back to the paintings on the wall. A year ago, he would have launched into a fight without hesitation over something like this. I don't know what it means that he's so subdued. I don't like it, even if I'm marginally grateful for it.

Charon hesitates but finally gives a sharp nod. "Fine."

I barely wait for him to close the front door behind him to turn to Orpheus. "Why are you here?"

"I came to apologize." He turns back to me slowly. His gaze flows over me, from the crown of my head to my bare feet and back again. There's something in his dark eyes that I can't quite define, but he shields it from me before I can figure it out. "I know it's far too little, too late, but I'm sorry that you were harmed because of my actions. I was a selfish little prick, and it never occurred to me that you might be in any danger when Zeus asked me for that favor."

"Would it have made a difference?" It's the question that's lingered through all these months, that's caused me to lose more sleep than I'll ever admit. Orpheus is selfish and conceited and occasionally cruel, but he was never violent. Then again, *he* wasn't the one who committed violence against me. Zeus's man did. Would Orpheus condone that if he thought it would feed his ambition and get him closer to the most powerful person in Olympus?

His eyes fly to mine. "Of course it would have made a difference." He sounds genuinely shocked I'm even asking. I don't *think* he's lying, but I can't quite be sure. Orpheus scrubs a hand over his face. "This won't earn me any points, but after your sister made a public fool of Zeus, I honestly thought all he wanted was to be photographed with you and use that to draw her back to the upper city."

I blink. "Surely you can't be that much a fool. You know where you told me to meet you." I shake my head, my heart sinking. "And even if you thought Zeus was the one meeting me, you know how he was with women." A monster. It's common knowledge that he most likely murdered all three of his wives, and he committed violence against no small number of women less powerful than him.

In Olympus, everyone is less powerful than Zeus.

That man is gone, fallen to his death from the top of Dodona Tower, and his son seems to be cut of slightly different cloth. Still a monster, but not one who hurts those weaker than himself. At least not without cause.

I shake my head again, trying to focus. "Gods, Orpheus."

"I know." He sinks onto the couch and hangs his head. "I fucking know. I don't deserve your forgiveness. I'm not asking for it. I'm here to give you whatever closure you need. I just…I don't know how to do it beyond apologizing."

The front door opens before I can form a reply. Charon steps inside, his gaze flicking between me and Orpheus. He passes me my clothes. "Here."

As much as I want to escape this situation, I don't quite trust them to be alone together. I yank on my panties and jeans. That will have to do. I feel slightly more centered once I have pants on. "I don't know what I'm supposed to say."

I don't know what I *want* to say.

Every time I look at him, it hurts, but that's not the only thing I feel. Something strums in my chest, a feeling of rightness that only seems to come when we're in the same room. It doesn't matter how much he hurt me, because that damned connection is still there. I thought for certain it would be gone, that I would have exorcised it along with all the other parts of me I can no longer stand.

It's not gone.

If anything, it's stronger than before.

"You don't have to say anything." Orpheus pushes slowly to his feet. I've never seen him look so defeated. His shoulders are bowed and his head down. "Like I said, I'm not here to ask anything of you. I've said what I came here to say. If at some point you want or need more, all you have to do is ask. We can talk or you can yell at me or whatever you need." He drags in a breath and glances at Charon. "More than that, I'm...I'm glad you're happy, Eurydice. I really am. Even if it's not with me."

I don't know what's happening to my chest. There's an awful fluttering, wrenching feeling that only gets worse as he starts for the door. If he walks through it now, this ends for good. That's what I thought I wanted, but now that it's happening, I'm panicking. "Wait."

Charon goes still. It's the same almost predatory lack of movement as last night. He doesn't contradict me though. He just looks at me and waits for whatever I'm about to say.

Orpheus is doing the same, but somehow it's so much worse. He's never been that good at hiding what he's feeling, and right now there's a blossoming hope in his eyes that only makes the feeling in my chest worse. I can't give him my heart again. I *can't*.

But I...don't want him to walk out that door—or out of my life.

Apparently I really am a fool who never learns from her mistakes. It's the only explanation, because this man may have brought me great joy, but he's also brought me the greatest sorrow of my life. I should be *happy* to see the last of him.

Instead, I find myself repeating, "Wait." I don't know what else to say. I don't know what else I want, just that I can't let him leave. Not yet. "Please."

Orpheus turns more fully to face me. "Whatever you want, Eurydice."

Whatever I want.

That's the ridiculous part of this. I don't know what I want. Once upon a time, I thought I did. I thought it would be him and me for the rest of our lives. Marriage. Children. Growing old together, surrounded by family. Riding the edges of the waves of power in this city without actively engaging with them.

I realize those were naive dreams. Orpheus had always had his sights set on something more than a mundane life. He wouldn't have sacrificed me if that weren't true.

But I can't quite release those dreams. Even with our history. Even with Charon here, watching us with an unreadable expression on his face.

He's the one who moves first. Of course he is. If left to our own devices, I have no doubt Orpheus and I would stand here all night, staring at each other and unable to say the words tangling up inside us. I don't know what I want, and I don't know what I need, but there's a part of me that longs to lash out at him, to hurt him the way he hurt me. Just like there's another part of me that doesn't want him to ever leave.

Charon steps between us. "It's late. Take the couch, Orpheus. We'll talk in the morning."

Orpheus opens his mouth, seeming about to argue, but finally nods. "Yeah. Sure. Okay."

I don't resist as Charon presses a hand to the small of my back and guides me down the hall to his room. I've been here dozens of times over the last couple months. He technically has a room in the main house, but he likes a little privacy at times, and he gave me an open invitation to stay here whenever I like. Whether he's present or not.

He closes the bedroom door behind us. Once again, it strikes me that we haven't had an opportunity to discuss what we did in the back seat. The intentions we declared with only the darkness as witness. My body flares with heat at the memory of how deliciously he stretched me. I shiver. "Charon—"

"Not yet, baby." He catches my wrist and turns me to face him. He's usually serious, but his expression is almost empty, it's so stoic right now. "Before we talk about us, we need to talk about him."

"What do you mean?" My voice squeaks a little.

He studies me. "You wanted closure, but things aren't closed. Seeing him opened up some shit."

He's not wrong, but I kind of hate that he's speaking the things I can barely admit to myself. I tug on my wrist, and he releases me. "I thought it would be gone." I wrap my arms around myself. "There was always this connection between us, and I thought what he did would sever it, but it's still there." Stronger, even.

"I see."

I *hate* how empty he sounds. I tighten my grip on myself. "We have a connection too, you know. It's just different. I meant everything I said both last night and tonight. I love you. I want to be with you if you can accept a damaged heart. I just…I didn't think I would feel like this if I saw him again."

"I know." Charon sighs, and all the tension leaks out of him. "This complicates things."

"What do you mean?"

For a long moment, I think he won't answer, but he leans back against the door with another sigh. "I meant what I said before too. The joy of being with you outweighs the potential pain of not having all of you. But now that he's here? We can't move on without dealing with him." He shakes his head slowly. "Maybe we can't move on without *him*."

The awful feeling inside me grows thorns that tear into me. Between one blink and the next, I'm back on that dark street, my breath sawing through my lungs, my feet screaming in pain, the fear so overwhelming that I was certain my heart would burst. "I don't see a future with him."

"No lies between us, baby." Charon pushes off the door and crosses to me. He moves slowly, carefully resting his hands on my hips. "You're still hurt and furious, but all those feelings haven't gone away."

"I wish they would," I whisper. I'm glad Orpheus felt the need to apologize, but that doesn't change the pain he caused. It doesn't take it away. "It would be so much easier."

"Life doesn't work like that." Charon's fingers pulse on my hips as if he can't quite help himself, but he releases me and steps back. "Give him a chance to make it right."

I jolt. "Excuse me?"

"If you send him away now, he'll always be between us." His blue eyes are so intense, I have to struggle to hold his gaze. "If he's going to be between us, I'd rather him *be* between us. It's easier to deal with the man himself than the memory."

I can't believe he's saying this. "We just had sex, and you want my ex to stick around."

"What I want is you." He slices a hand through the air. "*You*, Eurydice. Whatever that means, whoever that includes. If that means he comes too, then so be it."

"Just like that," I whisper. "Surely it's not that simple."

"It is for me." He finally lowers his gaze, releasing me. "He wants to pay penance, and you deserve to have penance paid. I don't give a fuck what that looks like. Stick a collar around his neck and walk him like a dog if that will make you happy. Fuck him. Sleep with him. Do what you need to do."

"But—"

He steps into me and catches my chin in a light, firm grip. "But make no mistake, none of that threatens *us*, baby. We crossed that bridge tonight, and there's no going back. You and me, we're endgame."

CHARON

MY PHONE RINGS WHILE EURYDICE IS IN THE SHOWER. I know who it will be even before I pick up—no one calls this late unless it's business. Sure enough, Hades's name scrolls across my screen. I glance at the door to the bathroom, refusing to feel guilty that I was fucking his sister-in-law in the back seat of my car a short time ago, and answer, "Yeah?"

"We have a problem." Hades isn't one for small talk, and that's only gotten more pronounced in the last two months since we found out Persephone is pregnant. He never fucked around with security when it came to her or the lower city, but now he's downright draconian. "I need you at the greenhouse. Take Medusa."

I raise my brows. Medusa has shifted almost seamlessly from her old career as Athena's knife-for-hire to working security for Hades, but there are times when her skills have come in handy. Not that Hades orders anyone killed. He doesn't. But some situations are more dangerous than others, and for him to specifically direct me to bring her means he thinks this will be one of those times. "I'll go now."

"Report to me directly with what you find." He hangs up without another word.

"Thanks, Hades. Appreciate all the information." I crack my neck and take the time to change into a clean set of clothing. Eurydice is still in the shower. I hesitate outside the door. She's rattled and right now isn't the time to press her, but I'm not leaving without letting her know what's going on.

I step into the bathroom. "Eurydice."

"Yes?" She turns off the shower and pokes her head out. She can't seem to decide if she wants to waltz out naked or be bashful, which I find unspeakably charming.

"I've been called in. I don't know when I'll be back." I hesitate. "Do you want me to drop you at the house?"

"No." She shakes her head and snags the closest towel. I like nice shit, and towels are included in that. It's a big fluffy thing that covers her from chest to knees as she steps out of the shower. "I don't want to have to explain to Persephone what's going on until it's resolved. If you're okay with it, I'd prefer to stay here."

If I'm okay with her staying in my town house and sleeping in my bed. I might laugh, but she'd read it the wrong way. "I'm good with that. Keep your phone on you."

She smiles faintly. "I always do."

We need to have about a dozen conversations, and we don't have labels or shit that would make me feel better, but I'll be damned before I leave without kissing her goodbye. I step forward and press my lips lightly to hers. "Sleep well, baby."

"I'll try." She lifts her fingers to her lips as I turn and leave the bathroom.

The lights in the living room are off, but I can clearly see Orpheus on the couch, shirtless with one arm flung over his eyes. I don't know if he's sleeping or just faking it, but I pause and allow myself to look at him.

He really is pretty. He's also not what I expected. I thought he'd come in here, all blustering and defensive, and instead he just seems sad and defeated. It's disconcerting. Throwing him out feels like kicking a dog, and I don't make a habit of hurting those who don't deserve it.

He *does* deserve it, but that doesn't change that my instincts are conflicted when it comes to him.

I turn without another word and leave the town house, making sure to lock the front door behind me. The street is just as quiet as it was when we arrived, but I still pause and look around.

Something feels...off.

It would be easy enough to brush the feeling away, but I find myself pulling my phone out of my pocket and dialing Minthe. She answers on the second ring, her voice groggy. "This better be good."

"I need someone on my street."

"What?" She yawns and, when she speaks again, sounds more awake. "Something going on?"

"I don't know." I turn a slow circle, but nothing seems to be out of place. "Just a feeling."

"Okay." Another yawn. "I'll be there in twenty."

"You don't have to do it personally."

"Yeah, I do. No reason to drag anyone else out of bed. Send someone to relieve me around breakfast."

Minthe can be a pain in the ass, but she's reliable as fuck. "Thanks."

"That's what friends are for." She hangs up without another word. Part of me is tempted to wait until she shows up to leave, but Hades wouldn't have summoned me to the greenhouse without good reason. Time is of the essence.

I call Medusa as I climb into my car and head out. I'm not surprised she's still awake, just like I'm not surprised that she doesn't ask any questions. She and her girlfriend, Calypso, seem to be night owls naturally. Either that, or Medusa bolts into wakefulness without any delay. Considering her former line of work that's just as likely.

The drive is short enough that I don't have much time to think. It's just as well; tonight took more turns than I could've ever anticipated. First with Eurydice instigating things between us, and us losing control in my back seat. Then with Orpheus showing up in the lower city *tonight* of all nights.

I don't want to think about Orpheus though.

I pull to a stop in front of the greenhouse. Technically, it's a flower shop that's been owned by the same family for several generations. Most businesses in the lower city are like that; they can trace their lineage parallel to the history of Olympus. Some of them are transplants. It's not common for people to move into the city from the greater world, but it's not entirely unheard of either.

Matthew's family has owned this flower shop, and the greenhouse above it, since the city was founded. He's the last of them now, except for a distant cousin who lives out near the warehouse district.

I don't know why anyone would fuck with Matthew or the flower shop. There's no money to be had here, and as far as I can tell, he doesn't house any flowers or plants that are rare enough to tempt someone to steal from him.

The only value this place holds is for the people who live in the lower city. Hades in particular comes here when he needs time and space to think. These days, Persephone comes with him.

All the lights are on as I climb out of my car and head toward the building. The big glass windows are untouched, but someone has thrown a brick through the glass door. Matthew is on his knees, trying to sweep the glass into a bin.

He looks up as I approach, and the sheer relief on his face makes me uneasy. "Thank the gods you're here."

We don't see much crime in the lower city, but it does exist. It's a city, after all. Still, Hades rules with a firm and fair hand, and most people are all too happy to obey the rules. I can't remember the last time I've seen something like this. Maybe a few years back when the last Zeus sent his people over the river to cause problems. He, of course, claimed innocence when confronted, but we all knew it was him.

I step carefully over the glass. Nothing else seems to be disturbed, which is a relief. Or it would be if Matthew didn't look like he was about to cry. I crouch down next to him. "Tell me what happened."

"Alarms went off about thirty minutes ago. I was asleep, so it took me a few minutes to get down here to figure out what was going on." He sniffles, and his hands shake where they hold the short broom. "Charon, they…" He looks to the door that leads up the narrow set of stairs to the greenhouse. I hadn't realized it was cracked until now. "They destroyed *everything*."

Oh, fuck.

I don't get a chance to respond, because Medusa walks through the front door. She's a tall white woman with close-cropped blond hair, and nearly as many muscles as me. Despite the cool temperature, she's wearing a T-shirt that leaves her arms exposed, revealing her scars and snake tattoos.

"Help him clean up, and keep watch." I rise to my feet and head toward the door to the second floor. "I need to assess the damage."

"Will do." She carefully nudges Matthew away from the broken glass and divests him of the broom and bin in such a smooth move that he's left blinking at her. Good. She's got things well in hand.

As bad as I was worried it would be, it's worse. The entire second floor of the building has been a greenhouse for generations. Now it's just a mess. The narrow aisles between the plants are covered with shattered glass, dirt, torn stems, and trampled flowers. I make my way around as best I can and pause in front of the sitting room that I'm nearly one hundred percent sure was created solely for Hades.

It's been entirely demolished.

The furniture is in pieces. They knocked over the bookshelf and took the time to rip several books to shreds. This wasn't a robbery, but then I knew that before I even arrived. Hades wouldn't have called me out of bed for something as simple as a robbery. No, this was a targeted attack.

Against Hades.

"Fuck." I drag my hand through my hair. A year ago, I would've assumed that Zeus was behind this, but our current Zeus isn't the type to pull some petty bullshit like this. Besides, he has bigger fish to fry.

Which is the problem. A year ago, the list of our enemies was long but finite. Now, the possibilities are endless. It may be one of the Thirteen, deciding to take advantage of the chaos to fuck with Hades. Or it may be some disgruntled citizen, either from the lower city or the upper city, who wasn't ballsy enough to attempt murder, but wanted to cause pain all the same.

Or it might be the enemy everyone is worried about.

Not Minos. He's watched too closely to pull something like this. But he works for someone, and we still haven't been able to figure out who. Theoretically, the boundary that separates Olympus from the rest of the world should also separate us from our enemies...but the boundary is failing.

It's possible people are slipping through. We can't take anything for granted these days.

I go through the place as thoroughly as I can, but there's nothing to find. Whoever caused all this destruction knew what they were about, and they left nothing to indicate their identity.

Eventually, exhaustion drags me down the stairs to where Medusa is waiting alone. The glass has long since been cleaned up, and she managed to find some wood from somewhere to nail to the doorframe to cover the space left by the broken glass.

"I made Matthew some tea and sent him to bed."

I raise my brows at that. "I'm surprised he agreed to go to bed. He was pretty distraught."

"Yeah." She shrugs. "But he didn't have much choice since I drugged him."

"Medusa!"

"What? He wasn't going to be able to relax. I helped."

Her tendency to drug people seems to be a little habit she picked up from her girlfriend. I sigh. "Did he consent to being drugged?"

"Oh...well..." She blushes, her pale skin turning bright pink. "I helped?" She sounds significantly less sure of herself this time.

I pinch the bridge of my nose and fight down my frustration. "We talked about this. You can't just drug people, even if it's technically helpful."

"Sorry." She almost sounds like she means it. She turns to look at the cash register. "He had a couple hundred bucks in there, but they didn't even bother to take it."

I suspected as much, but hearing the confirmation makes my stomach sink. Robbery is never a good thing. But this is worse. "Someone wanted to make an example."

"Example?" She frowns harder. "But they just smashed some shit."

There are times when I forget that Medusa used to kill people for a living. This certainly isn't one of them. "If they had hurt Matthew, that would be all the declaration of war. This is more insidious. This place is somewhere that Hades and Persephone, the rulers of the lower city, come to feel safe. By destroying this, they're saying they can get to them. They're saying that our leaders don't have safe spaces." I turned for the door, my mind already racing. There aren't many places where Hades and Persephone visit with any regularity.

Even so, I need to make some calls. Just because Matthew wasn't hurt this time doesn't mean someone won't be in the next attack. Because there *will* be a next attack.

I'd stake my life on it.

ORPHEUS

I WAKE TO THE SOUND OF SOMEONE MOVING AROUND the kitchen. There's absolutely no reason for me to expect it to be Eurydice, but even after nearly a year apart, I would know her soft footfall anywhere. Part of me wants to lie here with my eyes closed and prolong the moment before this all comes crashing down on me.

She may have been hesitant to see the back of me last night, but that was an emotional moment, and I had just shown up when she didn't expect me. I'd be a fool to hope that maybe she misses me even a fraction as much as I miss her.

I *am* a fool.

Still, it's better to get this over with. I sit up and climb to my feet. The kitchen is down the hall from the living room where I spent the night, so I follow the sounds of Eurydice puttering until I find my way.

I stop in the doorway and allow myself to drink in the sight of her. She looked good last night, of course. This morning she's like something out of a dream. Sunlight filters in through the window, giving the room an almost dreamlike quality. She's wearing an oversized T-shirt that must belong to Charon. It dwarfs her, but it only hits the tops of her thighs, leaving her long light-brown legs bare. I'm strangely delighted to discover she's painted her toenails a bright yellow.

I clear my throat to let her know that I'm here, but she doesn't even flinch. She just glances over her shoulder and gives me a tight smile. "Morning."

"Morning." I don't know what else to say. Do I apologize again? Do I turn around and quietly leave? The thought of doing the latter makes my feet feel as if they are filled with concrete. I don't care if she hates me, just as long as I don't have to leave her presence. Selfish. I'm so fucking selfish. Apparently I haven't learned anything at all.

Eurydice doesn't say anything else. It takes me a few seconds to realize what she's doing, and I take a step into the kitchen without thinking about it. "Pancakes?"

"I was in the mood."

This is so fucking awkward. It feels so good and yet hurts so badly, all at the same time. I find myself speaking without thinking it through. "I know coming back around has complicated things for you. I'm sorry. If you and Charon are—"

"Me and Charon have nothing to do with this." She sets the bowl on the counter with a little more force than necessary. "He's giving me the space to do what I need in order to get over you."

It feels like she just reached out and punched me in the stomach. "What do you need in order to get over me?"

"If I knew, that would make things so much easier." She sighs. "Charon had some suggestions."

Every word out of her mouth is a knife between my ribs, and yet I never want her to stop. At least she's talking to me. "What did he suggest?" I find myself asking.

Her lips twist, and for moment I think she won't answer me. But then she says, "He said he doesn't care if I put a collar on you and walk you like a dog, fuck you, or sleep with you. That he and I are endgame."

That strange feeling from last night is back, compounding in my chest until I can barely breathe past it. I hardly feel like myself as I sink to my knees before her. "Do it."

"What are you talking about?" She flutters her fingers at me. "Orpheus, get off the ground."

"I'm not saying you should fuck me. I would never presume after everything that happened." Even if I want her so desperately, it feels like I've been cursed, possessed, or have some kind of otherworldly influence over me. Maybe all three. I tap the front of my throat. "But if you want to collar me, I'm more than willing to pay penance that way."

"Orpheus, don't be ridiculous."

"He's not being ridiculous."

We both jump at Charon's voice. I hadn't heard him come in, and from the way Eurydice's eyes go wide, neither did she. She crosses her arms over her chest. "I don't care what you said last night—"

"Look at him, baby." Charon crosses the kitchen in slow steps that I don't hear but I can feel nonetheless. His big hand lands on the back of my neck. "If you're not going to set him free, then exorcise him."

"He's a *person*." But her gaze drops to the point where his fingers curl around my throat.

"No one's saying he isn't. You've spent enough time in the club to know better." There's a dangerous edge in Charon's voice, but I don't know him well enough to divine its source. He's not gripping me tightly at all, just letting me feel the weight of him while all his attention is on Eurydice, but I can't stop shivering.

I've messed around with kink in the past, but it never really did it for me. Bondage can be fun, and a little spanking spices things up, but that's not what this feels like.

It feels like Charon is *branding* me. The fact that he's doing it for her only heightens the experience. The muddied feeling that's plagued me for so many fucking months finally clears, the clouds parting for the space of a heartbeat. I want this.

I *need* this.

"Yes." My voice is hoarse. Even as I speak, part of me is all too eager to point out that this is just as selfish as everything I've ever done. Two birds, one stone, or something like that. I don't know. I can't think clearly. "I'll do it."

Charon's thumb strokes my throat, a tiny movement so brief I'm half-sure I imagined it. "What do you say, baby? He'll give you all the submission and pleasure to balance out all the fear and pain. Is it a bargain?"

She frowns at him, obviously searching his expression for answers. I don't know if she gets what she's looking for, because her gaze drops to me and goes complicated. "You've never submitted once in your life, Orpheus. You were a selfish lover and a selfish boyfriend. You're going to get tired of this within a day, maybe two, and go back to your life in the upper city."

She's wrong. I don't have much life to go back to. Saying as much won't convince her though. I don't know *what* will convince her, but ultimately this isn't something I want to bully her into doing. I never would have dreamed this was a possibility when I crossed the River Styx, but now I need her to say yes more than I need my next breath.

I hold my inhale, waiting.

Eurydice focuses on Charon once more. "You're sure about this."

"I meant what I said last night." His tone goes lower yet, downright sinful. "I saw the way you watched some scenes more intently than others. You've spent months watching, figuring out what interests you—in theory. Time to put it into practice."

She searches his expression. Some kind of silent communication flickers between them, a testament to their shared history and the strength of their relationship. I knew it was happening—he wouldn't have come to me to give her closure if he didn't care—but witnessing this small, intimate moment is a knife in my guts.

Eurydice shifts her attention to me. "You're sure about this."

There's only one correct answer. "Yes."

"So be it." She flicks a hand at me. "Orpheus, if you're going to insist on being on the floor, the least you can do is clean it."

Surprise flickers through me, quickly followed by my bruised pride. Clean the *floor*? I thought she was going to command me to lick her pussy or something. That, I would have been all too happy to do.

She arches a brow, and it's like a different woman stands before me. Gone is the innocent, sweet girl who used to stand at my side, replaced now by a proud queen. "But before we begin, you will pick a safe word. Use it at any time, and the scene stops."

"I don't need a safe word to do chores." I sound like a brat, but I can't quite help it. "If you wanted a maid—"

"Pick a safe word or this goes no further."

I bite down a curse. Either I meant what I said about penance or I didn't. I don't want to crawl around and clean the floors, but the only other option is going back to the upper city. Which is no option at all. I swallow hard. "*Grace.*"

"Good. Charon will show you where the cleaning supplies are." She turns back to the bowl of batter, effectively dismissing me.

It stings…but that sting feels almost good. Maybe this *is* the way. I can't time travel back into the past and change my behavior, and I can't battle all the invisible shit between us, but I can do this.

I jolt when I realize Charon still has his hand on the back of my neck. I look up to find him watching Eurydice with a thoughtful expression on his face. He glances down at me and squeezes, just a little, before releasing me. "This way."

I start to rise, but Eurydice's voice stops me. "Crawl, Orpheus. It's what good dogs do." She speaks without looking over her shoulder, but there's a new tension in her spine that makes me shiver.

Okay. I can do this. I don't know what the fuck is going on, but I can do this. I turn carefully and crawl after Charon to the closet tucked around the corner. He sets a bucket, cleaner, and a brand-new sponge in front of me.

I stare. A mop would be easier, but I suppose that isn't the point, is it? In the old stories my mother used to read me when I was a kid, there were always impossible tasks the heroes had to go through in order to get their just rewards. I don't know that I deserve a reward, but I can do the task.

Crawling with a bucket and cleaner is awkward as fuck, but I manage to get back to the kitchen and fill the bucket halfway with hot water. By the time I've started on one corner of the decently sized kitchen, Eurydice has finished cooking the pancakes and served them on two plates at the small dining table in the next room over.

Charon doesn't even look at me as he steps around me to take a seat across from her. "Thanks."

"I am not happy with you." But she nudges the syrup over to him. "Can you talk about last night?"

I keep scrubbing, giving myself over to the repetitive motion. The floor is already pretty clean, which means I don't have to pause in one spot too long. As I inch along, it strikes me that I've never done anything like this.

Oh, I've always picked up after myself, but even from the time I was a small child, we had a housekeeper. I might have been cut off from everything else in my normal life, but my mother has sent Thyia to me on a regular basis to assure herself I'm not wasting away in filth.

There's something...soothing about this.

Charon and Eurydice's conversation filters over me. He sighs. "Someone destroyed the greenhouse."

"What?" She gasps. "Why would someone do something like that?"

It's a good question. I don't know what this greenhouse is, but it's obviously got some import for her to react like that.

Instead of answering directly, Charon says, "Why don't you tell me?" He takes a couple bites of the pancakes while he waits.

Eurydice sips her coffee and considers him. After a moment

she says, "Hades and Persephone spend a lot of time there. It's not exactly advertised, but anyone who's familiar with the lower city is aware that the greenhouse functions as a refuge for both of them. It's a direct attack."

"And?"

She sighs. "I didn't realize this was a test."

"It's not a test." He takes another bite and chews slowly. "You're the daughter of one of the Thirteen, sister to another, and sister-in-law to two more. It's smart to reason through what moves your family's enemies will make."

"I know." Another sigh, this one almost playful. It strikes me that this is something of a teaching game they've played before. She sets her coffee mug down. "Okay, it's not a simple attack. If it was that, they would have actually *attacked*. Was Matthew okay?"

"Yes. Scared, but okay."

"Hmm." She nods. "If they hurt one of Hades's people, then he would seek them out and destroy them. It would be a direct conflict. This is more insidious."

"How?"

"I'm working on it." She points her fork at him. "If he can't even keep one of his refuges safe, then can he keep his people safe? It's more about sowing fear and distrust than about seeking a confrontation. One of his strengths is that he protects the lower city, and he wasn't able to do that this time."

"Yes." Charon takes a deep drink of his coffee. "It's a problem. They didn't leave a trail, and while we have cameras scattered about, they didn't pick up anything."

"So they studied the system before taking this step."

"Looks like it."

I mull that over as they move on to more mundane topics, talking about people I don't know. The upper city has seen increasing unrest in the last month. It makes sense that the lower city is seeing it as well, but it's interesting that it's not taking the same route. I don't know what that says about the people involved.

Apollo's warning rings through my head again. It's not just the Thirteen in danger these days. Triton might have been killed for other reasons, but there's really no way to tell for sure.

Is Eurydice in danger?

The thought makes me scrub harder, until my fingers cramp. I'm no warrior. Besides, with Charon at her side, she hardly needs more protection. That doesn't change the fact that I want to do whatever it takes to ensure she's safe.

No matter what that looks like.

EURYDICE

IT'S VERY HARD TO FOCUS ON WHAT CHARON IS SAYING when I can see Orpheus scrubbing the floor out of the corner of my eye. Up to this point, I've never participated in kink; I've only observed and read about it. But Charon is right in that I've spent a number of months in the club watching different scenes play out... and I've spent just as many months getting myself off to the fantasy of participating. Before this morning, I would have said I leaned more submissive.

There's no denying the pure bolt of power that went through me when I told Orpheus to crawl like a good dog. There's an element of wanting to humiliate him, but the surrender in his dark eyes went to my head faster than any alcohol I've ever drunk.

I need time to think about what that means, about the implications, but at this point I'm just feeling my way. I glance at Charon under my lashes. He hasn't looked at Orpheus once, but there's a tension in his shoulders that isn't normally present when it's just us.

And there's the way he put his hand around Orpheus's throat. I saw how Charon flushed, just a little. That wasn't all for me. We're in this mess up to our eyeballs, but it's strangely comforting that we're in it together.

Orpheus finishes the kitchen and takes the time to clean out the bucket—not an easy feat on his knees with the high counters—before returning it back to the closet it came from.

Charon glances at him and opens his mouth, but I know what comes next. Every scene has a different flow, a unique cadence. But one thing that is consistent is that a...submissive...needs to be taken care of. A good job should be rewarded. *A good dog should be praised.* I snap my fingers. "Come." I point to the spot right next to my chair. "Sit here."

Orpheus doesn't hesitate. The tile floors have to be killing his knees, but he doesn't complain as he crawls to me and kneels carefully at my side. He bows his head and a bolt of something sizzling and complicated goes through me.

I hesitate, but he didn't complain and he showed every evidence of doing exactly as I ordered to the best of his ability. It's the most natural thing in the world to place my hand on his head and guide it to my thigh. "Good boy."

His breath shudders out on my bare skin, and I fight down a shiver. It was satisfying to see him follow my command, but this... the heavy press of his head, his inhales and exhales ghosting over my thigh, his long hair soft beneath my fingers as I pet him.

Heat blossoms inside me. Desire. I won't do anything about it. Not now, maybe not ever. As much as I didn't want to see him go, I don't know if I'll survive letting him close enough to share my bed again. I don't intend to keep him, and if we have sex...I'll want to.

I look up to find Charon watching us. I don't know what I expect, maybe jealousy or anger, despite his words last night.

Instead, he's watching me with so much heat in his blue eyes, I have to fight not to shift in my seat. The desire surges higher, hotter. I lick my lips, and my voice comes out a little ragged when I finally manage to speak. "Charon?"

"I like you like this." He braces his elbows on the table. "You're steady on your feet."

That's exactly what it feels like. Even now, so many months later, there are plenty of times when I feel like the ground is moving beneath me. Not this morning, not since Orpheus knelt before me.

Not last night either, when I had my hand wrapped around Charon's cock.

I can't help it any longer. I press my thighs together, as if that will do anything to alleviate the ache that's begun in my core. Orpheus goes tense, which is the moment I realize he relaxed completely while I stroked his head.

Charon sees. Of course he sees.

He leans forward, gaze intent. "Does he deserve the reward of your body?" The question has a formal feel to it, which makes me realize the scene isn't over yet. Maybe it's only just beginning.

"No." The answer comes out too harshly, but it's too soon. I'm not ready.

"You're all achy and wet, aren't you, baby? He might not have earned access, but that doesn't mean you need to go without." Nothing changes in Charon's expression. "You want me to take care of it?" He doesn't even try to make the question subtle. He's so tense, I half expect him to leap over the table and grab me.

I want him to.

But...I glance down at Orpheus. Is it wrong that I want to fuck Charon when he's right here? It must be. How can I go from offering him comfort to wanting to twist the knife as if a switch flipped inside me? I don't know. I don't understand it, but I'm feeling my way at this point.

I give his head one last stroke. "You..." I drag in a breath. "You may watch if you'd like. No touching. Don't move." I can't believe I'm saying the words. Surely I'm not going to fuck my current... whatever Charon is to me right now...in front of my ex-boyfriend? Surely that's breaking some kind of rules.

How many nights did I spend haunting Orpheus's social media in the weeks following that night when everything changed? He certainly wasted no time being photographed with models and socialites and all manner of beautiful people. Surely he didn't go home alone most of those nights.

I *tormented* myself with visions of him fucking them, even though I knew it was technically none of my business because we were over. I'm petty enough to want him to feel even a sliver of that now. I might have done that before hurt to myself, but he's choosing to do it to himself now. A twisted kind of full circle.

A shudder works its way through Orpheus. He turns his face and presses a kiss to my thigh. It's a light touch, almost seeming accidental, but it shoots a trail of need straight to my pussy. He might have been a selfish lover in any number of ways, but he *loved* eating me out, and somewhere there's a series of small paintings of my pussy that he's promised never to share with anyone.

One promise he's actually kept.

He sits back carefully and presses his hands to his thighs. "I'll watch."

Oh gods, this is actually happening.

I sit quietly, my hand still buried in Orpheus's hair, as I watch Charon clear the table. He doesn't rush. I always knew he had a bit of a sadistic streak, but watching it play out in real time fucks with my head in the most delicious way possible. Because I know what's coming. I still ache from receiving it last night.

Just when I think I can stand it no longer, he takes the seat at the head of the table. Charon taps the wood in front of him, a clear, if silent, command. I don't rush to obey, but I waste no time nudging Orpheus aside and pushing to my feet. I don't look back to ensure my ex is watching me—I know he is.

I carefully perch on the table in front of Charon and spread my thighs. I didn't bother with panties this morning, mostly because I don't have anything clean to wear. It didn't occur to me that I might need to leave clothes here. Something I'll have to take into consideration for the future.

But then, I really like wearing Charon's clothes.

When he doesn't react, I set my feet on the arms of his chair, which spreads my thighs wider yet, and tug the hem of his shirt up to bare my pussy.

"Impatient," he murmurs.

He's teasing me, but I'm so turned on that I'm practically shaking. I bite my bottom lip and glance at Orpheus, who watches us with a rapt expression on his face. I've never seen him look like that before. I thought he was just going through the motions of submission in order to pay his penance, but that's obviously not the case.

This is doing something for him, the same way it's doing something for me. I might laugh if I had the space for breath. All that time together, all those shared orgasms, and somehow we never got to the core of need that we exposed in a few short minutes of arguing in Charon's kitchen.

"You asked if I wanted help with that. If you're not going to do it, then I suppose I'll have to do it myself." I start to reach between my thighs, but Charon catches my wrist.

"Oh no, you don't." He guides my hand back to the table on the outside of my hip. "You rushed me last night. You owe me, baby. Let me take my time."

"Are you trying to make me beg?" I'll do it. I won't even hesitate. I need him too badly to play more games right now, even if part of me enjoys the games immensely.

"Another time." He presses his fingers to the insides of my knees and urges my thighs wider yet. I'm so exposed that I can feel my pussy gaping. It makes me want to cover myself and give him more of a show, all at the same time. The feeling only gets stronger when Charon trails his fingers up my inner thighs. It's a light touch, meant to tease, and I get so wet that I'm afraid I'm leaving a puddle on the table.

Charon scoots his chair back, just a little, and bends down to cover my pussy with his mouth. It happens so fast that I don't even stop to think. My gaze flies to Orpheus. He's watching Charon eat me out as if he's been wandering for months in the desert and happened upon an oasis…only to find it's surrounded by an insur-mountable fence.

Charon drags his tongue up my center, finding my clit and giving it the same back-and-forth motion that I love so much. Suddenly, I'm not thinking about Orpheus at all. I dig my fingers into Charon's hair and moan as he feasts on me.

Because he *is* feasting. I may be on the verge of coming, but he goes after my pussy like it's his favorite delicacy and he might never get a chance to taste it again. Even as I tell myself to hold still, I can't help digging my heels into the arms of his chair and lifting my hips to meet his tongue.

"*Charon.*" Oh fuck, I'm going to come. It's happening too fast. I want this to be drawn out. A deep dark part of me wanted him to tease me until I really did beg. It's too late for that now. I orgasm so hard that I cry out, moaning his name as I grind myself against his mouth.

He doesn't stop.

He slows down a little, moving his attention to my folds and giving my clit a little time to recover. It feels a different kind of good. I feel drugged on my slowly easing orgasm, and I look again to my ex.

There are two spots of color high on his carved cheeks, and his dark eyes have gone heavy-lidded with pleasure. There's no anger on his face, and if there's jealousy, I can't quite divine its source. Acting on some impulse I refuse to put a name to, I catch the hem of my shirt and drag it slowly up my body. He watches it rise with his heart in his eyes. When I tug it over my head, baring my breasts to his gaze, he licks his lips and actually groans aloud. "Fuck, you look even better than I remember."

Charon lifts his head enough to look at me. Whatever he sees in my face makes him give a little growl that vibrates against my pussy. He nips my inner thigh and presses two fingers into me. The penetration bows my back and draws another cry from my lips. "More!"

"Not yet." He strokes me almost idly, his patience in this moment a direct counterpoint to the frenzy of last night. Both are unbearably sexy. That feeling only gets stronger when he withdraws his fingers and holds them down by his hip. "Come, Orpheus."

"What are you doing?" I whisper. But I don't stop him; instead, I watch, my clit throbbing as Orpheus crawls around the corner of the table and takes Charon's fingers into his mouth. "Oh, fuck."

Charon doesn't move. He doesn't force himself into Orpheus's mouth, and he doesn't take his hand back. As the seconds tick on, there's no doubt in my mind that my taste has left his skin. I bite my bottom lip as I watch Orpheus lick and suck at his fingers.

"Orpheus." I can't quite manage the same command in my voice that Charon seems to draw forth naturally, but Orpheus immediately releases his fingers and sits back on his heels. His cock is so hard that I can see the clear outline against the front of his jeans. He makes no move to touch himself though. He merely waits for my command.

It takes two tries to get the words out with both of them watching me. "If Charon fucks me, will you suck his cock clean?" Before this moment, I wouldn't have necessarily said that was something I'd seek out. Now, I *need* it.

I know that Charon has had boyfriends, and Orpheus has shared his bed with people of every variety. That doesn't mean what just happened will translate into either of them wanting more. "Do *you* want that?"

Charon sits back and palms his cock through his slacks. "I want what you want, baby." It's a cop-out, but I don't call him on it. I know him well enough to know that if he didn't want something, he would have no problem saying as much.

Orpheus licks his lips as if he can still taste me there. "I want you however you allow me to have you. If that's on his fingers? So be it. If it's on his cock?" He clears his throat and the blush in his cheeks brightens. "You gave me a safe word, Eurydice. I'll use it if I need to use it."

Charon strokes his hand on my thigh and covers my pussy with his palm. It's a light, possessive gesture. "Do *you* want that, baby? You want to watch him suck your come off my cock?"

Gods help me but I do. For so many reasons that I can't begin to put into words, even to myself. I feel like I'm in the middle of a fever dream, like nothing really matters in this moment, because there can be no consequences. I know better, but I have spent so goddamn long putting everyone else first. Being the easy one, the nice one, the sweet one. I need this, and I don't care if it's selfish. They're willing to give it to me, so I will take it. "Desperately."

Charon takes me at my word. He rises and scoops me into his arms easily. "Call your dog, baby."

I look over his shoulder as he carries me out of the room. Orpheus watches us with such heat in his gaze that I press my thighs together, hard. "Come, Orpheus."

It's not far to the living room, and Charon slows down so I can watch Orpheus crawl after us. I never thought something like this could be so hot. Charon walks to the couch and sets me carefully on it. I watch with my heart in my throat as he pulls his shirt off and his hands go to the front of his slacks.

"Let me."

For a moment I think he might argue, but his hands fall to his sides, and he allows me to undo the front of his slacks. I hook my fingers into his underwear and tug it down just enough to free his hard cock. My body trembles at the memory of what it feels like to be split wide open by him. Soon. But not yet.

Orpheus reaches us as I wrap a fist round Charon's cock. Without looking at him, I snap my fingers and point to the spot right next to us. And then I take Charon's cock into my mouth. My jaw starts to ache almost instantly. I relish the sensation and wedge him deeper, working to relax my throat and breathe through my nose.

He lets me have my way for a moment, but when my gag reflex gets the best of me, Charon digs his fingers in my hair and pulls me off his cock. His face has plenty of emotion now. He looks at me like a man possessed, like I've gotten into his blood, and he never wants to get me out.

"Your dog's famished, baby. Let's stop wasting time and feed him."

CHARON

I DIDN'T HAVE ANY PLANS FOR SEDUCTION WHEN I CAME home this morning. After a night of fruitless searching, my frustration was riding me hard. All I wanted was to see Eurydice and let her presence soothe me.

Then I walked in to find Orpheus kneeling on the ground at her feet.

I meant what I said last night. I will take Eurydice however I'm able to; after having her, I'll do anything to ensure I don't lose her. Even if that means sharing. I knew she needed closure with Orpheus, but even with all the time I spent studying her, I never anticipated the gleam of dominance in her eyes when she looked down at him. *Need* doesn't begin to cover it.

Even so, she's new enough at kink that I didn't think she would be able to take what she wanted for herself. The morning has been full of surprises.

Not that I'm complaining. Not with me sinking onto the couch and Eurydice naked and straddling me. She's flushed and so turned on that her pussy is practically dripping all over my lap. I love her like this. Needy and bossy and so desperate for what only I can give her.

Well, me and Orpheus.

I haven't quite let myself think about the mess I've gotten myself into. I won't pretend the flutter of attraction I felt for him is anything but the truth, but we're in a strange state right now where everything feels far too fluid. The past, the present, the future. All that melts together into a chaotic mess that is going to blow up in our faces.

I can't wait to get his mouth on my cock.

I don't know what the fuck that means. Probably something as simple as lust, though literally anyone else in the city would have been a safer choice. There's no use thinking about it now. Not when I have Eurydice grinding against the length of my cock.

She could move this along if she really wanted to, but she seems to enjoy the tease as much as I do. As good as it feels, it's obvious that she's also putting on a show. Whether that show is for me or Orpheus remains to be seen. Maybe it's for both of us. I find myself hoping it is.

I need her.

That's why I am the one to reach between us and position my cock at her entrance. She rises up on her knees to make room for me, and there's an imperious look in her dark eyes that makes my balls twitch. I've fallen in love with all the different facets of this woman, and it delights me to no end to continue to find new ones. Her attitude isn't quite bratty, but has a similar flavor.

"Don't tease us, baby." I don't push her though. I watch her drag her folds over the head of my cock, swirling her hips until I think I might lose my mind. "Take my cock."

She plants her hands on my shoulders and begins to lower herself. Her orgasm has made her slippery, but she still has to work to take me from this angle. It's hot as fuck to have her fighting her way down my length.

Without thinking, I look to Orpheus. His gaze is pinned to the point where my cock disappears into her pussy. There's a hunger there, written across his face, and I can't begin to say if that hunger is for me or for her...or both.

I shouldn't care. I meant what I said about us being endgame. Eurydice and me. When I spoke those words, there was no room in that vision for anyone else—especially him.

Now, I wonder.

It's nothing that needs to be decided tonight. We've all agreed to this scene, and that's enough for me. Eurydice slams the rest of the way down on me. The feeling of her pussy clamping around my cock nearly sends me to the moon. I jerk my gaze back to her face to find her glaring at me. "You're distracted."

"Not distracted, baby." That's not the word I'd use, but I don't feel like getting into it now. "Take care of your dog."

She glares for a moment longer but then snaps her fingers at Orpheus without looking at him. "Here, boy." She doesn't watch him to make sure he obeys her command, crawling to her and pressing his head to her palm...but I do. It's sexy as fuck. Eurydice pets him for a moment. "Now be a good boy and sit there silently. You'll get your reward soon enough."

Orpheus has the dazed look on his face of a sub deep in a scene. I'd been prepared to hate him for everything he's done—and part of me still does—but he's so fucking broken, I can't help wanting to pick up the pieces. My white knight complex is a bitch and a half. That, at least, is expected. What I *didn't* expect is the strange tenderness that makes me want to reach out and guide his face to my thigh, to offer him comfort.

It's not my place to offer him comfort. It's not my place to offer him anything at all.

With that in mind, I refocus on Eurydice. She's still got that bratty look on her face, but she doesn't quite pull it off, not when her eyes are so filled with emotions. I lean up and kiss her, just because I can. She's mine in every way that matters, even if we haven't ironed out all the details yet.

I've been hers for a long time.

She starts to move. Until the day I die, I don't think I'll see a more perfect picture than Eurydice, her hands propped behind her on my thighs, her lean body rolling as she rides my cock. I can't stop myself from running my hands up her thighs to catch her hips, though I don't try to take control. Not yet.

It's perfect. Too perfect. No matter how controlled I am, I'm still only human. I can't keep this up forever. I grab her hips and pull her down onto me, sealing us together and preventing her from moving. It's a mistake. This feels too fucking good. "Baby, please."

Her smile is slow, sweet, and a little evil. "Problem, Charon?"

"If you don't stop, I'm going to come, and then you can't play out your little game with your dog." I can feel Orpheus watching us intensely, but for once I'm not interested in looking at him. He can wait until it's time.

"So concerned about Orpheus." She strokes her fingers along my jaw. I can't tell if she's bothered by my words or not. Truth be told, I'm having a hard time stringing any thoughts together at all right now. It's everything I can do to stop myself from rolling us over and fucking her hard enough to make her forget her own damned name. *Another time.*

"It's not *Orpheus* who's about to make me blow my load."

"Very well." She sighs, her irritation not quite believable when she writhes a little on my cock and her nipples are hard points begging for my mouth. "If riding your cock isn't working out...I suppose I can ride your mouth."

A laugh bursts from me, making them both jump. "You *suppose* you'll ride my mouth. Come on, baby. Don't pretend you're not needy for my tongue."

"Don't gloat. It's unbecoming." She sounds so delightfully prissy that I laugh again. It takes no effort at all to lift her off my cock and haul her up to straddle my face. I like her squeak of surprise to find me supporting her weight like this. She wiggles, but I have a firm grasp on her and she's not going anywhere. "Charon, you're showing off."

Maybe a little.

Instead of answering with words, I pull her closer and drag my tongue up her center. Eurydice gives a sweet moan and snaps her fingers again. She can't quite manage a firm, bitchy tone with my tongue inside her, but she does a damn good job of trying. "Orpheus."

"Yes?" I can't see his face, but his voice has changed, deepened, gone rougher with need.

"Be a good boy and clean Charon's cock for me."

I have half a mind to turn her around so she can see him, but she reaches down and digs a hand into my hair, guiding my mouth up to her clit. Fuck, but I love her like this, riding my mouth and holding me to her as if she doesn't care if I suffocate. *Good girl, take your pleasure. You deserve it.*

I'm so focused on her, I almost forget her command to Orpheus. Or at least I do until his hands touch my thighs almost tentatively, a gentle pressure guiding me to spread for him. I expect... I don't know what I expect. For him to go after my cock like it's a chore to be suffered through. I should have known better. I saw how he cleaned my kitchen, after all. His mouth descending my length feels just like that looked.

Like worship.

The desire I was barely holding on to before comes roaring back. It's compounded by the taste of Eurydice on my tongue and the way she grinds herself against my face. Little sounds escape her lips and her movements go jerky. She's close.

Orpheus chooses that moment to cup my balls in one hand and press two fingers to the sensitive spot behind them as he sucks me deep and hard. I don't have the chance to brace for it, to resist the pleasure. I moan against Eurydice's pussy as I come, and he doesn't hesitate to drink me down.

He also...doesn't stop.

He gives me one last long suck, and then he begins licking his way down my length. Doing exactly as he was commanded, cleaning every inch of me. It's too much. I'm so sensitive that my thighs are shaking, but there's nowhere to go, pinned between him and Eurydice and the couch.

"Charon?" She twists a little in my hands. "Oh. *Oh.*"

I'm not sure who makes the decision to move, whether it's me sliding down or Orpheus tugging at my thighs, but somehow I end up flipping all three of us. Orpheus hits the ground on his back, and the little bastard has my cock in his mouth before I fully settle Eurydice onto the couch. He doesn't seem to care that I've gone soft. On the contrary, he seems delighted he can fit all of me into his mouth now.

I can't get distracted. Eurydice hasn't come yet, and I need her orgasm more than I need my next breath. I drag my tongue up her center and then back down, giving myself some time to get settled. There's a proper way to do this, calm and controlled and perfectly rhythmic. I'm not capable of it right now. This keeps fucking happening. The moment I get my hands or mouth on her, I lose control.

That truth is *not* being helped along by Orpheus. Not when his two fingers are making his intentions more than clear. I nip Eurydice's thigh in frustration. "Stop that shit, Orpheus."

He starts to obey me, but then Eurydice laughs. I look up at her, and she's never been more beautiful than in this moment. Her hair is wild around her face, and her skin is flushed with need and desire. She tugs at my hair with another laugh that edges toward a delicious kind of mean. "Whatever you're doing, Orpheus...don't stop."

"Baby, this is supposed to be about you." It's so fucking hard to focus, especially when Orpheus's fingers return, wet this time, and press into my ass. I can't stop myself from thrusting into his mouth. My cock isn't soft anymore, and while part of me loves this shit, another part of me wants to punish him for it.

Eurydice's smile goes soft in a way that makes my heart lurch.

"In what world would I not want to see you come apart, Charon? It's so sexy to see you lose control. I think I'm addicted to it."

I stare at her for a beat, but then Orpheus does something that makes my balls draw tight. If I don't hurry up, he's going to make me come again before I get Eurydice off. I don't think it's a competition right now, but the threat of one gets me moving again.

I press two fingers into her and go after her clit with my tongue. Her soft curse is music to my ears. This time, I don't mess around teasing her. This is a race to the finish. The challenge hits my blood, which only works against me. It's okay though; Eurydice was already almost all the way there. She tugs on my hair hard enough to make me groan in tormented pleasure, and then she's coming all over my face. I'm not far behind her. Again, Orpheus winds me up and then sucks me dry.

We end up in a messy pile half on the couch and half on the floor. I expect Eurydice to do something about Orpheus's hard cock pressing against the front of his pants, but she merely taps her thigh. He crawls to her and presses his face there with a look like bliss. *Penance.* It seems to be serving them both, and since no one is trying to get up and fuck up their aftercare, I haul myself onto the couch next to her. She sinks into my side with a happy sound. *I'm* happy. This feels too fucking good. I give her a soft kiss as our bodies cool and our heartbeats return to normal. Even as I tell myself not to, my hand drops to cover hers on Orpheus's head.

It's...perfect.

ORPHEUS

WHEN I CAME TO THE LOWER CITY, SOME PART OF ME really hoped I had a chance of getting Eurydice back, even as I told myself it was impossible. That there was nothing I could do to earn her forgiveness. I even believed it…until Eurydice told me to crawl.

Now, I'm not certain of anything.

And then there's Charon. He's a new component to the entire situation that I didn't anticipate. He's not trying to take charge. It's more that he's supplementing Eurydice's dominance. It's hot. I never thought that I would be happy on my knees, but there's something so incredibly peaceful about handing over the decision-making process.

For the first time in my life, I'm not thinking about what comes next, at least in those moments where I'm following orders. I'm not stressed about living up to the legacy my mother has created as one of the top models in the industry. I'm not worried about following my father's advice to live my life to the fullest and compromise nothing, because youth is fleeting and it's something he always regretted letting pass him by. He isn't quite trying to live through me, but it's close enough that he's always advising me to take the least stable path because "there's plenty of time to settle down—emphasis on *settle*—later."

That's not even getting into Apollo. He's a good brother, but he can't conceptualize how challenging it is to live in his shadow. He doesn't make mistakes. He's not greedy, or selfish, or malicious. He's a fucking paragon of virtue, and he casts a long shadow as a result.

I don't know how I'm supposed to go back. There's a clear line dividing my life—before last night and after last night. There's every chance that Eurydice will use me until she's purged every part of her that ever cared about me, and then she'll cast me out for good. It's even likely. I don't know what happens then. I feel adrift, floating mindlessly except for the tether that connects me to her.

My knees ache pleasantly as I kneel on the tile floor and watch her get ready. It's a ritual that I know by heart, and yet somewhere along the way I stopped appreciating the experience. I'm sure as shit appreciating it now. The long line of her throat as she tips back her head to put her hair into a high ponytail. The smooth curve of her shoulders, left bare by the tank top she pulls over her head. Her dainty feet, with that damned yellow nail polish.

My fingers twitch. The sensation catches me by surprise, and I stare at them as if I've never seen that before. Do I...want to paint? The question almost makes me laugh, but not in a kind way. Maybe Eurydice really is my muse. What a horrifying thought. Better to spend the rest of my life with that hollow spot where my creativity used to be than to get a glimpse of the way it could be again, only to have it ripped from my hands a second time.

I did it to myself. I know that, and yet it doesn't make it any easier to stomach.

Charon steps out of his closet, breaking my spiral. He's dressed in the way I've always seen him previously, his broad form clothed in a perfectly tailored suit. This one is a pleasant gray that manages to make his eyes look even stormier than normal. His gaze flicks to me and away. Does he feel as conflicted about this sequence of events as I do?

I want him. Of course I do. He's sexy as fuck, and there have been plenty of times in my past where I've enjoyed the particular kind of seduction that comes from coaxing the restrained partner into wild abandon. Charon would be a challenge. He *is* a challenge.

But this isn't a mere seduction where pleasure is the only thing on the line.

He drifts a big hand down Eurydice's spine. It's not quite a possessive gesture—more that he is amazed he's allowed to touch her at all. It makes my chest ache. Charon leans against the counter at her side. "What's on the agenda today?"

"I'm meeting up with Persephone for lunch." She lifts a hand. "Yes, we're going to the upper city. If the security is good enough for Hades, then I think we can both agree that it should be good enough for you."

He makes a face. "That's not a fair argument."

"What makes you think I have any interest in being fair?" Eurydice smiles at him in the mirror, her expression soft. "We're not doing anything particularly wild. We got word that Pan is out of the hospital and back in the Dryad. We just want to check up on him, and going to lunch seems the least pushy way to do that."

He looks like he wants to argue. I watch in fascination as he obviously talks himself down. His attention shifts to me again. "What about him?"

Eurydice takes a shuddering breath and turns to look at me as well. "Well?"

It takes me a few moments to realize she's talking to me. I roll my shoulders, trying to get my thoughts in order. For better or worse, the last twelve hours have created a strange little bubble around the three of us. Eurydice might not be willing to throw me off a bridge, but the same can't be said for the rest of her family. I have absolutely no desire to see Persephone, but this isn't about what I want. Not right now. "What do you want?"

She crosses her arms. "Listen, I know you're all about paying penance right now, and while I find immense satisfaction in having you crawl for me, you are still a person with thoughts and feelings and needs. Scenes end, Orpheus. Would you like to come with me, or would you rather stay here and wait for us to return?"

Part of me wishes she would make the choice for me. She's already made it clear that she won't though. I take a deep breath. Maybe it's foolish, but I can't shake the feeling that if I let her out of my sight, this will all end. Dealing with her sisters and their blatant hate is a small enough price to pay for spending time in Eurydice's presence. "I would like to come with you, if that's all right."

She studies me for a long moment and finally nods. "Okay."

Charon has his phone out and is typing away with his big fingers. "Medusa will be on your security detail. Are you going to see your mom as well or coming straight back?"

Eurydice sighs, and although the sound has plenty of

exasperation, there's more than a little fondness. "I was planning on coming straight back afterward."

"Then I'll send Minthe too."

"Charon."

He hesitates without looking away from this phone. "You know I worry about you."

"Medusa is more than formidable enough to ensure I'm safe. If you put too many people on my security, you might as well signal that I'm someone important. You'll make a target of me."

She's...manipulating him. She's not exactly lying, but it's clear that she has an agenda, and it's equally clear that hers is at odds with what Charon wants. I can't see a good reason not to have more security. As best I can tell, Eurydice hasn't spent much time in the upper city in the last year, but she has access to all the same sources of news that we do. She has to know how dangerous it is.

Why is she trying to have less security?

I open my mouth to ask, but Eurydice shoots me such a venomous look that I snap my jaw shut. Oh yeah, she knows exactly what she's doing. Curiosity unfurls inside me. She's up to something, but she's still willing to let me tag along.

Finding out what Eurydice doesn't want Charon to know is more than worth the price of an uncomfortable lunch.

She pushes away from the bathroom counter and waves a hand at me. "You'll need to wear something else."

I don't have anything else to wear. All three of us know it. Charon transfers his frown from his phone to me. "I think I have something that might fit."

That startles a laugh out of me. "There's no universe where

we're the same size." We're close enough in height, but he's built much wider and thicker than I am.

Charon ignores me, turning and heading back into the closet. He reappears a few minutes later with a pair of pants and a button-up shirt. I want to argue, but Eurydice sends me another of those sharp looks. It's not quite a command, but it might as well be. Which is how I find myself taking a quick shower and putting on Charon's clothes.

The biggest surprise comes from the fact that…they fit. I don't know if that means they don't belong to him, or if at some point he was significantly thinner, but I don't ask. In fact, I say nothing at all until Eurydice and I are leaving the apartment side by side. I wait two blocks before I ask the question that's been burning on the back of my tongue. "What are you hiding from him?"

"What makes you think I'm hiding something?"

I smile a little, though it feels bitter. "You forget, Eurydice. I might've been a shitty boyfriend, but I've known you half of my life. You never answer questions with a question unless you're trying to hide something."

She glares. "You always do that. We might've gone to school together, but it's not like we moved in the same circles. You don't get to act like you've known me for that long; you didn't even notice me when we were teenagers."

That's the thing that she's never understood; she sure as fuck never believed me when I tried to explain it. I always noticed her, from the moment that she and her sisters walked through the front doors of our private school. It was the fall after her mother had become Demeter, and they brought a novelty that legacy kids like me rarely saw. Most of my peers treated them as the enemy, and I won't

pretend I didn't go along with it at times, but Eurydice fascinated me
from the first moment I saw her. Delicate and beautiful and positive
in a way that I still don't understand. When everyone around me
was jaded, interacting with her always felt like a breath of fresh air.

It still does if I'm being honest.

Not that I'm interested in having this argument again. She won't
believe me now, just like she never believed me in the past. What I'm
more interested in is the fact that she's still dodging my questions. I
could press her on it, but I think I'll find more answers if I go along
with her today like a good little obedient submissive. Maybe I'll
learn something in the process.

The house she leads me to is exactly the sort of home I expect a
person who holds the title Hades to own. It doesn't match the rest
of the buildings in the lower city; it's a sprawling Victorian mansion
that takes up almost an entire city block. I have to pause and take
a few seconds to process what I'm seeing. It's beautiful in a creepy,
atmospheric kind of way. It also makes me wonder if it was built
solely to feed into the myth of Hades. For the last thirty years, his
name has functioned as a sort of boogeyman. Something to scare
children with. Before that though, the title Hades was not to be
fucked with. There's no other explanation for why Zeus targeted
it specifically.

Ultimately, it doesn't matter. That Zeus and that Hades are no
more. The men who hold the titles now are very different creatures.
It's some small consolation that they seem more intent dealing with
Olympus's enemies than in making enemies of each other.

At least for now.

EURYDICE

I PROBABLY SHOULD HAVE LEFT ORPHEUS BACK IN Charon's town house. Today promises to be a challenge even without him at my side, and his presence will make things more difficult. I'm not ready to explain what's happening between us. To be honest, I'm still not certain myself.

But I gave him a choice and he made it.

I lead the way up the wide stairs to the imposing front door. The first time I saw this building, I was scared out of my mind. Now, it's a second home. I know these hallways, with the thick carpet and dark color palette. I spent time in the sitting rooms we pass as we move deeper into the house. I even have a bedroom on the second floor that has slowly gained a significant portion of my clothing over the last year. I think most of my stuff is in the lower city now.

I hear the panting and yips before the trio of black dogs come barreling around the corner, Cerberus, Scylla, and Charybdis. Technically, they're barely more than puppies, but they must have some massive hunting dog breed mixed in with the rest, because they easily come up to my hip. Cerberus barks when he sees me and picks up his pace.

I can tell the exact moment that they noticed Orpheus. Their happy barks turn to growls and they surge forward, putting themselves between me and him. They press against my legs even as they bark, deep and feral and filled with warning. To his credit, Orpheus doesn't move.

"What's going on out here?" My sister steps out of a nearby room—the library—with one hand on her gently curved stomach. She looks good. Healthy. She would argue with me if I said as much, but pregnancy agrees with her. There's a glow to her skin, and she's never looked more like our mother than on days when she wears comfortable wrap dresses like the one she has on right now. Her long blond hair is braided back from her face, and her eyes narrow when she realizes who else is standing in her hallway. "What are *you* doing here?"

"Call off the dogs, Persephone." The dogs like me just fine, but they don't listen to my commands. They don't seem to listen to anyone except Hades and Persephone...and Georgie, the cook.

"No, I don't think I will." She crosses her arms and glares. "Explain, Eurydice. Now."

It's always like this with my siblings, to say nothing of my mother. They like to conveniently forget that I am an adult and have been for years now. Part of it is my fault; I knew they liked taking care of me, and so I allowed them to do so. It was easy and comfortable. I just had no idea I was digging myself into a hole it would be impossible to climb out of.

I cross my arms over my chest, mirroring her body language. "It's none of your business."

"You're my sister, and you're residing in my city, so I think you'll find that it is, in fact, my business." She transfers her glare from Orpheus to me. "Tell me you're not seeing this piece of shit again. You know what happened last time."

I haven't had much cause to regret calling Persephone for help that night, but there are moments like this where I wish I had done literally anything else. Not only because I acted the part of unwitting bait that put both my sister and Hades in danger, but because it's cemented me in their minds as the baby sister who is always in need of protection. They don't trust my strength. They sure as fuck don't trust my instincts.

I might understand their reasoning, but that doesn't mean I like it. "Call off the dogs, or I'm leaving right now."

Persephone glares, but while she might be the fearsome queen of the lower city to everyone else, she's still my big sister. I've seen that look before, and I know exactly how far she's willing to push it. I may not have been the object of her frustration often in our childhood—Callisto and Psyche hold that honor—but I've witnessed it enough to know her boundaries by heart. She's not going let me walk out of here with him, not without answers.

She snaps out a command, and the dogs immediately go silent and sit. They're still creating a barrier between me and Orpheus, but at least we can speak now without yelling. It's better that I get the drop on this so that I can control the conversation. I raise an eyebrow. "My relationships are my business. If I want your advice, I'll come to you for it, but unless you're willing to sit through several hours of our mother giving you all the pregnancy advice you never asked for, don't be a hypocrite."

She lifts her chin. "That's different. Mother hasn't been pregnant in over two decades. All of her information is outdated."

"Just like your information about Orpheus is outdated."

Persephone gives a truly impressive snarl that would do any of her dogs proud. "You can't honestly expect me to be okay with this...whatever this is."

Of course not. If our situations were reversed, I would be feeling the exact same thing. Gods, at this point I'm almost willing to shove our current Zeus out of the window just like the last Zeus in order to save Callisto from him. Only the fact that our eldest sister seems totally fine, even flourishing, as the new Hera has made me keep my silence.

"I expect you to respect my decisions," I snap.

Persephone stares at me for several beats. I brace for us to continue arguing, but she finally shakes her head and grimaces. "Fine. I will respect whatever it is you have going on here." She points a finger at Orpheus. "But don't think for a second that just because my sister has a soft heart, the same can be said for the rest of us. If you hurt her again, there won't be a body left to find."

"Persephone!"

For his part, Orpheus doesn't seem overly concerned. It's not that he's being arrogant—I've seen what that looks like on his gorgeous face. It's more that he is...looking to me to lead the way. It's not quite the expression he wore when he knelt at my feet, but it's similar enough that the thrill of pure power goes through me.

I didn't know it could be like this. I didn't even know that I *wanted* it to be like this.

Orpheus nods at me and then looks at my sister. "Eurydice is in full control. I won't hurt her again." I don't know if the words are for me or Persephone, but they warm me all the same. Maybe I'm a fool to be feeling soft feelings for him again. Maybe they never went away at all. I don't know which option is more terrifying.

Persephone shakes her head slowly. "I don't know what's going on, but I don't like it." She props her hands on her hips. "I suppose you want him to come to lunch with us?"

Truth be told, I hadn't thought about it in too much detail. I've been feeling my way with this from the start, and somehow I don't think that's going to change in the future. I'm reluctant to let Orpheus out of my sight, but it won't be a relaxing lunch with my sister if he's present. I worry my bottom lip for a moment until the solution lands right in my lap. "He'll wait in the car."

"He'll wait in the car," my sister repeats slowly.

"Yes." *Like a good dog.* I don't have to say the words aloud. Understanding is there in Orpheus's dark eyes, in the way they flare hot before he looks down at the floor. The slippery slope beneath my feet only gets more so. I...want him. I don't know why that's such a revelation, not when I've wanted him since we were teenagers. He likes to pretend that he always wanted me back, but it's not the truth. He was popular and universally beloved by our peers. Handsome, rich, from a legacy family. The only thing about him that didn't quite fit the cookie-cutter norm was his art, but that only made him more attractive to everyone around us.

It wasn't like that for me and my sisters. We grew up differently; our life in the countryside outside of the city proper was a simpler one. Oh, we've always had money and all the luxuries that come with it, but people don't play the same vicious politics out there. We were wholly unprepared for our move into Olympus.

Each of my sisters went about survival a little differently. Callisto was in so many fights that first month that her knuckles still bear the scars. Psyche let their shitty comments roll right off her like water off a duck's back, and then she turned around and played the game better than any of them. Persephone crafted a sunshine persona that was impenetrable.

And all three of my sisters stood between me and everyone else. Or at least they tried. The thing is, there are more than a few years between each of us, and so I spent plenty of time without them playing the part of my protectors. I learned my own lessons during those times. I'm not fierce like Callisto, or cunning like Psyche, or untouchable like Persephone.

In the end, I leaned into the parts of me that everyone around me saw. Fragile. Delicate. In need of protection. To some people, that made me a victim in waiting. But there were plenty of others who stepped into the gaps left by my sisters' absence. They were always louder and stronger than I was, and that's how I know Orpheus never actually saw me. I was always standing in the shadows of others. It was the only way I knew how to protect myself.

I'm not content to stand in the shadows of others any longer. "If you're done interrogating me, I'm famished."

My sister shakes her head. "Let's go."

The trip into the upper city isn't comfortable in the least. I sit between my sister and Orpheus, feeling like I'm being ripped in two by the silence. It's a relief when we pull up in front of the Dryad and Persephone climbs out of the car. I reach over and pull the door shut to give me a moment alone with Orpheus. "Are you okay waiting here?"

"You're asking me now?" He smiles as he says it. "It's fine. I don't want to ruin your lunch."

I don't know what to do with this new Orpheus. Without thinking, I take his hand. "Look, I get that you made a mistake last year, but that doesn't mean that you need to have an entire personality transplant. You're kind of freaking me out."

"I'm sorry." He turns his hand over and laces his fingers through mine. With our palms pressed together, I feel the fine shudder that moves through his body. He leans back against the seat and closes his eyes. "I understand what you're saying, but you have no idea what it's been like since we saw each other last. I'm not the same person I was, just like you're not quite the same woman you were. Part of that is because of what happened with you, and part of that is other shit going on that has nothing to do with you."

"You mean like Apollo cutting you off?"

He opens one eye and looks at me. "Yeah, that's part of it."

I have no business pressing him, and now isn't the time to do it, but I can't help asking, "And the rest of it?"

He squeezes my hand and gently slips free. "If you really want to know, ask your questions tonight. I don't think right now is the time for that conversation. Persephone is waiting for you."

He's right, but I still have to fight against the urge to lift my voice and tell Medusa to take us back to the lower city. Only the fact that I have other things I need to accomplish today keep me silent. "Very well. I'll ask my questions tonight." I lean forward until my breasts press against his arm. "And if you're a very, very good boy today, you'll get a reward."

"Fuck, Eurydice." He makes a helpless little sound that goes straight to my pussy. "You sure know how to motivate a man to be on his best behavior."

I catch his chin the same way Charon caught mine last night and tilt his face to mine. That delicious surge of power goes through me when his eyes flutter shut. I don't know that I want his submission in every area of life, but I can't deny that I love it right here, right now. I press my thumbnail to his lip, earning another of those sounds that make me clench my thighs together. "Think of me while I'm gone."

"I don't have a chance of doing anything else."

CHARON

I SEEK HADES OUT IN THE ROOM THAT'S BECOME HIS formal meeting place in the months since he married Persephone. I don't think he consciously made the choice to move; more that this room has a couch that Persephone likes to frequent while she watches Hades work. He does that sort of thing a lot, making space in his life for her to be at his side.

This room is significantly brighter than his old office. The windows at his back overlook the street below and allow him to survey the foot traffic. He's never said as much aloud, but I know he finds watching his people live their happy, healthy lives comforting. There are two bookshelves built into the walls on either side of the window, and they used to house some dusty old editions. These days, Persephone has been slowly filtering them out as she finishes books while she lounges on the luxurious green couch. The couch itself has acquired a knitted throw blanket from…somewhere. Pregnancy seems to come with a lot of naps, and Hades has ensured she's comfortable and close to him during those times.

I knock on the doorframe and wait for him to look up to say, "Busy?"

"Not with anything that can't wait." He looks exhausted, the circles beneath his eyes a deeper purple than they were a week ago. The lines bracketing his mouth are deeper too. He sits back in his chair and motions for me to take the seat across from him. "Any progress?"

I hate that my answer hasn't changed from the last time we spoke. "No. They knew where the cameras are. Our patrols too. No one saw anything, heard anything. The only reason Matthew knew it happened so quickly is because he installed that security system last month."

"And he didn't tell us," Hades murmurs.

"And he didn't tell us," I confirm. "He didn't want to bother us, but I think the real truth is that he didn't want to insult you by making it seem like he didn't trust your ability to protect him and his business."

Hades rubs a tired hand over his face. "He was right. I didn't protect him."

If he was any worse a leader, he would drag *me* over the coals for this. Hades might be the ruler of the lower city, but I'm his right-hand man. I'm the one in charge of security. I'm the one who oversees our patrols and ensures his will is done. "I dropped the ball."

He gives me a brief smile. "There's more than enough self-recrimination to go around. Let's focus on finding them." He picks up a pen and rolls it between his fingers, his dark eyes going distant. I wait for him to get to whatever destination he's headed toward. Hades has always been this way, someone who thinks things through before he acts. His only exception was Persephone, and instead of that emboldening him, he's only become more cautious as a result. "Do you think it's an inside job?" he finally asks.

I bite down on an instinctive denial. It *would* make the most sense if whoever destroyed the greenhouse has insider info... It's also the easiest answer. "It's possible." I take a deep breath. "But anyone who lives in the lower city would have that information. We don't keep our moves secret from our people." They've never given us cause to do so. I sure as fuck hope they're not behind this.

"I suppose you're right." He shakes his head. "Is it naive of me to hope that's the case? After Andreas..."

"Yeah." We don't talk about my uncle, the man who played the role of father to both of us. The old man's mind started to go years ago, but the truth neither of us could quite handle was the one he'd held back for thirty long years.

Hades's father, the man who held the title before him, the father who supposedly died in the fire alongside his mother? He is alive. He's *been* alive this whole time, ruling his own little kingdom in a city within drivable distance from Olympus.

Not that visiting was easy with the barrier, but best I can tell from all the things we don't say, both father and son thought the other was dead in the fire that scarred the man before me. It makes sense why Zeus allowed that to happen. He had a vested interest in weakening the lower city, and having a child inherit the title allowed him to shove Hades back into the realm of myth. What I don't understand—what Hades can't forgive—is that Andreas also knew the truth and kept it from him.

So many lies. So many betrayals.

I'm not an innocent. I know Andreas had a hard choice to make, and he made the best one for Olympus—specifically the lower city. And it *was* the best choice for the lower city. The Zeus who would go so far as to risk war to kill his rival wouldn't take kindly to that same rival returning to the city after being presumed dead by the public. Andreas let my Hades believe his father was dead...but he also let *that* Hades believe his son was dead. The only way to drive him from the city. The only way to keep them both safe.

I understand difficult choices. I even understand putting the greater good above the happiness of a single person. Or two people, as the case may be.

But that doesn't mean it was the right call for the kid I grew up idolizing. The boy who had to become a man much too soon, who had the weight of half of Olympus on his shoulders, while most teenagers were only worried about kissing pretty people beneath the bleachers.

"I would prefer to believe that all our people are above reproach, but I won't bet the life of my wife and unborn children on it. Look into everyone again. Prove that our trust is founded." He hesitates. "Please."

I don't remind him that I've personally picked and vetted everyone on Persephone's security team. He knows. He still needs me to do it again for his peace of mind. It's a small ask in the grand scheme of things. "I'll take care of it."

"Thank you." He lets me get almost all the way to the door before he speaks again. "How's Eurydice?"

I recognize a trap when it closes around me. Honestly, I'm

surprised it took him so long to circle around to this, but he's been understandably distracted. I close the door softly and turn to face him. "She's fine."

"She stayed over at your place last night."

I lift my brows. "Are you having me watched, Hades?"

He mirrors my expression. Not quite anger on his face, but a clear warning. "You took her to Minos's party without running it by me first. Did you think I'd let that decision slide without addressing it?"

"She's an adult."

"Funny. That's the argument she keeps giving my wife. I think you'll understand why both of us are...overprotective of her."

I get it. I even respect it. That doesn't mean I want the man who's part boss, part elder brother butting his head into my business. "I'll grant that Minos's party ended up more dangerous than expected, but Eurydice was with me. I kept her safe." I never would have let her be hurt. Andreas may have proved himself too ruthless to completely trust, but he trained me well. I didn't let my guard down once at that fucking party, not when the cost might be harm to Eurydice.

Knowing what we do now, she was never one of the targets. Minos wanted to set up his foster sons as members of the Thirteen, by virtue of the assassination clause. Only one out of two of them were successful, but that was one too many.

Hades barely blinks. "And last night?"

I try not to feel insulted that we're even having this conversation. Hades sees things clearly in every aspect of his life...except family. He went without it for too long, and part of him can't help overcompensating now that he has a wife and three sisters-in-law.

I highly doubt he extends that overprotectiveness to Demeter. She can take care of herself.

But it's a reminder that even if I see him as something of a brother, the same isn't necessarily true for him. "Last night was none of your business," I say firmly. "Eurydice was there because she wanted to be, and the second she stops wanting to be, she's more than free to end things."

Hades stares at me for a beat and then chuckles. "Lie to yourself if you must. Don't lie to me. I've seen the way you look at her when you think no one else is watching. You're not letting her go without a fight."

He's right, but that doesn't mean I'm going to admit as much aloud. The truth is exactly what I told Eurydice the other night: if she doesn't want me, then I'll go back to being her safe friend.

I don't know if that's possible after knowing how good her pussy tastes, how overwhelming the feeling of her coming on my cock is, but better that every moment with her be the sweet agony of knowing I'll never touch her again than to be cut out of her life entirely.

I don't know where Orpheus fits into that picture yet, but we'll come to some arrangement that suits everyone.

Ideally, without Hades and Persephone meddling.

"I respectfully request that you and your lovely wife stay out of it and let us figure things out like the adults we are."

"I make no promises." He chuckles again. "Godsspeed, Charon. You'll need all the luck and stubbornness you can come up with."

There's a part of me that mourns that it won't be a simple linear journey from meeting to friendship to love the way my parents' story was, but then their story ended in tragedy. There's a reason Andreas was the one to raise me.

I want to desire simplicity, but it's not actually what I crave. I knew things wouldn't be simple or easy with Eurydice. It doesn't matter. I want her. I *need* her.

But if I try to keep her confined to me, I'll lose her. I know that much. I don't know what the fuck is happening with Orpheus, but I don't need to know. Eurydice chose me. She'll keep choosing me as long as I don't *force* her to choose. At least I fucking hope she'll keep choosing me.

I glance at my phone as I leave Hades's office. There are no updates from Medusa, but that's a good thing. No news is good news in this line of work. Instead of checking in and micromanaging, I call Minthe. I barely wait for her to pick up to start talking. "We need to go over the security footage again."

She curses. "I already spent hours doing it. They dodged our cameras."

"The ones closest to the greenhouse, yes, but we need to widen the search." There's a feeling in my gut, an instinct demanding I follow it. I'll do as Hades asked and check our people again. It's smart to button up all avenues of investigation. I just don't think we'll find anything there. "They're not local. I'd bet good money that they're not even staying on this side of the river." It's risky. But they're not coming over the bridges, or we'd know about it. Even so, I can't afford to ignore any possibilities at this point. "No matter how good they are at dodging cameras, there's evidence of them *somewhere*."

She's silent for a beat. "What makes you so certain they're not local?"

A guess. An instinct. When I answer her, I speak slowly, feeling my way. "Remember that report we got from Hades two weeks ago? The one that came from Poseidon?"

"The one about Minos's missing shipping containers?"

"The containers weren't missing. Their contents, on the other hand, were." Contents that Poseidon claims he doesn't have any record of. I don't know if I believe him, but Hades does, and he would know more than I would. He interacts with the Thirteen directly. I only have secondhand information. "Someone unloaded them before Poseidon could act on the information we got."

"You think Triton had something to do with that?"

I hadn't really thought it through. Like so many other things that come from Hades's many meetings with his peers, it's a problem for the upper city. So much of that shit never crosses the river to bother us, so I only focus in on the information I need to keep our people safe.

I'm only now starting to realize what a mistake that assumption is. Just because no one has tried to kill Hades in an attempt to take his title—an impossible task since the legacy titles among the Thirteen are familial and therefore exempt from that clause—doesn't mean we are free from enemies in the lower city. Or enemies who will sneak across the river to sow fear.

That's what the attack on the greenhouse feels like. The action of an enemy.

"I think we can't take anything for granted," I finally say. "Search the cameras again, with a wider net this time. If they're not locals, someone has seen something. They're entering the lower city somewhere, if not by the bridges. They're moving around on the streets."

"What if someone's harboring them?"

Minthe has a way of speaking the things I'd rather not think about. It's incredibly frustrating but makes her an excellent part of the team. "Then we deal with it. It's a big job. Pull whoever you need for it."

"Was already planning on it, boss." She puts an ironic lilt on the last word. She might show a little more respect to Hades, but she and I have known each other too long to stand on ceremony. When we were teens and her parents were having a hard time accepting her identity, she moved into this big ass house with us. Her relationship with her parents has mended in the years since, but she never moved back out again.

A lot of people who work for Hades have similar stories. Minthe once joked that we're like the Island of Misfit Toys, and she's not wrong. Hades has a habit of collecting the desperate, the broken, and the hopeless. Then he gives us a home. Acceptance. Safety.

As a result, every one of us would die for him.

ORPHEUS

I SIT IN THE BACK OF THE CAR FOR A LONG TIME. OUR driver, a buff white woman with short blond hair and snake tattoos, grudgingly left the engine running for me before she followed Eurydice into the restaurant. I don't need the faint heat coursing from the vents, but I do appreciate the gesture. It gives me time to think. Up to this point, I've mostly been flying by feel. I would've done anything to prevent being sent away. I didn't expect to enjoy it so much though.

And now? After this morning, everything is crystallizing into a hope I never thought I would fulfill. I don't want this to end once I've paid penance to Eurydice's satisfaction. I didn't think it was possible to earn her trust again, but now I wonder.

And then there's Charon.

Every time I think of him, I expect to feel a stab of jealousy. Eurydice is beautiful; she always has been. There's something about her that makes people want to gather her up and put her on a shelf. I'm guilty of it myself. I wanted to hoard her time and her presence for me and me alone. She was my muse, after all. As much as I enjoyed the way people's gazes would linger on her whenever we were in public, there was a part of me that wanted to throw my coat over her and shield her from their attention.

I don't feel that way with Charon. Watching her ride his cock... his mouth...his hands...it pulls at parts of me I didn't know existed. Seeing her come on his tongue while he shoved his cock down my throat was an experience bordering on religious.

In the past, I preferred to put my own spin on reality in my paintings. A portrait where the subject is identifiable, yes, but I like to insert fantastical elements that deepen the meaning. I've never been overly drawn to Impressionism or any of the styles that leave too much up for interpretation though.

Sitting in this car, with the memory of last night flowing through my mind, my fingertips itch again. I don't know how to convey the tangled feeling in my chest into color and movement, but for the first time in so many months, I want to try.

I lean back and close my eyes. Eurydice has always felt a graceful blue to me, but with lust and need riding her hard—and that delicious thread of dominance—she bleeds over into magenta. She is all bold strokes and sensual curves. Charon, on the other hand, is a red so dark it's almost black. His desire is not anything as simple as lust. He wants me, he needs her, and he is the framework that holds this entire experience in place. He is both the grounding force and the boundary that keeps us safe. His presence won't stop us from cascading into ruin, but it would be all but guaranteed without him involved.

And me? I've never been one for self-portraits, but this image would not be complete without my presence. A fragile lacework of pale blue twined with lilac morphing into red at the edges.

I can't quite see how the three fit together seamlessly, but the threads are there all the same. In this moment, I hope with all my heart that life can imitate art. But then, I haven't painted this yet, have I? I don't know if I'm even capable of doing it anymore.

The door opens, startling me. I open my eyes to find Eurydice leaning down to catch my gaze. She glances over her shoulder, looking almost guilty. "Let's go."

It's on the tip of my tongue to ask her where her sister is, or at least her security detail. I don't. I have a feeling that to ask is to be left behind. She's allowing me to come with her, trusting me this much, and I won't do anything to make her doubt that decision. I scramble out of the back seat and follow her down the sidewalk at a quick clip. We're not quite running, but it's increasingly obvious that she's going rogue. "Charon's not going to like this," I murmur.

"I'll deal with him when I get back to the lower city." We turn the corner, and she slows down enough for me to catch up without rushing. She shoots me a sharp look. "Tattling won't earn you any points with anyone."

I hold up my hands in surrender. "I am a vault. Take me where you will." The words come out a little more serious than I intend, but I don't take them back. It's only been two days back in her presence, and I'm willing to do a whole lot more than crawl in order not to be sent away.

"We'll see."

We walk three more blocks before she flags down a taxi. I follow her into the back seat and wait for the car to pull away from the curb to ask, "Where are we going?"

"I need to see a woman about a thing." For a long moment, I think she'll leave it there, but she sighs and slouches against the seat. "How caught up on current events are you?"

"Enough. Most of what I know comes from the gossip magazines, but it's easy enough to read between the lines. Minos is the enemy, or at least the first wave of the enemy. It seems like his foster son went rogue when he relinquished the Hephaestus title, but the family has still done a damn good job of destabilizing the city."

Eurydice gives me a pointed look. "Not just a pretty face."

A year ago I would've made a quip about her thinking I'm pretty, but I just shrug and give a pained smile. "I am Apollo's brother, after all."

"Yes, but you've always been his brother. You've never paid attention to politics that don't directly affect you before now." She tucks her hair behind her ears and lowers her voice. "After Minos's party, Eris approached me with some information. Ariadne isn't as on board with her father's plans as it would seem. She's also far cleverer than anyone notices. She sees things, hears things that will be incredibly useful to us if she'll share that information."

I consider that as the cab pulls to a stop in front of the university. If it's easy enough to read between the lines of current gossip, Eurydice might as well have lit up a neon sign over her head. "No one except Eris knows you're doing this, do they?"

"It's a long shot, and Ariadne is easily spooked. Better that I try on my own. If I'm successful, then my sisters can yell at me about it later. If I fail, no one needs to know."

"Except me."

"Except you."

It's the smallest trust, but it is trust. Even so, I can't entirely celebrate. Eurydice is meeting with the daughter of the enemy, and while I think she's smarter than anyone gives her credit for, that doesn't mean that she can't get in over her head. If Ariadne is as clever she says, she might be laying a trap. It's been done before, after all. "It's not safe."

"It's Olympus. There's nothing about the city that's safe. I know that better than anyone." She climbs out of the cab and starts toward the gardens that the university boasts on its grounds.

I told myself I wouldn't push her, but I can't let that statement stand. I pay the cab driver and hurry after her, my guilt so thick that it chokes the breath from my lungs. I catch up to her just as she enters the gardens. "I'm sorry. I know words don't mean a goddamn thing when you experienced harm, but I'm so fucking sorry, Eurydice. I should've known that there was more going on, but I was so selfish that it never even occurred to me until…" Until I'd seen the headlines. I may play the part of the pretty fool, but I've always prided myself on seeing the rhythm of things. Of understanding what isn't being said. There wasn't a single positive reason that Eurydice would be in the lower city. Only negative ones. By the time I realized it the next day, it was too late.

"I know."

Her quiet confidence stops me short, and then I have to scramble to catch up again. "What do you mean you know?"

"You're right—you were a selfish prick. Maybe you still are, but the only thing you ever harmed was my heart. I don't believe that you would have set me up if you knew what Zeus really planned."

Maybe her words should reassure me, but somehow they make it so much worse. Because she's right; I did harm her heart. "I didn't say I was a prick."

"Am I wrong?"

Well…no. "I don't understand how you can even look me in the face. Why didn't you turn away when I came to you on the bridge?"

She slows her pace, and we take several turns through the gardens in silence. I haven't come here since I graduated, but I used to spend a lot of time haunting these pathways. No matter what time of year it is, the gardens are a riot of inspiration.

They have nothing on Eurydice.

She finally stops and turns to face me. "I loved you."

"Loved. Past tense."

"What do you want from me, Orpheus?" She crosses her arms over her chest and glares at me. "I have a lot of conflicting emotions right now, all campaigning for supremacy. I don't know what I'm feeling at any given moment. Sometimes I still love you. Sometimes I really would like to run you over with a car. It varies."

I know I should be focusing on her wanting to run me over with a car, but all I can hear is those four words. *I still love you.* The fledgling hope in my chest sprouts a second set of wings and beats madly as if trying to escape my rib cage. "I still love you too."

She curses and throws up her hands. "You are one of the most infuriating people I've ever met."

I grin. Her irritation only increases my joy. We have a chance. We have *better* than a chance. If the love is still there, then we can figure out the rest. I may not always be the smartest person in the room, but even I know better than to say that out loud. "I'm sorry." I do my best to sound meek and repentant. From the look she gives me, both irritated and amused, I don't do a good job of it.

Her phone pings, and then pings again and again and again. Eurydice pulls it out of her purse and her expression goes waxen. "Oh, fuck. We need to hurry."

I almost asked her who we're meeting, but the risk of her sending me away if I irritate her too much is too high. I'll find out my answers soon enough.

Eurydice hurries through the pathways, moving with an assurance that tells me she's definitely been here recently. She's not going to school here right now. From my understanding, she dropped out at the start of winter quarter last year. Another fault to lay at my feet. I've cost her so much, she must be a damned goddess to still love me after it all.

Most days *I* don't even love me.

I get my answers as we walk through the doors to the greenhouse and into balmy heat. I shake out my hands, which instantly start prickling from the change in temperature. If the gardens outside reflect the change in seasons, the various plants readying themselves for winter, in here it's a permanent summer.

The woman who steps into view is one I haven't met personally, but after a few seconds, I place her. Ariadne. She's only been photographed with her father a handful of times since arriving in Olympus, but the woman in front of me hardly looks like the same person. Oh, she has the same light-brown skin, curvy body, and straight black hair, but she's wearing a pair of leggings and a long sweatshirt that clings to her hips and waist and chest. She also doesn't have on a drop of makeup, and it's clear she hasn't been sleeping well by the circles under her dark eyes.

Those eyes take me in with suspicion, which she turns on Eurydice. "You were supposed to come alone."

"Consider Orpheus an extension of me." Her sharp tone softens, and she takes a step forward. "What's going on? You said we wouldn't be able to meet for a while, but your texts seemed pretty panicked."

"Yeah." Her full lower lip quivers. "I need you to get me out, Eurydice. I need you to do it right now."

EURYDICE

16

THERE'S NO GOOD WAY TO GET ARIADNE TO SAFETY WITH-
out exposing what I've been doing with her up to this point. Maybe
if Eris was answering her phone, things would be different, but after
the third time I get sent to voicemail, I know it's a lost cause. I almost
call my mother, but the only people my mother looks out for are
herself and her daughters. She might extend an offer of sanctuary,
but she's not above going back on her word if it suits her end goals.
I promised Ariadne that she would be safe. That means there's only
one person I can call.

I'm about to be in so much trouble.

The woman standing next to me hardly seems to have the same
bubbly personality that I've interacted with previously. I don't know
what happened, but she's scared out of her mind. She keeps flinching
every time Orpheus moves. I don't think it's him personally that's
causing the reaction. It's more that he's fidgeting, and the movement repeatedly startles her. Either way, it has my nerves fried.
"Orpheus," I snap. "Go stand watch by the door."

For a second, he looks like he wants to argue, but he finally gives a short nod and moves toward the door. We're not so deep into the greenhouse that he's soon out of sight though, and even though he's not trained the same way that Charon is, I find his presence comforting.

I turn back to Ariadne. "I need to know what I'm dealing with. I promised to help you, and I will, but I need all the details in order to make sure I keep my word to the best of my ability."

She wraps her arms around herself tightly, as if afraid that she'll shatter into a million pieces. When she speaks, it's so soft that I have to strain to understand her. "I'm pregnant. I need an abortion. As soon as feasibly possible."

I stare. Who...? But then, it doesn't matter, does it? I'm doubly glad I chose not to call my mother now, because I can't guarantee what she would do with this information. The pregnancy has to be caused by someone in Minos's household, and I highly doubt it's Theseus. Of the other three men left living with her, two of them are related to Ariadne. While I can't rule anything out, I don't think Minos is guilty of *that*. And Icarus certainly isn't.

Which leaves the Minotaur.

My mother wouldn't hesitate to use a pregnancy as leverage to attempt to bring the Minotaur over to our side. Even at the expense of Ariadne. I won't let her do it. I take Ariadne's hands and squeeze until she meets my gaze. "I have to call someone for help. I know this is scary, but we'll go to a clinic right now. I will stay with you the whole time."

The relief on her face makes me feel a little weak. I'm nearly certain Hades won't make the same call my mother would, but if I have to fight him and the rest of the Thirteen, then so be it. "After that, we'll set you up somewhere safe and talk about the future."

"Okay." She slowly pulls her hands from mine and nods. "Okay," she repeats.

I pull up my phone. It's tempting to take the cowardly route and call my sister instead, but in this I can't trust Persephone any more that I can trust my mother. I don't *think* she would force me to go back on my word, but I can't be certain. All the women in my family can be remarkably ruthless when those they care about are on the line. If Persephone thought that handing over Ariadne would protect her husband, her family, her unborn children? She'd feel guilty for doing it, but she'd make that call.

I take a deep breath and dial Hades.

He picks up on the second ring. "Eurydice? Is everything okay? Did something happen to Persephone?"

Guilt threatens to rise, but I muscle it down. "Persephone is fine. She's with Medusa and the rest of the security team."

He's silent for a beat, and when he speaks again, he sounds much more like himself. Calm and cold and perfectly collected. "In that case, what can I help you with?"

Here it is. The point of no return. Once I ask for his help, I have to live with the consequences, and so does Ariadne. I take a deep breath. "I need your help. I don't really have the time to explain everything right now, but I need sanctuary for someone, and that person needs an abortion. Today."

Again, he's silent for several moments. My heart beats faster as I have to face the very real possibility that he might tell me no. And if Hades denies me, then I can't ask Charon for help either. It wouldn't be fair to put him in that position—and I don't think I'd recover from reaching out for help and having him turn away in response. Better to not put either of us in that position to begin with.

"Are you the friend who needs these things?"

A surprised laugh bursts free, though it has an edge of hysteria. "If it was, I wouldn't have come to you for help. No offense, but my sisters and mother have my back before anyone else. Even you."

"Fair enough." Amusement filters in his tone but quickly fades. "You understand that I had to ask."

"I understand." If he went behind Persephone's back to help me, it would piss her off something fierce. Worse in so many ways, it would upset her. Right now, no one wants to upset Persephone.

Something I should've thought about before I ditched her at the Dryad.

"I'll arrange everything, including transport. Your friend will be well taken care of."

Relief threatens to make me lightheaded, but we're not out of the woods yet. "Sanctuary and the procedure. Today. Your word that both will happen."

"You have my word, Eurydice. I promise."

It has to be good enough. Once he's given his word, he won't break it. Not for anyone…even his wife. I take a shuddering breath. The next part won't be any easier, because I know exactly who he'll send as transport. That's a battle to fight later. First, I have to see to Ariadne. "We're at the university in the upper city. In the greenhouse."

"I see. Stay there until Charon texts you that he's arrived. Be safe, Eurydice."

"I will." I slip my phone back into my purse and turn to Ariadne. "You know that there will be a cost for the help."

"I'm aware." She tucks her hair behind her ears with shaking hands. "I know better than to expect anyone to help me out of the kindness of their hearts. I have the information you're looking for, for all the good it will do you."

There's nothing to say to that. It's not my job to decide whether or not her information is worth the cost of getting her away from Minos. Truth be told, I would do it for free, but that's not how Olympus works. Especially now when the price of failure is so high. "Is there anything else I need to know that can't wait until you're settled?"

"Only that my father will be looking for me." She presses her lips together. "Not just my father."

The Minotaur. I should leave it alone, but I can't help taking her hand. "Did he force you?" I don't have the power to command his death, but that won't stop me from calling in whatever favors I can come up with if he hurt her.

"What? *No.* It was nothing like that." She shakes her head sharply. "But if he knows I'm pregnant, then he's going to get the wrong idea. I can't let that happen."

He's going to get the wrong idea. I'm not sure what I'm supposed to make of that statement, so I set it aside. At this point I have to take her at her word. I don't know what would inspire a woman like Ariadne to climb into bed with a man like the Minotaur, but then I didn't think I would be commanding Orpheus to scrub Charon's kitchen either. People contain multitudes.

I try to keep her engaged and distracted, but after three attempts at conversation, I give up and settle down to wait. It's hard not to run scenarios about what happens when I have to face Hades and my sister...and Charon. None of them are going to be happy with me.

My phone pings. I dig it out of my purse to find the Charon has texted me. My stomach twists a little at the two blunt words. I'm here. He's fucking furious with me, and I can't even claim the high ground this time. I essentially lied to him. "Let's go."

Ariadne presses herself to my side as we head for the door. Orpheus has a strange look on his face, but he keeps his silence. He merely holds the door open for us and falls into step behind. There's no reason for us to be in active danger right now, not when Ariadne has proven herself adept at slipping her father's leash for short times during the last couple weeks, but I can't help but search the paths around us, trying to see through the bushes to ensure no one is following.

Charon waits for us by the curb, standing next to a nondescript black sedan. The tension in his shoulders reflects what I'm feeling. "Get in." He holds open the back door. I usher Ariadne in ahead of me. Charon grabs my wrist in a gentle yet unbreakable clasp before I can follow her. "We *will* be discussing this later."

"I know." I don't have it in me to dredge up any self-righteousness this time. The end might justify the means for most people in Olympus, but that's not how Charon functions. He would *never* allow me to put myself in danger to serve this city. The fact that I chose to put myself in danger, at least in his eyes, has to be driving him up the wall.

He turns that harsh look on Orpheus. "You didn't do a damn thing to keep her out of trouble, did you?"

Orpheus shrugs. "I figured it was better that one of us accompanied her. If I started arguing, she would've made me stay in the car."

"A good dog *protects*." He doesn't give either of us a chance to respond to that before he pushes me into the back seat and slams the door. Apparently Orpheus gets the front seat. Lucky him.

"I don't think he likes me very much." Ariadne huddles in her seat, her fear saturating the air in the enclosed space.

I put aside all thoughts of later. Charon and I will have it out, and apparently Orpheus too, but none of that matters right now. I take her hand and try not to wince when she tightens her grip to painful levels. "You're safe. Hades gave his word, and he never breaks it." And Charon serves Hades. His isn't an unquestioning obedience—Hades would never expect that—but he has no reason to question *this* order. We're helping Ariadne...and serving the lower city in the process.

"How novel." She gives herself a shake. When she speaks again, she's managed to dampen some of the brittleness that has me so worried. "I'm sorry to drag you into this. I really did plan on helping you even without asking for anything but a safe place to stay, but when the test came back positive, I didn't know who else to call."

Her family has only lived in Olympus for a couple months at this point, and I wouldn't say that they've made actual friends. Allies? Possibly. But even then, it doesn't apply to the entire family. Minos is the one charming people and making connections. Aside from his house party, he hasn't brought his daughter—or his son, for that matter—out.

Still...

"Why didn't you reach out to Theseus?" He might have had

one of the shortest runs for the Hephaestus title in our history, and I still might not trust him all that much despite the fact that he's apparently on our side, but he *is* her foster brother.

She's already shaking her head. "He doesn't like me, and he wouldn't hesitate to throw me to the wolves if he thought it would help him and Pandora. The only person I would trust with this is Icarus, but he doesn't know where to go in order to make this happen without it being broadcast across MuseWatch."

It's a fair concern. Nothing is sacred when it comes to the gossip sites. And Minos's only daughter being seen entering a facility known for this kind of procedure? They would be sharks scenting blood in the water. "The paparazzi don't find the lower city as welcoming. You won't be photographed. I promise." I've made more promises today than I have in the last six months. I really hope that I'm not about to break them.

Hades gave his word. I have to trust that.

Charon and Orpheus climb into the car, and then there's no more time for talking. I hold Ariadne's hand as we drive through the upper city to the Cypress Bridge. I wish I could breathe a sigh of relief as we cross over to the lower city, but although it's painful to cross the River Styx without an invitation, it's not impossible. Orpheus is proof of that.

Somehow, I don't think even horrendous pain will be enough to dissuade the Minotaur if he decides to come hunting.

CHARON

IT TAKES EVERYTHING I HAVE TO KEEP MY TEMPER LOCKED down through the next few hours. I have my orders though. Eurydice is safe enough when I deliver her and Ariadne to the small private clinic Hades ensures stays funded so that its services are available to anyone who needs them. It's also staffed by security people Minthe personally chose. It doesn't get the same attention the clinics like it in the upper city do, but we installed the best security system money can buy just in case. There is absolutely no reason for me to see the women past the front door. They're safe.

Too bad my instincts don't give a shit.

All I can focus on is the fact that Eurydice lied to me. She stood there and assured me that she would keep Medusa with her the entire time she was in the upper city, and the first chance she got, she was running off to put herself in direct danger. I don't need to know the details of Ariadne's pregnancy in order to know that. *She's* throwing herself on Hades's sanctuary, and she wouldn't do that if she wasn't desperate. Which means Minos, and anyone he can bring to bear, will be out tracking his daughter. Considering the current climate in Olympus, I don't think he would hesitate to hurt Eurydice if he thought she helped Ariadne.

And *that* is what I cannot forgive.

At least not until I have her in my arms and can reassure myself that she's actually fine.

With nothing else to do, I turn my fury and frustration on the easiest target. Orpheus. "I hope you're fucking happy."

"Hardly." He leans against the car next to me, his dark gaze pinned to the front door of the clinic. "But if she's keeping secrets from you, proving myself to be untrustworthy just means she'll be keeping secrets from me too."

I understand what he saying, but that doesn't make me want to strangle him any less. "You keep talking like we're a team. We're not." It doesn't matter that I decided I'm good with Orpheus being a package deal with Eurydice. What does matter is that she put herself in danger and he didn't try to stop it.

"If we're not a team, then why are you mad at me?"

I open my mouth, but no words come out. He has a point. I don't like it, but he does. "You weren't there the night she was chased through the warehouse district, terrified out of her fucking mind, and then attacked in plain sight of the lower city banks. You weren't there when she pieced herself together over months, until she felt strong enough to go out on her own. If you had been, you would understand why I am so angry right now."

"You're right. I wasn't there. I have so many fucking regrets about what happened that night, and how things fell out afterward.

I'm glad she had you. Truly, I am." He turns to face me, his body language still far too relaxed for my liking. "I know you're scared shitless at the thought of her getting hurt. I am too. I'm not a fighter like you, but I would still put myself between her and any danger without hesitation."

I don't know if I believe him.

I don't know if it matters.

We shouldn't get too into shit without her here, but there's something that needs to be said, and it's better to get it out of the way now. "You mean to stay."

Orpheus tilts his head back, giving me a good look at the line of his throat. I have the nearly overwhelming urge to set my teeth to that unmarked skin. He speaks before I can do or say something I'll regret. "That's up to Eurydice."

It's as good as saying yes. I respect him for not pussyfooting around the subject. "Are you planning to try to steal her back to the upper city?" My voice is deceptively mild, covering up the sudden shift inside me. I may have decided on her—and Orpheus—but that doesn't mean either of them feel the same way. What if Eurydice only saw this year in the lower city as a pause, a moment to catch her breath before flinging herself back into the glittering poison seeped into the other side of the River Styx?

I can't stand in her way. Doing so would mean clipping her wings, and I'd die before trapping her like that. Even if she takes my heart with her when she goes.

"I don't know." He sighs. "I didn't exactly have a plan when I accepted your...invitation...to cross the River Styx. All I wanted was to apologize and to find a way to *live* again instead of just existing. I didn't expect to have even a chance with her again." His lips quirk. "I didn't expect you either."

I know what he means, but I'm still pissed about everything, and I'm not willing to meet him halfway. Not right now. "I don't know what you're talking about."

"Don't you?" He moves faster than I would have believed possible and snags my wrist. One moment he's standing beside me, and the next he's in front of me, chest to chest. "So we're just going to pretend I wasn't choking on your cock a few hours ago?"

He smells really fucking good. I could push him off easily, but I let him press us harder against the car. The contact grounds something in me that's been spinning out since Hades called and told me to go to the upper city to pick up Eurydice, who was *not* where she was supposed to be. I take a slow, deep breath. "You were there for the taste of her."

Orpheus raises his brows. He really is pretty in a way that makes me want to smudge him up a bit. His lips curve. "Keep telling yourself that if you want." His gaze drops to my mouth, and for a moment I really fucking hope he'll kiss me. His smile fades, and he steps back slowly, almost as if he craves the contact as much as I do. "I might have come here for her, but plans change."

I have to swallow down my desire before I can speak with anything resembling a normal voice. Only the fact that he's suffering the same tempers the experience. "She might still send you away."

"Yeah, I know." He drags a hand through his hair. "Not a whole lot I can do about that. If she tells me to get lost, then I'll respect her decision."

"I don't understand you," I say softly. "I know your reputation, and I know what she's told me about you in the moments when she was willing to talk about *before*, but you're not acting like I expected."

He shrugs, though there's a new tension in his shoulders. "Both Eurydice and I have changed a lot in the last year."

That's the damn truth. Even as I tell myself now isn't the time, I can't help thinking about what we did this morning. Of her riding my mouth as he sucked my cock. A perfectly choreographed dance of three. There was no clashing of egos or friction to slow us down. I don't know if we can get that synergy outside the bedroom, but if we can...

A car pulls up before I can finish that thought. I tense as Hades steps out. Gone is the relaxed man I talked to in the study earlier today. Instead, this is the lord of the lower city, the holder of one of the three legacy titles of the Thirteen. Two other cars pull up and Thanatos climbs out of one. He looks at me, and something almost like fear crosses his expression, but before he can say anything, someone starts cursing behind him, and he's unceremoniously pushed aside.

Calypso takes his place. She's a beautiful plus-sized woman with long dark hair and a mean streak longer than the River Styx. She's also a gigantic pain in my ass. It looks like she's going to keep that trend today.

"Please tell me you're not all planning on standing out here like the firing squad."

Hades gives her a cold look. "She claimed sanctuary."

"Exactly." She props her hands on her broad hips and glares. "No matter how she feels about what's happening in there, she's going to have a lot of conflict going on in her head when she walks out that door. The lot of you are going to scare the shit out of her."

Sometimes I wonder what Medusa sees in her, but what do I know? The only parts of Calypso I ever witness are influenced by the fact that she doesn't particularly like me much. She doesn't seem to like *anyone* much. I try to take it as a compliment, since she wouldn't have dared be honest about her feelings while living in the upper city, but it's hard to appreciate the sharp side of her tongue.

For his part, Hades is mostly unaffected. "You have a suggestion, I'm sure."

"We'll take her." She holds up a hand, even though no one is jumping in to offer a different option. "You don't mean to, but you scare people, Hades."

"Who says he doesn't mean to?" Thanatos mutters.

"She'll be safe enough with me and Medusa. We'll give her a couple days to find her feet, and then bring her to you." She raises a brow. "And then you can truthfully say you don't have her when the rest of the peacocks come rattling your door."

Hades considers that for several long moments. He finally nods slowly. "What you're saying makes sense."

"Gee, thanks."

His lips quirk, but the smile dies before it can fully appear. He nods at Thanatos. "Escort them home, and wait until Medusa gets there. Have someone watch the street through the night."

Calypso glares. "That's not necessary."

"I say it is." He crosses to me and lowers his voice. "Did you know about this?"

I hate admitting the truth; it burns my throat. "No. She was supposed to go to lunch with Persephone and then come back to the lower city."

"I see." He glances at the door again. "Do you want to handle that, or should I?"

I have to clench my jaw to avoid telling him that there's no fucking way I'll let him *handle* Eurydice. It's not a normal reaction, and I know Hades well enough that such a statement shouldn't have me fighting not to punch him in the face. What the fuck is wrong with me? I clear my throat. "I'll take care of it."

"I expect a report in the morning." It's a testament to Hades's insight that he's giving me the night. Since I desperately want to put Eurydice over my knee—not that I'd admit as much to *him*—it's a good call. He swivels enough to look at Orpheus, and what little warmth there was in his dark eyes disappears. "I did not invite you to the lower city. I highly doubt my wife did either."

Orpheus meets his gaze steadily. A flicker of admiration ignites inside me; it's not easy to hold Hades's eyes when he's got *that* expression on his face. Orpheus says, "No, you didn't invite me."

"And yet here you are." Hades shifts a little closer, the move threatening. "Give me one good reason I shouldn't toss you into the River Styx for the harm you've done."

I expect Orpheus to fold. He did the moment Eurydice snarled at him, and while he hasn't shown me his throat, he also hasn't challenged me directly. But he doesn't. He just squares his shoulders a little. "With respect, Hades, that's between me and Eurydice." His gaze flicks to me. "And Charon."

It's nothing more than he said when we were alone, but having him publicly acknowledge me and the possibility of a relationship rocks me back on my heels. I keep underestimating Orpheus. I can't guarantee that he's not the selfish prick that I always believed him to be, but he's also more than that.

For the first time, I look at him and feel desire that has nothing to do with Eurydice.

ORPHEUS

EURYDICE ISN'T HAPPY ABOUT THE ARRANGEMENTS Charon made. Her anger is written across the lines of her gorgeous face and the tension in her shoulders. "She should come with us."

To his credit, Charon doesn't flinch in response to her sharp words. "Whoever hosts her will automatically be in danger. Medusa and Calypso are far better qualified to handle anything that will arise as a result of her procedure today—and eliminate any external threat."

I don't know much about Medusa, aside from her reputation and the fact that today she watched me like she was a wolf about to rip into a particularly tasty bunny. People never really spoke openly about the fact that she was Athena's knife in the dark for many years, or about how she disappeared unexpectedly a while back and was never seen again. Calypso, on the other hand, used to move in circles that I'm familiar with. She is a few years older than me, but it was well known that she was Odysseus's mistress. At least until she, too, disappeared. I hadn't realized that they'd run off together. *Good for them.*

"He's right," I find myself saying. I almost regret speaking up when she turns that anger on me, but Charon had a point earlier. I might be willing to let her walk me like a dog, but that doesn't mean I have to be submissive in every aspect of our interactions. There's a serious risk that if I piss her off, she'll send me away, but better to know that will be the end result now. Otherwise I'll fall even deeper into the trap of hope, only to have it ripped away later on. "You did your part and got her here. She'll be taken care of, and you can go see her tomorrow if you'd like."

"If I wanted your opinion, I'd fucking ask." She drags her hands across her face. "I really don't like that you're both ganging up on me."

I don't move toward her, because I'm still not entirely sure what the parameters of our relationship are, but I soften my tone. "We're just trying to take care of you, Eurydice." That, at least, is the truth both Charon and I can agree on.

She glances to where Calypso is ushering Ariadne into a black sedan that is identical to the one Charon drives. Medusa arrived a few minutes ago, and she doesn't look any happier than anyone else about this turn of events. She glares at Eurydice, her muscular arms crossed over her chest.

Eurydice shivers. "I know when I've been outplayed. Fine. You win this time. Let's go home."

Home. I know she doesn't intend the word to have any deeper meaning, but that damned hope flutters in my chest all the harder. I want it to mean something. I'm not foolish enough to believe that I've done anywhere near enough penance to make things right, but I have a direction and a goal now. That's more than I've had for the last year.

It certainly feels like home on the silent drive to Charon's town house and through the tense meal where no one quite looks at each other. Not exactly what I was hoping for when she said those three magic words, but it's familiar enough in its own way. My parents have been together for something like thirty-five years, though they never bothered to get around to the marriage part. While they definitely care about each other, there have been whole years where I was certain they didn't like each other even a little bit. This dinner feels a little too close to that for my peace of mind.

At least it does until Charon sets down his silverware and leans back in his chair. Eurydice tenses, obviously expecting him to start in on her about ditching her security detail today. But he turns those hard blue eyes in my direction. "Why don't you paint anymore?"

It's an effort not to shrink down in my chair. I am rich, handsome, and from a legacy family, but none of those things have anything to do with me. I didn't earn them. They are mine through an accident of birth. But painting? That's something I always felt good taking credit for. It's a craft I worked hard to develop, and my career exists because of that skill set.

A skill set I haven't been able to deploy for nearly a year.

I have a dozen answers to that question, ones I've given repeatedly in the months since I stopped painting. None of them are the truth. Even as I call myself seven kinds of fool, I give an honest answer. "I lost my muse, and after that my world went gray. It's hard to find inspiration in a world without color."

Eurydice sucks in a sharp breath, but I can't make myself look at her. Not when it feels like I just laid my heart on the table before us. For his part, Charon merely seems thoughtful. He finally says, "I've decided how you can make things right, Eurydice."

She sputters. "I didn't do anything wrong…"

He turns his head slowly to look at her, and her words die out. Charon leans forward and props his elbows on the table. "You want to try that again?"

She opens her mouth like she wants to continue arguing, but then her shoulders drop and her head bows. "Look, I was never in any danger, and this needed to be done for the benefit of the city as a whole."

"Your sister and Hades might buy that line of bullshit, but I know better. I don't give a fuck about Olympus. You made me a promise, and you broke it."

It's fascinating to watch her expressions flicker over her face. I don't get the feeling that she and Charon argue often. Based on what they've both said in the last couple days, it seems like he's taken the role of the supportive protector. He made her feel safe enough to find her feet, and that doesn't necessarily happen by kicking them out from beneath her the way he is now. It's enough to make me wonder how many times he's bitten his tongue until it bled to keep his worry inside. I bet it's happened more than once.

She finally sighs. "You can't expect me to move around wrapped in bubble wrap. This city has always been a dangerous place, and it's only getting more so as time goes on. If you put me in a cage, I'll wither away to nothing."

Charon shakes his head slowly, his lips curving just a bit. "That's a nice little straw man argument you came up with, baby. The city being dangerous isn't the problem. You making a call that will no doubt benefit the Thirteen in the ongoing conflict doesn't matter. What matters is that you lied."

She curses and flops back against her seat. "Okay, fine. I lied. I told you I wouldn't go anywhere without a security detail, and I had every intention of slipping them the first chance I got. Are you happy now?"

"Fuck no, I'm not happy. But at least we're getting somewhere." He turns to me. "I want to see what you've got."

"What?" He jumped subjects so quickly, I can't keep up. "What are you talking about?"

"Eurydice owes me an apology. Truth be told, she owes you one too, because she put you in a position where you couldn't talk back without fear of her leaving you behind. As her punishment, I want you to paint her."

I'm already shaking my head. "I just got done telling you that I don't paint anymore." Even if I have started to feel the first glimmer of inspiration in the last two days. It's not enough, not to do anything resembling the kind of work I used to be capable of.

"I'm not telling you to make a painting *of* her, Orpheus. I want you to paint her body. And Eurydice? You will be good and sit perfectly still for the duration. At the end, if we're both satisfied, you'll be forgiven."

Heat licks through me. I turn just in time to see Eurydice's eyes go wide. "You can't be serious."

"You don't know how agonizing the drive was to pick you up today. Hades didn't give me any information except that you needed help and needed it as soon as possible. A little bit of sensual agony won't hurt you, baby. I think it's more than a fair trade."

She narrows her eyes. "You're not going to let this go, are you?"

"Absolutely not."

"So be it." She motions at me. "What paint do you need?"

Charon pushes slowly to his feet. "I already have the materials." He doesn't give either of us a chance to argue before he turns and walks out of the dining room. A few seconds later, his footsteps ascend the staircase and move in the direction of the bedroom. He didn't technically give us an order to follow, but the intent is clear all the same.

Eurydice looks shaken. "Did you two talk about this beforehand?"

I shake my head, feeling just as rattled as she looks. "No. We talked a little, while you were in the clinic, but not about this. I don't know when the fuck he had the time to get body paint." Assuming those are the materials he's talking about. Theoretically, other paints would be safe to put on the skin, but I don't feel comfortable getting experimental. Body paint exists for a reason.

We rise at the same time and follow Charon up the stairs to his room. I can't help sneaking glances at Eurydice all the while. There are plenty of nerves present, but she shows the same antic-ipation I feel curling through my stomach. It's happening again, that strange alchemy that seems to pop up when the three of us are together.

Once in Charon's room, we find him laying a dark sheet over the bed. I still can't believe his audacity. He had no doubt in his mind that we would both obey. He was right; here we are, obediently waiting for our next command. I can't help but lift my brows when he pulls out a bucket of previously opened body paint. "You're just full of surprises."

It's hard to tell in the low light, but I think Charon might be blushing. "There was a party several months ago where a particular kind of costume was highly recommended."

Next to me, Eurydice frowns. "I don't remember any party."

"That's because you weren't invited." Before she can do more than tense a little, he continues, "Hades and Persephone presided over the revelry."

"Oh. *Oh.*" She looks at the body paint with new interest. "What was the theme?"

"We are not discussing it." He sets the bucket on the ground by the bed and focuses on me. "I don't have much in the way of brushes. We'll just have to make do." He holds up two brushes that have seen better days. They're still better than I expected.

"Those will work. I'll be right back." I leave the room and head down to the kitchen to grab a plate from the cabinet. It takes me a few tries to find the right one, and by the time I get back up to the bedroom, Eurydice is in the process of taking off her clothes. I busy myself with examining the paint colors and dosing out a little bit of each onto the plate in a half circle. I might not have used this particular product before, but there's some comfort in the familiarity of this process.

The brush feels strange my hand. For a moment I have the panicked thought that maybe I really don't know how to paint anymore. Maybe it's like everyone says—if you don't use your skills, you'll lose them. I sure as fuck haven't been using it.

They aren't expecting me to create a masterpiece though. Or rather, it will be a masterpiece that no one but the three of us will see. One meant to be destroyed in the shower later. In the past, the idea of creating art that disappears without an audience would have me turning away from the project. Tonight, it removes some of the pressure I didn't realize I was feeling.

Charon climbs onto the bed and leans back against the headboard. He pats the mattress next to him. "Come here, baby. Lie down and give him a good canvas to work with."

"I don't see how this is much of a punishment." She obeys though. I get a devastating look at her ass as she climbs onto the bed and arranges herself where he directed. Then they both look at me, and my heart drops into my stomach. I want this so desperately.

Intent solidifies inside me. Up until this point, I've been a passive party, willing to let Eurydice do as she would. If she had sent me away, I would've gone. But the time for that has passed.

I'll do anything to stay. No matter the cost.

EURYDICE

WHEN CHARON SAID HE WANTED ME TO EARN HIS FOR-
giveness, I expected something more traditional. Bondage, or maybe
him putting me over his knee and spanking me until I begged him to
fuck me. I was even anticipating it. Somehow, despite my bravado,
this is so much worse.

It's absolutely agonizing watching Orpheus mix the paint. He's
got a look on his face that I'm intimately familiar with. Once upon
a time, I used to love to watch him work. He wasn't precious about
being alone while he was painting, so I was able to watch him whenever I wanted to. And I always wanted to.

I don't know if I believe in magic, but when Orpheus sinks
into his creative zone and draws forth beauty from nothing...that's
magic. I always felt special because he allowed me to witness it.

I'm not the same woman, grateful to even be in the room. The
person I am now would never be satisfied with only witnessing
magic. I want to be the one creating it. I don't know what that looks
like for me. I'm not an artist like Orpheus, or a designer like Juliette,

or even a photographer like Psyche—my sister would never call herself that, but it's the truth.

I'm still figuring out where I fit in, which should make this experience particularly uncomfortable, because Charon is effectively shoving me back into a role I no longer want. Except…

It's different.

I'm not a passive observer this time. Not when I'm stretched out with my head on Charon's thigh. Not when Orpheus is joining us on the bed.

He looks at us for several beats and then takes up a position next to my hip closest to the head of the bed. "May I?"

I'm about to answer when I realize that he's not looking at me. He's waiting for Charon's permission. I tense, not sure how I feel about that…except I do know, don't I? It's there in the deep pulse of heat spreading through me. As much as I like being the one to give commands, this is unbearably sexy too. I turn my head just enough to see Charon, to watch the hunger grow in his dark eyes. Not just hunger for me. He wants Orpheus. He wants *us*.

"By all means."

Orpheus smiles and goes about nudging me into the position he wants me. One arm gets draped back over Charon's thighs. He grabs a pillow and stuffs it under my hip so I'm tilted toward him. His hands don't linger on my body, and every time he touches me, I have to fight not to arch into the weight of his fingertips against my skin. He's treating me as gently and remotely as he would any of his canvases. It's agonizing and so hot, I can barely stand it, and he hasn't even *done* anything yet.

Then he begins to paint.

I try to stay relaxed, but the first drag of the wet brush along my heated skin is almost more than I can bear. It's such a small sensation. Somehow that only makes it worse. This is going to go on for a very long time.

"Hold still." Orpheus has a distraction to his tone that I recognize well.

He barely waits for me to force myself to stop shifting before he dips his brush in paint and continues. He doesn't paint particularly thickly, so he makes quick work of coating my skin with a base layer that starts at my collarbone and curves down around my breasts to my stomach and hips and upper thighs. The cool air from the room makes the paint feel colder than it is. Honestly, it's a welcome relief. I'm so hot I feel like I might die from it.

Orpheus leans down and blows slightly against my skin. I jolt to find him grinning at me. The jerk is tormenting me on purpose. I glare. "You're enjoying this."

"Very much."

I have to crane my neck to see Charon, and I get distracted halfway through when I realize his hard cock is only a couple inches from my face. He's obviously enjoying the show, but he makes no move to touch himself or hurry things along. I shift toward his cock, and that's when he *does* move, weaving his fingers through my hair and holding me firmly in place. "Your punishment is still in play, Eurydice."

Out of the corner of my eye, Orpheus picks up his brush again. I lick my lips. "Can't we fast-track this? I'll suck your cock, then I'll suck his cock, then you can stop been irritated with me."

He chuckles, but not in a way that makes me think I'll get what

I want. "One word, Eurydice. *Punishment.* You're not the one who gets to decide if it's fast-tracked or not, and there's no easy way out of this. You will lie there and be still while Orpheus paints you to his satisfaction...and then we'll see how we're feeling."

I'm about to argue when Orpheus starts painting again. When I used to watch him, I was always slightly envious of the canvas. His slow, methodical brushstrokes seemed like the most relaxing thing in the entire world. I was a fool. There's nothing relaxing about this. It's pure agony to have him so focused on my body and yet not focused on my body at all. I am merely the medium for his genius.

Charon chose his punishment well.

On Orpheus's third layer, I break. I'm so turned on, I can't stop shaking. I'm pretty sure I've left an embarrassing wet spot on the mattress, and my nipples are so tight I don't know if they'll ever be the same again. "Please."

"Please?" At least Charon sounds as if he's in as much agony as I am. He just covers it better. He still has his fingers in my hair, but he allows me to turn my face toward him. Gods, his cock looks even bigger than it did earlier. I can't help licking my lips again, and he gives my hair a sharp tug in response. "Eurydice, you were in the process of begging. Don't get distracted now."

I forget myself and start to reach for him, but Orpheus barks out a sharp "Do *not* move."

I freeze. He's focused on my ribs right by my left breast, doing something that requires tiny light brushstrokes.

"Orpheus, please. I need you to touch me; I need you both to touch me."

His color is high on his sharp cheekbones, but his dark eyes are perfectly focused. "Not until I'm finished."

"Orpheus." I've never heard Charon sound like this, almost playful. "She's suffering mightily."

"You created this punishment." He lifts his gaze to Charon—or tries to. In reality, his attention is snagged somewhere between his cock and thighs and neck. "It looks like you're punishing yourself."

The tension builds between them, heartbeat by heartbeat, until I'm certain I can feel it on my skin the same way I can feel the drying paint. Charon finally smiles, a slow happy curving of his lips. "I can handle waiting. All the same, I would love to accommodate you." He flicks his fingers at Orpheus's hips, which is when I notice that he's just as hard as Charon.

"Accommodate."

Charon's fingers go soft in my hair, but he's still not looking at me. "You seem pretty focused on your art."

Orpheus narrows his eyes. "Even on such a beautiful canvas, you have to be careful. It's…been a long time since I've felt like this. Of course I'm focused."

"Not even Eurydice can distract you?" He reaches for the pillow next to them. "It's enough to make me wonder just how far we can push you."

Orpheus watches him carefully wedge a pillow between my head and the bed, replacing Charon's thick thigh. "I was under the impression that we were punishing Eurydice."

"We are." Charon climbs off the bed and circles around to the other side of Orpheus. "Consider this just a bit of fun."

I watch Charon arrange himself, his thighs bracketing Orpheus, his chest to the other man's back. He's big enough that I can still see him clearly. The expression on his face makes me shiver with anticipation. I swallow hard. "I know I have the smallest sadistic streak, but yours puts mine to shame."

"I like what I like." He snakes an arm around Orpheus's waist and presses a hand to his lower stomach. It's hard to tell from this angle, but I think Orpheus's hard cock is pressed against Charon's knuckles. I bite my bottom lip and fight the urge to shift so I can see better. Charon leans close to Orpheus's ear, and though he lowers his voice, it still carries clearly to me. "Do you want to use your safe word?"

Orpheus chokes out a laugh. "Not even a little bit."

"Let me know if that changes." Charon wraps his first around Orpheus's cock, and I nearly come on the spot. "I've wanted to get my hands on you since last night." He kisses Orpheus's neck. "Don't stop painting."

I hold my breath as Orpheus leans forward and braces one hand next to my hip. Charon mirrors his movement so that they're basically on all fours above me. I can feel the air displacement where Charon slowly jacks Orpheus's cock. He's not touching me, but the possibility that he might, that he might do us both at the same time…I want it so badly, I have to put all of my will into not arching up to close the distance between us. Compare that with the light touch of Orpheus painting me, and I'm about to go out of my mind with need.

"Okay," I gasp. "You've proven your point. I'm very, very sorry. I promise never to scare you like that again, or slip my security detail, or do…anything! Just touch me. *Please*."

"See. Isn't she particularly sweet when she begs?"

It takes Orpheus a few seconds to answer. When he does, he hardly sounds like himself. "Yeah. I like it. A lot."

"Me too." Charon kisses Orpheus. For some reason, I almost expect it to be rough, but I couldn't be further from the truth. The kiss starts off light and sweet, almost as if he's asking for permission. That only lasts a heartbeat though. Orpheus drops the brush, and then his fingers are in Charon's hair, and he's toppling the other man back to the bed.

It's the purest agony to watch them fall into each other, their hands a frenzy on each other's bodies, as if they can't get close enough, can't touch each other hard enough, can't believe this is real. I'm both devastatingly jealous and so fucking privileged to be able to witness this.

Charon breaks the kiss slowly, Orpheus's bottom lip between his teeth. I can actually see him bite down a little before he releases Orpheus. "You're terrible at multitasking."

"Guilty." Orpheus kisses him again, a quick, hard contact that makes my toes curl. "Can you blame me?"

"Not even a little bit." Charon nudges him until he's facing me again. "Get back to painting."

Orpheus looks a little dazed, but he obeys. He fumbles to pick up the brush and palette. When he refocuses on me, it's clear that half of his attention is on the man at his back. For his part, Charon resumes his teasing. Except this time, he takes it up a notch.

He slides down the bed until his face is even with our hips. He's close enough that I get a clear view when he leans up and takes Orpheus's cock into his mouth. It's just as slow and teasing as his hand was earlier. I don't know if that'll make a difference. My whole body clenches in jealousy and need at the way he sucks Orpheus deep and then eases back to flick his slit with his tongue.

Orpheus's brush skitters across my skin. "If you want this to look right, you need to stop doing that right now."

Instead of answering with words, Charon snakes a hand under my thigh and strokes my pussy. I'm so wet, there's no resistance as he slides two fingers into me. He strokes me idly as he sucks Orpheus off, and it takes my pleasure-drunk brain several seconds to realize he's fucking us in the same rhythm. Normally, I need more clitoral stimulation in order to orgasm, but I'm so turned on right now I think I'm going to get there just from the penetration alone. "Oh gods, Charon. Please don't stop doing that."

I should've known better.

He wedges a third finger into me...and then he stops. I'm so close, I can't stop shaking, but I need more to get over the edge. "You are an absolute *bastard*."

"I've been accused of worse."

Orpheus closes his eyes and lets loose a string of curses I've never heard him say before. He carefully sets down his palette and his brush. Then he laces his fingers through Charon's hair. "It's as done as it's going to be. Now finish what you started."

ORPHEUS

UP UNTIL RECENTLY, I WAS PRETTY SURE CHARON HATED me. Now I know it for a lie. I've fucked people who hate me. I don't make a habit of it, but self-loathing is an intoxicating drug, and sometimes it got the best of me. This moment, with his mouth around my cock, is nothing like those rare times with people who actually feel that way. It's a long way from love, but I'll take what I can get.

Next to us, Eurydice looks ready to explode. Charon has his fingers buried in her pussy, but it's clear he's not doing much to get her off. The man really does have a sadistic streak. It's hard to focus on that with him sucking me down like his redemption is on the other side of my cock. I don't know if this is payback for last time or just simple lust, but all I can do is tighten my grip on his hair and hang on for dear life.

Just when I'm on the verge of losing control, when my balls have drawn up and I can't stop myself from thrusting into his mouth… he eases back.

I stare down at him blankly. "You've got to be kidding me."

He licks his lips. Watching that movement is almost enough to push me over the edge. Charon clears his throat. "Eurydice has more than served her punishment, don't you think?"

I look down at her, allowing myself to drink in the sight of my paint on her skin. It's not my finest work as such things go, and yet I'll never be able to recreate the masterpiece because it's *her*. Eurydice. The woman I've loved and lost and found again. The blue and purple flowers I've painted on her skin, framing her breasts and pussy, only accentuate her beauty. They sure as fuck can't compare to it.

I still don't know if I'm allowed to touch her. With so much hanging in the balance, I'm afraid to take that step or assume anything. Doing so might fuck this all up.

Charon understands. Of course he does. He withdraws his fingers from her and presses them to my lips, fucking my mouth slowly and coating my tongue with the taste of her desire. It's exquisite torment. I can't get enough.

He brushes a quick kiss to my lips and then looks down at her. "What do you say, baby? He's been putting in a lot of work. Don't you think he deserves a little taste?"

I'm not sure Eurydice is even hearing us clearly right now. Her eyes are glazed with need, and little tremors work through her body at regular intervals. One lick, maybe two, and she's going to come apart. She turns her head to us. It takes her a few tries before she's able to form words. "Make me come, Orpheus. Now. *Please*." Her voice breaks on the last word.

"You heard her." Charon trails two fingers down my spine, stopping at the small of my back. "Make her come so hard that she's begging for your cock. And when you give it to her, I'll give you mine."

There's no mistaking his meaning. I'll fuck her. He'll fuck me. I'd like to pretend it's both of us continuing to top her, but it wouldn't be the truth. I'll be stuck between them, helpless to do anything but take what they give me. I want that so desperately I almost agree immediately.

But that would be a mistake, and I'm working very hard not to continue making mistakes when it comes to Eurydice. I clear my throat. "Are you okay with that?"

"Yes. Now hurry up. I need your tongue."

It might just be the sex talking, and maybe I really am just as much a selfish bastard as I've always believed, because I don't ask again. I've been dreaming about the taste of Eurydice for months, and the taste I got from Charon's cock was nowhere near enough. I don't know if I've earned the right to touch her, but I'm not going to question her need.

I shift down her body and make myself comfortable. This part of her is as much a work of art as the rest. At one point late in our relationship, I convinced her to pose for me with her legs spread and her pussy on display.

I never did get around to finishing the painting.

She's so wet she glistens in the low light of the bedroom. I can see her clit clearly, hard and needy for my tongue. I don't know why I'm hesitating. Maybe I really do have a masochistic streak, because this moment of waiting is agony, and yet it's making me so hard I'm a little afraid I might come against the sheets before I properly taste her.

"Orpheus. Fuck me with your tongue. Right. Now."

This time, she isn't begging. She's ordering.

Somehow, that makes all the difference. My hesitation melts away. It's my choice to submit, but I'm not the one in the driver's seat of this interaction. Eurydice is. Charon is. And I'm only too happy to follow where they lead.

I lick my way up her center. She might have ordered me to fuck her with my tongue, but it's been a year since I've had my mouth on this woman, and I'm not about to be rushed. Her taste is exquisite. Exactly as I remember. I pause at the top of her pussy and cover her with my mouth, pulsing my tongue against her clit.

She makes the sweetest whimper. In the same moment, Charon sets his teeth against the top curve of my ass. It's not quite a bite, more the promise of one. I'm shocked at how desperately I want that. I press my forehead to Eurydice's lower stomach and gasp for breath. "Are you going to mark me?"

"Do you want me to?"

Eurydice writhes her hips, searching for my mouth. I have to grab her thighs to hold her in place. It's so hard to think with the scent and taste and feel of her consuming my senses. Do I even need to think, though? I knew the answer as soon as Charon voiced the question. "Yes."

I go back to eating her pussy as he palms my ass. He's a big guy. His hands nearly cover me as he squeezes, pressing me together and then parting me in a rhythmic motion. It makes me think of fucking. No doubt that's the intention.

It's hard to focus on what Charon's doing behind me when Eurydice has her fingers in my hair and is grinding herself against my face. When we had sex before, she wasn't exactly a passive lover, but she was almost shy at times about asking for what she wanted. There's no shyness in this. I love it.

Instead of trying to take control, I go where she guides me. She doesn't hesitate to position me exactly where she needs me. She lets me fuck her with my tongue for several beats, and then she guides me up to her clit. I remember exactly what she likes. How could I not when I tormented myself with the memories of our time together for a year straight? I waste no time giving her exactly that now. Every cry she makes spurs me forward. I want her to come over my face. I want that clear mark of ownership, even if it won't last forever.

Her body goes tight. A wave of satisfaction hits me, so strong that I shake. I am so caught up in how her thighs clench around my head that I almost forget about Charon behind me. As the last tremor works its way through Eurydice's body, Charon bites me.

The pain is sudden and deep. Its ache radiates out from the point of contact and has me thrusting against the sheets despite myself. I try to stop. To get control of myself. But then Charon's wet fingers press against my ass...press *into* my ass.

I lose it.

In desperation, I go after Eurydice's pussy again, thrusting my tongue into her in time with my own hips grinding against the bed. Each movement I make pushes me back on Charon's fingers, pressing him deeper. Her cries mingle with a desperate sound coming out of my throat. *Fuck, I'm going to come.*

Charon wedges one hand between me and the mattress, and wraps his fingers around the base of my cock, squeezing harshly. My breath shudders out. It's painful to be pulled back from the edge of orgasm like this, but I'm pathetically grateful all the same. He keeps fucking my ass with his fingers, and I belatedly register that his mouth is still against the bite, his tongue soothing my aching flesh.

Eurydice digs her fingers into my hair and pulls my face away from her pussy. She looks down at me with glazed eyes and bites her bottom lip. "Orpheus." My name sounds like a promise. She tugs my hair again and looks over my head at Charon. I don't know what she sees there—he sure as fuck hasn't stopped what he's doing to me. Her thighs shake on either side of my head. "Fuck me. I need your cock pressing into me and stretching me wide. I'm done waiting."

I want that too. But the only thing keeping me from coming on the spot is Charon's fingers gripping my cock. Humiliation washes over me. I don't know what it says about me that it only makes my desire burn hotter. I lick my lips, tasting her there. "If I fuck you right now, I'm going to come too fast."

"You'd disappoint me like that?" Her voice is low and almost dangerous. "Don't you want to be my good boy, Orpheus? Don't you want to please me?"

"Yes," I gasp. "More than anything."

Charon, the bastard, nips the bite mark on my ass. "You're not coming until I let you. Stop making excuses and do as our woman says. Fuck her properly."

It's slow work to move up the bed with Charon still at my back. I don't tell him it would be a lot easier to concentrate if he didn't have his fingers in my ass. It might be true, but it feels too good to stop. Besides, I trust him. He's not going to let me come until I give Eurydice what she needs.

It's Charon who guides my cock to her entrance, and it's Charon who sets the pace. I almost feel like a puppet on his strings. It's strangely comforting. And hot. Really fucking hot. But we're not finished. He shifts behind me, easing his fingers from my ass and pausing to spread lube on his cock. And then he's there, his broad head pressing against me…pressing *into* me.

I haven't had a partner since the chaotic aftermath of losing Eurydice, when I realized that no amount of sex or alcohol would fill the gaping wound left by her absence. Charon isn't a small man. I have to concentrate on relaxing, on taking what he gives me. He goes slow. No matter how brutal he is in some ways, it's clear he takes care of his partners. He's taking care of me right now.

Eurydice seems to know it too. She's shaking beneath me, but she waits patiently until Charon has filled me completely. They share another of those looks filled with too many things. I can't see him, but her heart is in her eyes.

I knew she loved him. Now I'm seeing it in real time.

Strange how it doesn't hurt as much as I expected. How can it when I'm between them like this? When they've folded me into the possibility of *us*?

We surge together in a rhythm as old as time. Every thought left in my head fades away against the pounding pleasure. Charon keeps his fingers wrapped tightly around my cock, preventing me from losing control. It's a good thing too. With him filling me, and Eurydice soft and desperate beneath me…without some assistance, I would've come on the second stroke.

She tangles one hand in my hair and reaches past me to do the same with Charon. "More. Harder."

Charon's lips touch my ear. "She wants *more* and *harder*, Orpheus. Can you handle giving it to her?"

If I can't, I'm going to die trying. The thought is suitably dramatic enough to focus me. I'm distantly aware of Charon moving back the tiniest bit, giving me space to plant my hands on either side of Eurydice's shoulders. And then I start to fuck her exactly like she needs.

Giving her more.

Giving it to her harder.

I slam into her again and again, each withdrawal driving me back on Charon's cock. Too much. Holy fuck, it's too much.

Just when I think I can't stand it any longer, when I'm going to beg him to let me come, Eurydice clenches around me. Her whole body goes tight, and she lets loose a cry I'll hold close until my dying day. She's still fluttering around my cock when Charon releases me. After that, it's over quickly. It takes me less than four strokes before I'm surging forward and filling her. I collapse half on top of her... which is when I realize that it's not over yet. And that Charon's been holding back.

He's not holding back now.

He wedges one big arm beneath my hips, lifting my ass to the angle he wants. And then he plunders me. There's no other word for it. He takes my ass as if he owns it, as if I've been his all along, and I'm only now coming to terms with it.

As he pulls out of me and comes across my back in hot sticky spurts, I'm not sure he's wrong.

CHARON

I EXPECTED THE SUMMONS, SO I'M NOT SURPRISED TO find a text from Hades when I wake up in the morning. What *does* surprise me is that he wants Eurydice to attend. Maybe it shouldn't. For better or worse, she's the reason that we have Ariadne in the lower city. I have a feeling that Ariadne might be hesitant to share the information she possesses if the person she reached out to for help isn't present. That doesn't mean I want Eurydice involved in this any more than she already is.

Not that anyone has asked me what I want. I won't be consulted when it comes to *this* situation. Hades might have all but explicitly agreed to let me figure things out between me and Eurydice, but that courtesy doesn't apply to anything that will officially affect Olympus.

I sit up and drag my hands through my hair. My whole body aches after last night, a pleasant reminder of just how good it is when the three of us get out of our own way. At some point we need to have an actual conversation, because no matter how good the sex is, it's only one part of the equation that creates a healthy relationship.

That's what I want. With Eurydice...and Orpheus. The bond between them remains strong, even if there's plenty of baggage to go along with it. The wound between them never properly healed, and I don't know if having me in the mix is enough to keep it from festering further. Shit is complicated.

Either way, I can't chase down those answers right now. As much as I want to prioritize Eurydice over politics, the fact remains that she inserted herself into said politics. I would have preferred to keep her away from all the bullshit and danger, but she's also made it incredibly clear that she won't be kept out of anything. Not even for her own safety. With that in mind, I reach over Orpheus's sleeping body and lightly tap her hip. "Wake up, baby. It's time to pay the piper."

She stretches slowly, arching her back until the sheets slide off her breasts. I don't think she's doing it on purpose, but it's incredibly distracting. Still, it's best not to keep Hades waiting. I haul myself out of bed and make quick work of a shower before anyone can think to join me. Eurydice walks into the bathroom as I wrap a towel around my waist. She won't be fully coherent until she has some coffee. I enjoy the soft, sleepy look on her face. There's a trust inherent in witnessing these early morning moments, and I don't want to lose the intimacy.

She makes a beeline for the sink and grabs her toothbrush. "I know for a fact that both my sister and Hades are night owls. Why are we being summoned this early in the morning?"

"You kicked the hornets' nest, baby. The sooner we get things squared away with Ariadne, the better." I haven't heard of any other attacks since the ones on Triton and Poseidon, but that doesn't mean they haven't happened. Minos might not have been directly responsible for most of the recent assassination attempts—possibly excepting Triton—but he's still a danger.

The problem is that he's no longer the only danger.

I don't know how we, as a city, deal with the now-public knowledge that there's an assassination clause. I would love to think that it's an upper city problem that has no bearing on the lower city, but for better or worse, we are one city. What happens here affects the upper city, and vice versa.

The thirteen positions of power that were previously considered unassailable now appear all too accessible for those willing to get their hands dirty. I don't know how we move on from that.

I don't have an answer as I get dressed. It's above my pay grade. Normally that would be enough to have me put the problem aside entirely, but the ever-present worry that someone will attempt to kill Hades makes it my problem.

For whatever reason, Eurydice decides not to dress up for the meeting. Instead, she pulls on a pair of jeans that are more holes than fabric, and a knitted sweater that's seen better days. She slicks her hair back into a ponytail, dabs on a bit of makeup that seems like nothing but makes her look well rested, and announces herself ready to go.

We walk back into the bedroom together to find Orpheus awake. He makes no move to get out of bed, just watches us with a tense look on his face. "Morning."

I'm still deciding how to handle the situation when Eurydice props a knee on the bed and presses a light kiss to his lips. "We have to go to a meeting, but we'll bring lunch when we get back. You should probably call your brother."

Orpheus makes a face. "I don't need to report to him like I'm a child."

"I know. Just like I know Apollo worries. Be a good boy and throw him a bone."

His expression goes slack for a moment, and then he chuckles. "It's hard to argue when you say things like that."

"How strange. I had no idea." She grins and heads for the door.

I take a step to follow, but then half turn to him. "Go back to bed, Orpheus. You need to rest." He doesn't look as hopeless as he did when he first showed up on our side of the river, but we've been running him ragged, and he wasn't particularly well rested before. "We'll talk when we get back."

"I'd like that."

"Me too." I turn and head downstairs. I find Eurydice standing out by my car. "Next time, wait inside the front door." I want to believe the lower city is still safe, but the growing unrest in Olympus and the attack on the greenhouse proves otherwise. Until we figure out who's causing problems in the lower city, I don't want her going anywhere alone. Even the sidewalk in front of my town house.

Eurydice takes one look at my face and wisely decides not to argue with me about this. "Okay."

"Thank you." I open the door for her and move around to the driver's seat. It takes no time at all to drive from my place to Hades's residence. I park but make no move to get out of the car. "We're going to talk today. Really talk. I want everything out in the air so we can deal with it, one way or another."

"I would rather not." She doesn't look at me when she says it.

Yeah, I'm not surprised by that. "You don't get the cocks without the men attached, baby. If we don't iron our shit out, it's going to blow up in our faces. I don't want that for you, I don't want that for me, and I don't want that for Orpheus either. I know this shit isn't easy for you, but it's necessary."

She seems to consider that for a moment and then reaches for the door. "Let's go."

I don't press her. There will be plenty of time for that later, and she's right that there's no benefit to us putting off what comes next. When we make it to Hades's office, I'm not remotely surprised to find Persephone there as well. The person who *does* surprise me, though, is Hera. She sits next to her sister on the couch, perfectly coiled rage in a pretty package. She and Persephone might share their mother's coloring, but Persephone and Eurydice actually look a lot more like each other if you were to line the sisters up. Callisto—now Hera—is a blade sheathed in beauty. I don't know what possessed her to marry Zeus, and frankly I don't need to know, but the thing that no one seems to understand is that she was already one of the most dangerous people in Olympus before she took the title of Hera.

Eurydice crosses to her sisters, and they rise to meet her. They exchange hugs and kisses on the cheek, but the tension in the room doesn't decrease in the least. When she's done greeting them, I expect her to sit on the couch between them—clearly, they expect it as well. She doesn't. Eurydice moves back to stand with me in front of the desk. A soldier ready to report. The comparison isn't lost on me. A quick glance around the room says it's not lost on anyone else present either.

"Persephone, if you would be so kind." Hades motions to the door. He waits until she obeys and returns to her spot to pin us with his dark gaze. "I do not appreciate being cornered into giving my word without all the information. While I will not go back on it, I would like a full report. Now." Even though he speaks mildly, his displeasure colors the air.

He's *furious*.

I open my mouth, but Eurydice gets there first. She straightens her shoulders and lifts her chin, her voice calm and collected. "When I met Ariadne at the house party, we had an instant connection. I know that Apollo thinks she has more information than she's sharing, so I took it upon myself to make friends with her in an effort to gather that information. We've been speaking secretly since then, and so when she came to me for help, it was the opportunity I couldn't ignore."

I don't look at her, sure that any sharp expression would give away that she's not telling the full truth. I don't know what her motivation is for covering for the former Aphrodite, but I don't like it. Now's the time to speak, to let everyone in the room know that she's still not telling the full truth.

I don't. Maybe that makes me a traitor. I don't know. At the end of the day, Eurydice has shared the relevant information. Hades isn't a fool; he knows better than to trust other members of the Thirteen, and he has even less reason to trust Eris and her new husband, Theseus. Eurydice keeping Eris's name out of this ultimately won't change anything.

I *will* be asking her why she is still lying later. If I don't like her answer, I'll be the one to tell Hades the full truth.

Persephone starts to say something, but Hades holds up his hand, commanding silence. "You took an unnecessary risk."

"It paid off."

"That changes nothing. It was still a risk. Don't do it again." He steeples his hands before his mouth. "But I will give credit where credit is due. You've managed to pull off something no one else even got close to. If you can get the information out of Ariadne that we need to meet the threat that Minos's benefactor presents, then I'll seriously consider not tossing you to your mother's mercy."

Eurydice startles. "Excuse me?"

"Your sisters and I aren't the only ones you answer to, Eurydice. I haven't informed Demeter of this little stunt, but that doesn't mean I won't." He raises his brows. "How do *you* think she'll react when she hears about the risks you took?"

"That's not fair," she whispers. "What if Ariadne doesn't know anything?"

"You took this risk, and so the consequences are yours. One way or another."

Persephone makes an angry noise. "That's not fair, Hades. She needs more security, and—"

"No." He still doesn't raise his voice. "I understand you wanting to protect your little sister, and I respect the desire. But she wants to play in the dangerous arena of politics. She'll do it with or without our blessing, little siren. Which means we go about this in the proper way."

EURYDICE

22

I DON'T KNOW WHETHER TO BE ELATED OR TERRIFIED. IT feels like I fought so hard to be taken seriously, but now that it's happening, I don't know where to look. Persephone isn't happy. It's written there in the tenseness around her mouth and the sharpness in her hazel eyes. Strangely enough, Callisto isn't looking for a knife to sharpen. She merely watches our brother-in-law with a strange expression on her face.

I realize they're waiting for a response and clear my throat. "What is the proper way?"

"As the protected younger sister of my wife, you've been given a gratuitous amount of leniency. I've allowed you to come and go from the upper city with no restraint while you recovered from last year's events. We have devoted resources to keeping you safe without asking for anything in return."

"*Hades*." My sister's voice snaps into the space between us. "We were happy to help."

"Yes, we were." He nods to Persephone. "Understand that I

don't hold that time against you. My assistance was freely offered without strings. However, if you intend to immerse yourself in the politics and dangers of Olympus, then there are conditions to be met in order to maintain the protection I've offered you."

In all the time I've known him, part of me has always wondered why he is so feared. He is one of the kindest men I've ever met, and as he said he has offered me safety and freedom with no stipulations. He's been a soft older brother, totally and completely nonthreatening.

That's not who is standing in front of me right now.

This man is the king of the lower city. He's the one so many people in the upper city fear, and with good reason. I'm having a hard time not wrapping my arms around myself. He's right. I've been a treasured guest for the last year. I have a feeling that if I told everyone in this room that I had made a mistake and I had no intention of doing it again, I could go back to being that guest. A flower in a glass vase, never able to put down roots or reach my full potential.

He's giving me a chance to take that potential…to *earn* it.

I lift my chin and hope no one in the room notices that I'm shaking. "What are those conditions?" I don't offer to agree to them without hearing what he has to say. I'll do damn near anything to not go back to the way things were, but that doesn't mean I have to be foolish. Hades might be ruthless when it comes to protecting the lower city, but he's not without a heart. His conditions will be fair, even if I don't like them.

"You're connected to too many of the Thirteen. Daughter of Demeter. Sister of Hera. Sister-in-law of Hades and Zeus. When you were essentially a civilian, it didn't matter, but if you're going to stay in the lower city, you *will* be loyal to me."

All of the air rushes out of my body. "You're saying I can't go back to the upper city."

"I am saying that if you stay in the lower city, you will become an official member of my household and be employed by me."

If I agree to this, it will change things. No, not *things*; it will change *everything*. Oh, I don't expect my mother to just turn me out, or for Callisto to decide that she never wants to see me again, but what about the rest of the implications?

If I agree to this, it means I will be answering to Charon in an official capacity. I've been in the lower city long enough to know that Hades doesn't have any rules against fraternization, but all of those relationships are between staff. For as long as I've been here, Charon has never indulged. Not until me.

That's not something I'm going to ask about right here, right now. Not with my sisters looking on. "I understand, but what does that mean practically?"

"I don't expect you to suddenly be part of the security team, but your connections make you uniquely suited for information gathering."

Next to me, Charon doesn't seem to be breathing. Hades obviously didn't talk to him about this beforehand. Persephone holds her pregnant stomach, glaring daggers at her husband. It's a testament to their relationship that she won't challenge him, even in a relatively private setting with only family present...well, family and Charon.

And Callisto?

She has a small smile on her face that I don't like one bit. It's the same expression she gets when she's about to start shit that will drag everyone into the mess. She would never do something to directly harm me or either of our other sisters, but that doesn't mean she would hesitate to get us into a whole shit ton of trouble. She doesn't say a single word.

Really, I was only ever going to have one answer to this. I don't know what it looks like answering to someone in the official capacity, but I've been searching for a role to call my own, and that's exactly what he's offering me. "I agree."

"Good." His gaze flicks to Charon. "She needs a permanent security detail. One person should be good enough."

I half expect Charon to argue. He's done everything in his power to keep me out of danger, and no matter how protected I am, working for Hades is dangerous. Especially in current times. But he surprises me and just nods. "I'll put Minthe on her."

"Good. Eurydice, I want you to check in with Ariadne this afternoon. She made a bargain with you in exchange for help that I provided, and while I am sympathetic to her current condition, time is of the essence. We need that information, and we need it now."

I'm not sure what to say, so I go with a generic, "Yes, sir."

He raises a single brow. "We don't stand on that kind of formality here."

I flush when I realize what I've said. I've been to his club. I know what my sister calls him when they do their scenes. That's not what I was intending, even if a little snark bled into my tone. I clear my throat. "Sorry, I mean, I'll handle that and report back."

"Dismissed."

It takes me a second to realize he's talking to me. I flush as I turn and walk out the door. Little shakes work through my body.

It's not that I'm scared of my brother-in-law—I'm not—but there's no going back now. For better or worse, I am now employed by Hades.

I suppose I should ask him about wages at some point.

That thought is enough to make me laugh a little. It's not until I've made it four steps down the hallway that I realize I'm not alone. I glance over at Callisto. She has her hands tucked into her gray duster, and it kicks out around her long legs with every step. It's an incredibly dramatic piece, drawing the eye and giving the impression of a gunslinger about to engage in a duel. I don't know if my sister would've worn it six months ago.

"I suppose you have thoughts about what just happened." I expect all of my family will.

She glances at me, her expression unreadable. "Hades takes care of his own better than any of the other Thirteen do."

She doesn't sound like herself. A frisson of fear shoots down my spine. "Better than you?"

"Don't you know, little sister? I don't have people."

I stop walking. "That's not true, Callisto. You have us. You've always had us, and you always will have us."

She turns to face me. I still can't read her expression, and that scares the shit out of me. My oldest sister has never been one for politics, and she's never bothered to hide exactly what she's thinking or feeling.

She's hiding both now.

"Stay in the lower city," she finally says. "Let yourself fall in love with that man who watches you with his heart in his eyes. Have a happy life. You deserve it."

My fear transforms into alarm. It almost sounds like she's saying goodbye. "What's going on? Why are you talking like that?"

"When you talk to Ariadne, she's going to tell you that something's coming. Something catastrophic. Something I don't think most of the upper city will survive, at least those peacocks in the legacy families. I need you to promise me that you will stay in the lower city. I want to hear you say it."

What could she possibly know? Everyone in Olympus has been working overtime to figure out what Minos's endgame is, but my sister speaks like she already knows it. Who could...?

"Have you been talking to Hermes?" In the two months since Minos's party, Hermes hasn't been around much. It's more than her stopping her unannounced visits to this house to pester Hades. Even MuseWatch has noticed her absence enough to comment on it. She was supposedly even seen slipping through the boundary a few weeks back, which shouldn't be possible on her own. "She's a traitor."

"Maybe. Or maybe she's doing what it takes to survive. We could all take some notes on that." It's clear she won't budge on her determination to get a promise from me.

It's easy enough to do, except for... "What about the family dinners?" *What about Psyche?* I don't voice the last question. Considering our sister is married to a mostly former hit man, she should be safe enough, no matter what happens. Eros will make sure of it. Or at least I hope he will.

"I don't expect we'll have them for the next little while." She looks away. "Don't worry about Mother, or Psyche for that matter. They can both take care of themselves better than you and

Persephone, and I'm doing everything I can to ensure our family is protected."

"What does that mean?" I take a step toward her. "What are you doing? What have you done?"

Instead of answering, she says, "I'll have your promise now, Eurydice."

Later today, I'll talk to Charon and see what he thinks. I don't believe he would keep something so important from me if he had information about a threat against the upper city. Or at least more of a threat than they are already experiencing. I don't think so… but I'm not entirely certain. "Fine. I promise not to go to the upper city for a little while."

From her narrowed eyes, she's all too aware of the limit I put on that promise. "Good."

I watch my sister walk away. Few people are aware of how dangerous she is, and not just because she punches first and asks questions never. Everyone in my family is fiercely loyal, but it goes to a greater depth with Callisto. I always understood that on some level, but it wasn't until she went behind everyone's back and arranged a marriage with Zeus in order to protect Psyche—and me—that I started to realize exactly the lengths she would go. My sister doesn't care about the city. She sure as fuck doesn't care about the Thirteen or gathering power for herself.

What is she up to?

I have a feeling I won't find the answer to *that* until it's far too late, but at least I can find other answers. If Callisto knows exactly what's coming for us, then it's all the more important I talk to Ariadne and get that information to Hades. I pull my phone out and glance at the time. It's not technically afternoon yet, but it's late enough that showing up to Medusa's house isn't out of the question.

I head for the door but stop short when I turn the corner and find Minthe waiting for me. She's a tall white woman with long brown hair, impeccable fashion sense, and a sleek, muscular form that I envy. No one looks at her and thinks *breakable*. She holds up a hand, which is when I notice that she has my coat captive. "Going somewhere?"

Yesterday, I would've answered evasively. Today, I am in Hades's employ. Just like Minthe. "I want to check on Ariadne to see if she feels well enough to tell me everything she knows."

Yesterday, she would've asked if I had Charon's permission. Today, she just shrugs and jerks her thumb at the door. "Let's go."

Clearly, my change in status has already been conveyed to her. I half expect to choke on being babysat, but this doesn't feel like that at all. This feels like I'm finally a member of the team. Like I have value. Like I'm an asset.

I will do everything in my power to prove that I'm worthy of Hades's trust.

CHARON

I BARELY WAIT FOR THE DOOR TO CLOSE BEHIND EURYDICE before I spin on Hades to demand to know what the fuck he thinks he's trying to pull. Persephone gets there first. She marches around the desk and gets right in his face. "What do you think you're doing?"

"I think I was rather clear about my intentions."

"Hades," I cut in. "She has no training. She's going to get hurt."

The look he gives me is calculating. "Ensure that she doesn't."

"I don't understand why you're doing this." Persephone lifts a hand as if she'll touch him but takes a step back instead. "That's my baby sister. Charon's right—she's going to get hurt."

He drags his hand over his face. "I wish the two of you would give me a little more credit...and would see things more clearly. She needs a purpose. She's all but begging to have one. She'll be safer here than doing this back-and-forth thing she's had going for the last year. If she decides it's not what she wants, I'll release her from my employ. But in the meantime, she'll stay in the lower city."

Understanding flares. Again, Persephone speaks before I can. "You sneaky motherfucker, you let her take this job because you knew she wouldn't agree to stay on this side of the River Styx otherwise."

"Yes, in part." He turns to look out the window. "She managed to pull off something that no one else could. If Ariadne really has the information she promised, it may be invaluable." He sighs. "Or it might already be too late."

"You can't think like that."

"I can't afford to think any other way."

My phone chooses that moment to buzz in my pocket. I send an apologetic look to Hades and Persephone, and dig it out. Thankfully, it's not Minthe or Eurydice, but that doesn't mean it's good news. Thanatos's name appears on the screen. "I have to get this."

"Take it in here."

I nod to show I understand and put the call on speaker. "I'm here."

"We have a problem. I need you to come down to the club." His voice is rough and raspy as if he just smoked an entire pack of cigarettes. "Hurry."

I exchange a look with Hades. We both know what that tone means. Trouble in the worst way. Thanatos didn't tell me to put the house on lockdown though, which means he believes it's already finished and the danger has passed.

I wish I could believe that too.

Hades turns to Persephone and takes her hands. "I need you to go to our room and lock yourself in until I call you." She tries to pull her hands from his, but he tightens his grip. "Do this for me, little siren. I need to make sure we're safe, and I can't do that if I'm worried about you and the babies. Please."

Persephone curses softly but presses a quick kiss to his lips. "Be safe."

"I will. I promise."

We walk Persephone as far as the curving staircase that leads to the second floor. I don't comment on the fact that he waits until she disappears from sight before he moves with purpose toward the part of the house the connects with the club. He's not that much taller than me, but I still have to focus on keeping up with him. "Someone attacked the club."

"Undoubtedly." A deep anger comes off him in waves. Even during the most tumultuous time with the past Zeus, his club was always safe. It was a proving ground and a theater, but not a single one of the rest of the Thirteen ever dared threaten it. To do so would mean revoking access to Hades. Though most of them weren't brave enough to come to the lower city themselves, they had plenty of spies they sent to keep tabs on him. Hades knew about every single one of them and chose to allow it.

That careful balance is *sacred*.

We reach the black door that leads from the house to the club. I've never really understood why Hades invested what he must've in that door. It's abnormally large, and its surface is so glossy it almost looks like liquid. As if you could press your hand against it and slide right through. It's dramatic as fuck, and no one sees it except Hades and Persephone. I don't even bring Eurydice through this door on the nights when we visit the club.

I don't comment on the fact that Hades is blatantly bracing

himself before he opens the door and steps through. I follow on his heels, only to stop short in horror. My brain shies away from what I'm seeing. The only word I can come up with is *ruin*.

The club has only been closed for a couple hours, and the cleaners we employ should just be wrapping up. I've been here plenty of times during off hours, when the lights are high and the mystique is nowhere to be found. Even then the luxury and beauty of this place are on full display. Not now.

The front doors have been blasted open and hang off the hinges. I stare at them for a long moment. That had to be noisy, but that doesn't mean a damn thing. There's a lot of soundproofing that went into the construction of this place. The club keeps late hours, and no one wants the music or activities to disturb the rest of the house's occupants. I move to the nearest couch and run my fingers over the torn fabric. "They shot the place up."

"Yes." Hades still hasn't moved from his spot near the door. I can't read his expression as he surveys this place that has been so important to him for so long. The attack on the greenhouse was a private attack, meant to go straight to the very heart of him. This is a direct fucking *challenge*.

I turn as Thanatos hurries up. Half his face is covered in blood, and he's limping, but he doesn't seem to be otherwise seriously injured. He glances at Hades and must see the same thing I do, because he turns back to me to give his report. "They came through just as we were locking up after the cleaners left. Bashed me over the head and then locked Hypnos in the office. They wore masks and didn't speak, and they were in and out before I could get my feet."

We suspected they were professionals. This proves it. They

knew our schedule. It's not exactly something we hide, but to have things narrowed down to that tight window, they had to have been watching us for some time. More, they didn't kill anyone. I don't know what to make of that. I want to appreciate that I have no one to mourn, but it feels particularly sinister. Intentional in a way that raises the small hairs on the back of my neck.

I step closer to Thanatos and lower my voice. "How badly are you hurt?"

"I'm fine." Even as he speaks, he weaves a little, and I have to jump forward to catch him before he slams to the floor. He clears his throat and blinks at me. "I'm mostly fine."

I guide him over to the nearest couch and try not to notice just how destroyed it is. This is the same couch Eurydice sat on when she challenged me... Was that only a couple days ago? It feels like another life. Impossible to look at the space and not picture the harm that would come to her if she'd been here when they attacked.

The lower city isn't nearly as safe as we want it to be.

I send a quick text summoning the doctor we have on staff. Hades still hasn't moved. Worry tightens the muscles along my spine. He's been more sensitive since Persephone got pregnant. It's understandable, but it makes him unpredictable. That's dangerous. The Hades I grew up with would never strike out without reason. But this man, the one who feels that his wife and unborn children are threatened? I don't know what he'll do.

After making sure that Thanatos won't fall right off the couch, I stand and move to Hades's side. "We'll find them."

He exhales, slow and steady and perfectly controlled. That's scarier than if he'd cursed and thrown things. He doesn't look at me as he speaks. "I want them on their knees before me. You have two days, Charon. Otherwise I'm going hunting on my own."

I jerk back. "You can't. We need you here." I hesitate, but I don't like the empty look in his eyes. "Persephone needs you here."

"Don't tell me what my wife needs. Two days." He turns and walks back through the door, closing it softly behind him. The click sounds unnaturally loud in the silence he leaves in his wake.

We are so fucked.

I turn to Thanatos to see the exact same realization dawning on his handsome face. He drops his head against the back of the couch and whistles. "This is bad."

"Really bad," I agree. "Where is your sibling?"

"Guarding the door."

I head across the club to the front doors, pausing to look again at how they've been blown off the hinges. How the fuck did they manage that? Worse, the hinges themselves are warped, which means we won't be able to close the doors until we replace them. Considering they were custom made, I don't think that's going to happen quickly.

Hades's club is out of business.

The number of people who would've noticed the attack on the greenhouse is minuscule. We were able to get the glass doors replaced pretty quickly, so Matthew's customers might have recognized the upgrade, but not the reason for it. They won't know what happened upstairs. No one except Matthew and Hades go up to the greenhouse itself. It's not open to the public. Plenty of people know Hades spends time there, but they're all very good at respecting the fact that it's a private place.

The club isn't like that. Hades holds court here, the same way that Zeus holds court in Dodona Tower. They might not be official rulers, but these are their courts all the same. People come to this club from both sides of the River Styx to beg for favors, or just for the chance to see him in person. To watch the boogeyman of Olympus dote on his pretty sunshine wife. Tonight, they will come here to find the doors barred.

And then the whispers will start.

I'm head of security. I know the ways in which we fight our enemies. Some of our most important battles are fought through public perception. This is bad. It will weaken him in a way that the greenhouse didn't, at least as far as the upper city is concerned. Our people won't see it as a failing that he wasn't able to protect this club. Our people aren't the ones we need to worry about.

If those fools in the upper city who are so intent on murdering their way into becoming members of the Thirteen start to turn greedy eyes on this side of the river...

It will be a bloodbath.

I find Hypnos leaning against the wall just outside the doors. Technically, zir's a club manager, but everyone who works directly for Hades is required to go through very specific kinds of training. Hypnos is more than capable of using the shotgun in zir hands.

Ze doesn't take zir gaze off the street. "How's Thanatos?"

I don't demand a report first. I appreciate the fact that ze had the forethought to act as guard, even though ze is obviously worried about zir brother. "He's going to have a wicked headache, but I think he'll be fine. We're having the doctor look him over regardless."

"Okay." Zir shoulders slump. "They came in too fast. I barely realized we were under attack before they slammed the office door shut and barricaded me in. By the time I loaded the shotgun and blasted my way out, they were gone."

It's nothing more than what Thanatos said, but I appreciate the confirmation all the same. "What can you tell me about them?" I lean closer. "And don't think I missed the fact that your shotgun was unloaded in the office. We've talked about this."

"It's a safety issue."

"I agree wholeheartedly, which is why it should be loaded." I see the resistance on zir face but keep going. "I'm not asking you to hand it to a toddler. The office is locked when you're not in there, and the gun should be secured regardless, but in a situation like this, seconds count."

Hypnos sighs. "If you think I could've fought off three professionals, then you're out of your damn mind."

Understanding dawns, and I curse myself for not realizing exactly what zir being locked in the office means. "We have security footage."

"I already uploaded it to a file and sent it to you. It's still on the computer in the office though, if you want to look at it now."

"Well done." I start to turn for the door but pause. "Reinforcements are on their way. We'll get this sorted."

I head to the office and close the door softly behind me. Or I try. Hypnos blasted through the door and took out a good chunk of the doorframe in the process. Another thing we'll have to replace. I sink into the chair and turn to the computer to find that Hypnos anticipated my needs. The security footage is pulled up and ready to play. I brace myself and push the button.

It happened so fucking fast.

Our patrons think we don't have sound recording in place, but Hades doesn't trust them that much. I listen to an explosion that's strangely muted. There's a soft popping sound and a faint billow of smoke, and then they're in the room tearing it up. I suspected they were professionals, but seeing their well-coordinated movements only confirms it. They don't speak. They merely charge into the room, open fire, and then disappear a minute later.

I play the recording through three more times, my unease growing with each time through. I finally pause it on the few seconds where all three of them are in the frame. They wear black masks, black tactical gear, black gloves and boots. They've even blacked out the skin around their eyes and mouth that was left exposed by the masks so there isn't a single identifying feature to latch on to. The tactical gear is bulky enough that is impossible to tell gender too. They could be literally anyone.

Fuck.

EURYDICE

MINTHE MUST HAVE CALLED AHEAD, BECAUSE THEY'RE ready for us when we arrive. The apartment Medusa and Calypso share is a charming little space tucked into the neighborhood on the other side of the winter market. It's close enough to walk, which we do despite the cold weather. Winter is more than just a promise; it's here.

The situation seems relaxed enough as Calypso lets us through the front door and guides us into the living room. I'm pretty sure this space came furnished when they initially rented it, but evidence of the way that they've made it home is everywhere. On the kitchen counter, there's a wide array of tea in neatly labeled canisters. The corner of the living room has been converted into an office space for Calypso. There's a small desk scattered with papers covered in various stages of design. Curiosity flares, but that's not what I'm here for, so I focus on Ariadne.

She looks muted. I can't tell if it's in relief or despair. She does manage to give me a small smile as I sink into the chair across from her. I lean forward. "How are you feeling?"

"Complicated." She tugs on the throw blanket wrapped around her shoulders until it covers her more completely. "Mostly relieved, though I'm playing the part of betrayer to my father, even if he is an unmitigated ass. Conflicted, because I didn't tell…" She shrugs. "Like I said, it's complicated."

I can't imagine the courage she must've had to reach out and ask for help, let alone trust us enough to actually follow through on that offer of help. It's hard not to feel like a monster for pressing her when she's so obviously feeling fragile, but I have my orders. I want this role that Hades gave me, and that means doing what's necessary. "I know that you just went through an ordeal, but—"

"I have my bargain to fulfill," she finishes for me.

"Yes."

She looks down at her hands, and although impatience pricks at me, I keep my silence. It doesn't take long for her to work through whatever thorny past she's seeing. She's certainly not looking at anything in this room, or even this day. When she finally speaks, her voice is soft and steady. "I don't know if my father was always so ambitious that it poisoned everything about him, or if something happened to make him this way, but I do know he wasn't always a bad father. I have many happy memories from my childhood in Aeaea."

"What changed?" I should probably be silent and let her talk her way through this, but I'm supposed to be gathering information, and every little detail is important.

"*She* came to the island."

I don't move. I'm pretty sure I don't even breathe. According to Eris, Cassandra heard Hermes and Minos talking at the party right before everything went off the rails. In that conversation, they talked about his benefactor, a mysterious woman Hermes seems to have some connection to. Is this the same woman?

"You have to understand. Our island is almost as isolated as Olympus is, but we don't have a magical barrier enforcing it. People just have no reason to come; we work very hard not to give them a reason. Aeaea watched tourism take the communities around us and turn them into mockeries of themselves. The council—not the current council, but the one from a couple generations ago—put laws into place ensuring that we couldn't follow in the path of our neighbors." The sadness in her voice tells me just as much as her words do.

"The community started to die," I guess.

Her smile wobbles around the edges. "You've heard the story before."

"Not this one, but there's historical precedent. It's horrible to watch a community wilt, but I don't see what that has to do with our current situation."

"That's what I'm trying to say—fifteen years ago, this woman appeared on our island, walked right into the council meeting, and promised that if they put her in charge, it would pave the way to a glorious and prosperous future for our island."

What she's saying sounds like something out of a storybook. I narrow my eyes. "From everything you've just said, you have a community that is wary of outsiders, if not downright hostile. What conceivable reason would they have to listen to the stranger?"

"Because she promised them Olympus." She must see the pure disbelief on my face because she shakes her head slowly. "Yeah, that was my initial reaction when I started digging through my father's computer to find out why he suddenly started acting so strangely. It's true. Ever since that day, Aeaea dances to her tune."

This is a fascinating, but I don't see how it helps the situation we're in now. We already knew that Minos had a benefactor. This is just a little history lesson explaining that. "Okay," I say slowly.

"It's okay; I didn't get it at first either. It wasn't until she and my father started planning his entrance into Olympus so that Theseus and Aster—the Minotaur—could compete for the title of Ares that I was able to hack into her systems. Then I realized the scope of what they're planning."

I blink. "You did *what?*"

She won't quite meet my eyes. "Like I said, my father wasn't always neglectful and too busy with his master plan to worry about being an actual father. But ten years is plenty of time to learn any skill, including hacking. It's not like it's hard."

I would beg to differ, but it's not really my place to argue with her on the subject. "Are you going to keep me in suspense or tell me what you found?"

Her smile steadies a little. "The trouble was that I thought she gave us a fake name, so I wasted a lot of time trying to figure out who she really was. It's a rookie mistake. Usually the simplest answer is the correct one." She pulls her knees to her chest and wraps her arms around them. "She didn't have all this information about Olympus because she was like my father, someone on the outside desperately looking in. She had it because she's *from* Olympus."

I jolt. "What?" Even living in the country before my mother became Demeter, we should've heard about an exile. They are exceedingly rare, with the last Aphrodite being the only one in the last twenty years...or so I thought.

The thing is, once you exile someone, they stop being under your purview. Apollo might have technology to ensure that the former Aphrodite can't be a danger to us, but was that technology in place fifteen years ago?

Maybe they killed the people they exiled...

The thought makes me shudder. I could ask my mother about this, except no, I can't, because I agreed that I am working for Hades, which means all my reports will go to him. My mother can no longer be the main authority in my life.

"Does the name Circe ring any bells?"

———

I feel strange as I head back to the house with Minthe at my side. She hasn't said anything since we arrived at Calypso and Medusa's apartment. She played the part of the silent guard, but I know that she's Charon's second-in-command, which means she must have thoughts about what we just heard. I open my mouth to ask her but stop before a single word escapes. I'm not sure what the protocol is surrounding something like this. She heard everything I did, but are we allowed to talk about it? I don't know.

Better to report directly to Hades and sidestep any potential errors.

We find him still in his office with a stack of untouched paperwork in front of him. There's a strange look on my brother-in-law's face that I've never seen before. It's frightening. I don't know what happened in the time since I saw him last and now, and I don't know if I'm allowed to ask.

He looks up as I knock on the doorframe. "Did you get the information we need?"

"I think so."

"Come in and shut the door. Minthe, report to Charon."

Minthe squeezes my shoulder and then heads down the hall. I may have known Hades for over a year, but it still takes more courage than I'll ever admit to step into the office and close the door behind me. I follow his silent command to take the chair across the desk from him.

The silence gets to me immediately. Maybe I'm supposed to start? "Her name is Circe. I think she was exiled from Olympus fifteen years ago, and she apparently went straight to Aeaea and offered them Olympus on a platter. Ariadne was kept out of the actual nitty-gritty plans, so most of the information she has is what she could glean from her father's emails and conversations she overheard."

Hades steeples his fingers in front of his face and leans forward. "Go on."

"The gist of it is that Minos was intended to soften up the city and sow chaos, as well as undermine the power of the Thirteen. He was to destroy public confidence in them. Then, after an undisclosed amount of time had passed, they would bring the barrier down."

"How? Not even Apollo is entirely certain of how it works—or why it's failing."

I feel absolutely sick over what I have to say next, and I would do anything not to be the messenger that delivers this information. But he has to know. They all have to know. "It started failing fifteen years ago. It may have taken us longer to realize it, but that's when the process began."

"You can't know that." He leans back. "Circe may have claimed that she's behind that, but it's impossible."

I wish he was right, because it'd mean Apollo has a way to fix the barrier. "Unfortunately, it's not. She took a piece with her when she left. Ariadne couldn't tell me what it looks like, or how it functions, but it was the proof the council on Aeaea needed in order to go along with Circe's plan." I shiver. "The barrier will fall, and when it does, she will be waiting there with an army."

"We have scouts monitoring the perimeter. There hasn't been any movement on that front." The words sound like he doesn't believe me, but his tone isn't dismissive. More like he's musing to himself, mulling over the information I brought him. "That doesn't mean Ariadne's lying though. Just that Circe is smart enough not to show her hand before she's ready to strike."

"What do we do?"

He gives himself a shake and finally focuses on me. "Leave that up to us, Eurydice. You did a fine job getting that information. We'll hold up our end of the bargain with Ariadne, but for now it's time for you to go home."

It's not until I'm walking out the front door that I realize he didn't tell me to go to the room that I usually keep in this house. He told me to go *home*, and there's no way he meant the upper city.

He meant Charon's town house.

I'm not even surprised when Minthe pulls up in one of Hades's nondescript black sedans. I climb into the passenger seat and sit back with a sigh. I don't mean to speak, but I have too many emotions tangled up inside me, and Minthe will understand. I hope. "I thought the information would fix things, but it only made them worse. We are in a lot of trouble."

"Welcome to the lower city." She laughs a little. "But seriously, you did good work today. You handled her perfectly and got every bit of information that she had. It was well done."

Warmth takes up residence in my chest. It's one thing to think that I might have something to offer, but it's entirely another to have it confirmed by someone who has no reason to lie to me. Minthe isn't related to me, even by marriage. She's not interested in getting in my pants. She's essentially a coworker who's giving me a pat on the back for a job well done, and that feels so damn valuable. "Thanks."

"Now that we have that out of the way, I have something you need to hear."

The warmth in my chest dims. "Okay."

"We didn't get a chance to talk about it this morning, but I'd like to make one thing clear." She weaves through the light traffic with an ease I envy. "Medusa is still adjusting to how we do things in the lower city. She sees things in a very black-and-white way, which means your previous role as honored guest who isn't technically a citizen of the lower city created a gray area you were able to manipulate her through. Don't think that I will allow you to do the same to me."

I jerk back. "I never manipulated her." That sounds insidious. Evil, even.

"How many times have you slipped her security detail? No, you don't have to answer, because I already know. Seven times in the last year. That shit won't fly with me."

"I had my reasons."

"I literally do not care." She glances at me. Considering her words, I expect to see anger on her face, but there's just a calm resolve. "You're on the staff now, and you're officially a citizen of the lower city. If you try to slip my security detail, I will track you down and drag you back to Hades and Charon by your hair. No hard feelings; it's just business. You want to go somewhere, you talk to me about it, and we figure out a way to do it safely. If we can't do it safely, then we go to Charon and see if he has extra resources to lend. There's a proper way to do things, Eurydice, and I expect you to hold the line."

I swallow my instinctive angry response and force myself to really think about the words she saying. She's not treating me like a child. She's laying out clear boundaries and expecting me to hold them. I can do that. "I understand. You have my word that I'll talk to you before doing anything that might be dangerous."

It's not until she stops at the curb in front of the town house that the events of the afternoon catch up to me. Events of the last couple days, really. I haven't gotten a good night's sleep in days. The stress feels like it's wearing me down to a single thread that might snap at any moment. Ariadne's words keep circling around in my head. They all add up to one conclusion. *War.* The one thing that we thought we were all safe from, and it's coming knocking on our door, sooner rather than later.

I don't know how we're going to survive it.

ORPHEUS

I KNOW SOMETHING'S WRONG THE MOMENT EURYDICE walks through the door. There's a slant to her shoulders that I don't like, as if she's carrying the world on them. I rush to her but stop before making contact. We might have shared a bed last night, but that doesn't mean that she'll welcome comfort from me. "Eurydice?"

"It's bad," she whispers. "It's really bad."

Slowly, tentatively, I lift my arms a little. An invitation. She doesn't hesitate. Eurydice throws herself into my arms and wraps me up tight. She buries her face in my neck. I rub her back with one hand and cup the base of her skull with the other, massaging little circles into the spots behind her ears. "You don't have to tell me, but if you want to talk about it, I'm here."

"I knew we were in trouble, but…" Her voice is muffled, but still clear enough. "I mean, Theseus *killed* the last Hephaestus at Minos's party. I thought I understood the stakes. I was wrong. We're *all* in danger."

A shiver of fear works its way through me. It's been bad enough with the Thirteen walking around with targets painted on their chests. It sounds like she's talking about something more, something that will affect every single citizen in Olympus. My parents. My brother. Cassandra. "You reported to Hades?"

"Yes."

It's on the tip of my tongue to ask what Hades intends to do, but he has no reason to have shared that information with her. Eurydice and I might be related to members of the Thirteen, but that doesn't mean we're part of the group that rules Olympus. Most of the time we find out information when the rest of the population does. That's never bothered me before, but right now all I want to do is call my brother and demand answers. Apollo is a good man. If he thought our parents were in danger, he would make whatever moves were necessary in order to protect them. I believe that with my whole heart.

But what if he doesn't know all the details?

"Eurydice, I have to tell my brother."

She hesitates. "Please give it a day. Hades isn't like the rest—or at least the rest beyond your brother. He's a good person. He won't let our families be hurt for something as meaningless as politics."

I might laugh if I didn't feel so shitty. "Right, because it's not just my family at risk. I should have thought of that. Your sister and your mother are both in the Thirteen, and Psyche lives in the upper city. Sorry. I keep trying to not be a selfish prick, but I guess some things take longer to unlearn."

"Oh, Orpheus, no." She cups my face with her hands. "I had the same thought when I first heard what Ariadne had to say. I wanted to call my mother immediately. But there's a right way to go about these things and...well...Hades essentially hired me. I answer to him first now."

I stare at her, not sure what to think. There's a part of me that wants to tell her she's out of her mind for thinking that she can operate in Charon's league. She's going to get hurt. Except...what if she doesn't? I don't know Hades beyond his reputation for being fair. He's married to Persephone, who is one of Eurydice's most overprotective sisters. He wouldn't have hired her if he didn't believe she was more than capable of doing the job.

More, I'm not going to be the one to dim the light in her eyes. Not again.

The need to call my brother is almost overwhelming, but I wrestle it down. The information about this danger might be new, but the danger itself isn't. Apollo is on alert. He won't be caught flat-footed, and I highly suspect that he already hired guards to monitor our parents. It seems like the kind of thing he'd do.

Or maybe I'm just making excuses to do what I want. Just like I always do. I have Eurydice in my arms, and even with a threat against the entire city bearing down, I don't want to leave her side. Disgusted with myself, I pull away with a bitter laugh.

At least, I try to. Eurydice tightens her hold on me. "Orpheus. Where did you go in your head just now?"

"Nowhere. I've been here the whole time."

"No, you haven't." She presses her fingers against my temples. "You were okay, and then you got this look on your face, and I don't think it was directed at me."

I should move away again, but I can't make myself. Not with her touching me. Instead I close my eyes. "After you left, there was a time when I thought I was better off. Then I realized that I was living in a world without color; you took the entire palette with you when you walked out of my life."

"Orpheus—"

"Please let me finish." I hesitate for a few moments, but she doesn't keep speaking. I almost wish she would. Better to focus on her, but that's just my self-pity talking. "I've been a selfish prick. Even losing you wasn't enough, initially, to snap me out of that. I essentially went through the stages of grief. When I first believed you were gone for good, I was angry at you for blaming me for Zeus's actions. That stage lasted until Apollo stepped in and cut me off. I tried bargaining with my brother afterward. I'm sure you can imagine how well that went. I spent the next six months depressed, barely able to get through my day." I curse and shake my head sharply enough to dislodge her fingers. "Fuck, I'm *still doing it*. I don't know how the fuck to stop being so selfish. I try. I swear to the gods that I'm trying. I just keep fucking failing. How can you and Charon stand to be around me?"

"Orpheus, look at me."

I don't want to open my eyes. It's a childish fear, as if by keeping my eyes closed, the heartbreaking truth won't be real. As long as I don't see her expression, I don't have to acknowledge the anger and recrimination there. Maybe she could pretend that I'd changed, but after what I just told her, she'll know I haven't. That I might not be *capable* of changing. Now's the moment she will send me away, and I deserve nothing less. Keeping my eyes closed won't change that.

But she told me to open my eyes with that bite in her tone that I can't disobey.

Eurydice isn't looking at me with anger. The emotion she's wearing is far too complex for that. There's some anger there, to be sure, along with sadness and bitterness and even a little pity. But mostly it's...*sorrow*, my mind supplies. What I'm seeing is...sorrow.

She doesn't step away for me. "It hurt. That night when everything happened, the physical pain I experienced was nothing compared to the knowledge that you valued me so little you were willing to let me die for your ambition."

Horror closes around my chest. "I didn't—"

"I know. At least I know that now. I didn't know anything that night, not beyond the kind of fear that made me worried my heart would burst." She looks away. "I forgive you. I'm not saying you didn't share plenty of blame for what happened, but for all the time leading up to that night? It took two of us to get there. I was just so happy to be standing in your sunlight, I didn't care there was nothing left of me. I didn't know who I was, Orpheus. I wasn't confident enough to tell you when you did something that made me feel small."

The feeling in my chest sprouts fangs and claws. "I never wanted you to feel small. Not even on my worst day."

"I know." Slowly, she presses her hand to my chest. "I guess my point is that we both have changed quite a bit in the last year, but some things are really hard to unlearn. More than that, I don't think you're nearly as selfish now as you were when we dated the first time. That man would never have even considered noticing he was being selfish, let alone worrying about it. And, for the record, you're *not* being selfish to worry about your family. I'll say that as many times as it takes for you to believe me."

Ironically, her words make me feel better...and worse. "I don't understand why you don't hate me. Things made more sense when I was scrubbing Charon's floor." Penance. I haven't paid nearly enough of it, no matter what she thinks. If Charon was here, he would understand.

Her nails prick my chest through my shirt. "If you want some degradation, I'm happy to oblige. But only because it's something you *want*, not because it's something you deserve."

"Eurydice—"

"Don't you get it? Your whole fucking life right now is penance, Orpheus. You haven't been painting, which was the one thing that brought you pure joy. Best I can tell, you lost all your friends."

"Turns out, they weren't much of friends to begin with," I mutter.

Her smile is sad and a little sharp. "I know. Now you know too. Your brother cut you off from the family purse. You've been miserable for months. It doesn't change what you did, but it makes it a lot easier to forgive you. I can't demand you forgive yourself—I wouldn't dream of doing so—but you might want to try it on for size. Especially if you're serious about wanting to build a life here."

"Build a life here," I echo. "Is that actually an option?"

"We'll talk about it when Charon gets home."

Because he is the other corner to our triangle. He's a good portion of the reason why Eurydice has found her feet. He sure as fuck is the reason why I came to the lower city in the first place. He gave us the framework for this thing. I don't know that we'd be having this conversation at all if not for him. "Okay." I cover her hand with mine. "What can I do in the meantime to make you feel better?"

"I think we both could use a little comfort right now." She turns her hand to interlace her fingers through mine. "Come on."

As she leads me up the stairs, my heart starts to pound. Wasn't I just thinking that Charon is the other corner of our triangle? Being sexual with Eurydice while he was present felt...safer. I wasn't as worried about us bruising each other on our sharp edges. Not when he could step in at any moment.

It isn't to the bedroom that Eurydice leads me. She takes me down a small hallway that I haven't explored to a closed door. The look she shoots me is almost guilty, and I understand why the moment she pulls me inside.

It's an art studio.

An unused one. I drop Eurydice's hand and move about the space, my mind empty of thought. It's not an exact replica of the one in my old apartment, but all the pieces are there. The easel with the oversized canvas I prefer to paint on. The oil paints in my favorite brand, all unopened and untouched. A slightly smaller selection of brushes than I normally use, but all of my favorite ones are there.

I turned to look at her. "What is this?"

"An...invitation. I know this is high-handed, and I'm only slightly sorry for it. You need something to do, Orpheus. You need *this*. I saw your face when you had the brush in your hand last night."

I feel exposed. There's an impulse to strike out, to do something to burst this fragile moment where she sees me all too clearly. But then, Eurydice has always seen me more clearly than others. Before, I was arrogant enough to think it made me almost godlike in her eyes. Now I understand that, for all the good she sees, she is equally aware of my flaws and dark underbelly. All the things I would hide from the world, laid out for her perusal. "You spent too much." That, at least, is a reasonable response.

"It might've been my idea, but this gift isn't from me." She moves to the comfortable-looking chaise positioned in such a way that someone sitting on it can watch the person at the canvas while still being out of the way. "If you want to throw a fit about it, take it up with Charon."

I turn slowly, taking in the room through new eyes. "Charon did this?"

"I suggested we collect your things from your apartment in the upper city, but he muttered something about new beginnings. I provided the information about the products you prefer to work with, but he did the rest. Or rather, he sent one of his people to do the rest."

I don't know if that changes things or not. I don't know how to feel at all.

Without meaning to, I run my fingers over the plastic that covers the canvas. It's been so long. I don't know if I even know how to paint anymore. Last night was as much about Eurydice and caring for her as it was about the paint itself, but she's right. It felt good to have a brush in my hand again. I turn to find her perched on the chaise, watching me closely. "You didn't really answer my question, you know. About what would make you feel better while we wait for Charon."

Her smile is soft and sweet. "I thought it was obvious—I'd like to watch you paint."

Something almost like fear tears through me. What if I've

forgotten everything? Surely painting is just like any other skill—use it or you lose it, or however that saying goes. Can a person lose their inherent talent? I'm sure it's possible, even probable.

"Could I paint you?" The question's out before I can think of all the reasons she'll tell me no. Before, the only way she'd agree to it was if I promised no one would see those pieces but the two of us. I held to that promise, even at my most selfish. Truth be told, that impulse was selfish too. I didn't want to share her with the world.

Eurydice stares at me, and there's a moment of perfect understanding between us. We can never change the past that got us to this place, can never erase the scars she has because of my carelessness. But right here, right now, we can begin again. Maybe we can even do it right this time.

She smiles. "Yes."

CHARON

26

I KNOW MY LONG DAY IS ABOUT TO GET EVEN LONGER when I'm summoned to Hades's office again. I walk through the door to find him glaring at his computer, which only means one thing—he's about to meet with the rest of the Thirteen. Since the new Zeus took over the position, Hades has been venturing into the upper city for these meetings. I will admit more than a little relief about the fact that he's not doing it tonight. After the attack on the club, we need to lock down.

He won't give that order. Not until he absolutely has to. He doesn't normally care about public perception the same way the others seem to, but he's certainly more aware of it since he married Persephone.

"I want you sitting in on this meeting. I'm sorry I'm not able to give you an update before I deal with the rest of them, but time is of the essence."

"Of course." I take position just off his right shoulder where I can hear what's said and see the screen, but no one on the screen can see me.

He pulls up the software to initiate a video call, and then hesitates. "Eurydice has been safely escorted back to your town house. Minthe arranged for someone to relieve her when her shift ends. They're not inside the house, but they are keeping watch."

Relief twines with alarm. "You don't normally take this kind of interest in nitty-gritty things like schedules."

He gives me a slashing look. "We *are* talking about my sister-in-law. The reason I don't take an overt interest in details like scheduling is because that's your job, and I'm not interested in stepping on your toes. You're my second-in-command for a reason, Charon. I'm informing you so you can focus on this meeting without worrying about Eurydice. She's safe."

This is about the information Ariadne gave. He's expecting me to have an extremely negative response to it. I take a slow breath. "I appreciate that." There's nothing else to say. We don't have that kind of relationship anyways. We're friends as such things go, but until Hades met Persephone, he attempted to keep a thick icy wall between him and anyone else. Things might've thawed in the last year, but old habits are hard to break.

Hades scrubs his hands over his face and smooths back his hair. It's the only sign of nerves he gives. When he pushes the button to initiate the call, his shoulders are straight and his face is a cold mask. One by one, squares pop up with various members of the Thirteen. There's Zeus and Hera, sitting a very careful distance apart. There's Poseidon, looking like he hasn't slept in days. They aren't who I'm interested in. My gaze skips over Hephaestus and Aphrodite, both newly appointed barely a month ago when the last two stepped down.

Finally Hermes arrives. She appears to be on a mobile phone, walking somewhere quick enough to give me motion sickness. Her dark-brown skin gleams with perspiration in the low light, and sometime since I saw her last, she's put her hair in braids.

I'm not the only one who's waiting for her to arrive. Zeus leans forward as if he can reach right through the screen and throttle her. "Hermes. You haven't reported for the last month's worth of meetings. Where are you?"

"Here and there, hither and yon. You know, the usual." She grins, but it doesn't quite have her usual carefree vibe. "This meeting wasn't called to talk about me, was it? Why are you so obsessed with me?" She laughs.

"Maybe because you're a fucking traitor." Artemis doesn't yell. She doesn't have to. Her words cut through the tension like a knife. "For all we know, you're working for the enemy."

"How very dramatic." She opens her mouth, no doubt to continue needling Artemis, but Zeus cuts in before she can continue.

"This meeting wasn't called by you—either of you. Hades, you have something to say?"

I feel a twinge of sympathy for Hades. It can't be comfortable having twelve pairs of cold dangerous eyes staring at him, waiting for him to give them what is inevitably bad news. He doesn't flinch. "One of my people has been in contact with Minos's daughter, Ariadne. They were able to turn her to our side in exchange for several things that I will not disclose at this time, but suffice to say that those things do not endanger Olympus. The information she passed on, however, does."

Apollo flinches. I've seen him before, of course, but considering that his little brother is back in my town house and was in my bed last night, I study him with new interest. He and Orpheus share the same coloring, with their dark eyes and black hair, but Apollo has more of his father in him. He's built broader than Orpheus, and his jaw is nearly as square as Zeus's.

When he speaks, his tone is careful. "Someone was able to turn Ariadne?"

"Who?" This comes from Demeter, mother to Eurydice, Persephone, Psyche, and our current Hera. She's a middle-aged white woman who's started to go soft in a way that has nothing to do with weakness. I've seen pictures of her from her youth, and she looks just like Eurydice and Persephone. In the decade since she won the title of Demeter by popular vote in Olympus, she has truly embraced the matronly earth mother persona.

She's also one of the scariest people I've ever encountered.

Hades doesn't flinch in the face of her suspicion. "It's immaterial. The information I have, however, isn't."

"Tell us." Zeus sits back. He's a cold motherfucker, and right now is no exception. I can't read anything on his face. The last Zeus was charismatic and boisterous, always the biggest personality in any room he walked into. His son either doesn't have the skill to manipulate people like that, or doesn't have the interest. I know which I would prefer to deal with, but the people of Olympus have been raking him over the coals for being so unlikable. He won't play the game, and they resent him for it.

"Does the name Circe mean anything to you?"

I search the faces on the screen, looking for recognition. I don't know who this person is, but I can connect the dots when they're laid out in front of me. She is Minos's benefactor. Which means she's the enemy. I'm not comforted by the confused looks on everyone's faces—except three. Zeus, Ares...

And Hermes.

Hermes bursts out laughing. "Gods, it took you long enough to figure it out. I thought I was going to have to send a carrier pigeon." There's a sound in the background, sharp and booming, and she looks over her shoulder. "Oh damn, I have to run. Have fun, darlings." A second later her square disappears.

Hades sits back with a sigh. "Apparently some of you are in on the secret. Her name is unfamiliar to me."

Zeus shakes his head, and for the first time, something resembling an actual expression appears on his face. "What you're saying is impossible. Circe is dead. She died fifteen years ago."

Ares is so pale, she looks like she might pass out. "Perseus, her body was never recovered. At the time, I thought it was Father covering things up, but..."

"*But?*" Aphrodite stops short and seems to try to compose themself. "What are you talking about? Who is Circe?"

"You wouldn't recognize the name because she's not from one of the legacy families. It happened so fast, everybody was focused on who she became, rather than who she was." Ares tucks her hair behind her ears with shaking hands. "She was only a couple years older than me at the time, but it was pretty clear right off the bat that Father bit off more than he could chew. He didn't wait long to make his move."

Pieces fall into place, one by one. I see my suspicions reflected in the faces of the people in the meeting, in the sudden tension in

Hades's shoulders. The last Zeus had a reputation as a wife killer. His first wife, mother to his four children, died from an unfortunate fall down the stairs. An accident, Zeus claimed, and supposedly he wasn't anywhere in the house when it happened. His third wife died from a rumored overdose. The official story is that she accidentally mixed meds and had an adverse reaction, but whether that was intentional on her part—or her husband's part—is anyone's guess.

But the second wife?

A drowning accident during a romantic trip to the coast during their honeymoon.

Hades leans forward and props his elbows on the desk. "Are you saying that Circe, Minos's benefactor, enemy to Olympus, is the previous Zeus's second wife?"

"It's understandable that her real name doesn't ring any bells." Zeus smiles, but not like anything is funny. "When you would've known her, her name was Hera."

Things devolve pretty quickly after that. Hades manages to get out the rest of his information, including the fact that apparently when Circe slipped out of Olympus, she took a piece of the barrier with her. *She's* the reason it's failing. No one has a good solution. Athena offers to send one of her people to take care of the problem quietly, but Zeus tells her that the situation is already beyond that point. Artemis refuses to believe that a Hera could be the source of all these problems. The new Hephaestus promises to take a look at the barrier, certain that xe can find a solution that no one else has managed to before now.

In short, it's a fucking mess.

Two hours later, when Hades cuts off the call and sits back with a groan, no solutions have been solidified. He rotates his chair so he can look at me. "What do you think?"

"There was always a possibility that the enemy originated from the city. The information Minos had was too specific to come from an outsider. The assassination clause is too cleverly hidden. This mostly confirms what we already knew." I drag my hand over my face. "If she was married to the last Zeus, even for a short time, she has more than reason enough to hate the city. Everyone stood by and let him do whatever the fuck he wanted for far too long. Can't blame her for wanting revenge."

Hades nods slowly. "No, I can't blame her for wanting revenge, but I *can* blame her for all the violence and suffering her plans have caused. If she had only come back and killed him, I would have shaken her hand and been done with it. She's responsible for a number of deaths and an increasing amount of unrest that means the violence is just beginning."

"Not to mention the attacks on the greenhouse and the club." She *has* to be behind it. It's the only thing that makes sense. Ultimately, it doesn't matter if she gave the order directly or if Minos did, because she is his benefactor.

"Not to mention the attack on the greenhouse and the club," Hades agrees. "She softened us up so much, I don't know if we can manage to bring together enough people for a standing army to defend the city. Ares has her soldiers, but there's only so many of them, and their experience leans more toward bodyguard work than actual battle."

We don't have even that much in the lower city. The last Zeus never would've stood for that kind of gathering of power, even if

Hades was interested in it, and it hasn't been a high priority in the year since that Zeus died. We have a couple dozen people on staff, and another couple dozen rotating in periodically as needed. Not enough. Nowhere near enough.

"What do we do?"

He stares at the now-blank screen of his computer for several moments. "We keep doing exactly what we were doing before this. We drive the enemy from the lower city."

It should be enough, but I can't help pressing him. "And after that?"

"I...don't know."

That scares me more than anything else that's happened today.

EURYDICE

WATCHING ORPHEUS PAINT HAS ALWAYS UNWOUND something in me. For a man who is so present in every room he walks into, when he paints it looks like he's in another world entirely. After today, I would like to be in another world entirely too. I know there are hurried meetings happening behind closed doors concerning the threat against the city. Part of me wishes that I could be listening in.

The rest of me knows better.

I did my part. Now my responsibility is ensuring Hades keeps his word to Ariadne. I don't expect he'll go back on it, but even if I don't understand the full implications of her information, this reveal is about to do the equivalent of kicking a hornets' nest. He's going to have so much to worry about, it will be easy to let the promises to Ariadne go unfulfilled. The potential oversight is understandable, and not a reflection on him, but that doesn't mean I'm going to let him get away with it. Ariadne put herself in great danger to help us, and I want to ensure that we actually help her back.

But not tonight.

Tonight, I'm going to lie here and let Orpheus paint me. We'll release some of the pain still lingering between us. It's strange to realize I had already started to forgive him before he ever made the journey to the lower city. The fact that he came, that he's so invested in penance and doing whatever it takes to make things right...it means a lot. The man he used to be never would've considered apologizing, let alone engaging in the kind of things we've done since he arrived.

Watching him now, doing an activity I'm intimately familiar with, he should look like the old Orpheus. But he doesn't. There is a heaviness to him, a weight he's willingly caring around. Some people might call it maturity. I don't know if that's exactly the right word, but he seems content enough with the burden.

"Do you want to talk about what happened today?"

I concentrate on maintaining the position where he's arranged me on the chaise, with one arm draped over my head and my body stretched out. He ensured I would be comfortable, propping me up with pillows so I can hold the position for an extended period of time. It still takes effort not to move. "You don't normally like a lot of chatter when you paint."

"There isn't a lot left in my life that's 'normal.' If you want to talk, I'm happy to listen."

His words scratch at me, an itch I can't quite reach. It takes me several long beats before I realize the problem. "What about what you want?"

"What I want doesn't matter."

I tense but remind myself to relax at the last minute. Even though we're speaking, his brush moves at a steady pace, making the trip from paint to canvas and back again. "That's bullshit, Orpheus. I understand you feel guilty for fucking up, and that's why you're paying penance, but that doesn't mean it has to become your entire personality. You're a whole human with thoughts and feelings and needs."

"Am I?" His brush hesitates, and then goes back to the canvas. "I thought I was your dog."

I glare. "Don't do that. Don't dirty what we shared in the last couple days. You enjoy being on your knees as much as I enjoy putting you there, but that isn't the entirety of our relationship, and you know it. You've wronged me, but I've forgiven you for it. To keep hauling around your guilt is selfish."

He flinches as if I reached out and struck him. "Well, we've already established I'm a selfish asshole. I guess I continue to play to type."

"Stop. Doing. That." I have to concentrate to stop gritting my teeth. "I don't want to be the albatross you string around your neck for the rest of your life. Can you see how that would be more of a burden than anything else? You've always had hopes and dreams and ambitions, Orpheus. Those didn't just go away in the last year, even if you buried them deep."

He sits back with a sigh. "If you want an honest answer to this question, it's going to prove just how selfish and worthless I am."

No matter what else is true, I don't like seeing him in pain. But if we have any chance at a future, we need to get this kind of thing figured out now. If Orpheus is more in love with the idea of paying penance to me than he is in love with me as a person, it will never work. I don't know if that fear is irrational or not, but his reluctance to name the things that he personally wants worries me. "Tell me."

He stares at his painting for a very long time, so long that I think he's trying to get out of answering the question. I'm about to press him again when he says, "I just want to paint. That's all I've ever wanted. I only did all the other shit, the networking and the partying and playing the golden boy to the legacy families, because it made my mother happy. She loves me—and it's not a conditional love, either—but I think there's a part of her that can't help wanting me to mirror her ambitions and take the family further than she did."

I can see that. Calliope used her modeling as a way to open doors for her, and later her family, into the upper tiers of the legacy families. She was never shy about wearing her ambition on her sleeve. In Olympus, that's practically a virtue. I'm nearly certain that her positioning helped her eldest son become Apollo. He deserves the title, and he's one of the best of the Thirteen in my personal opinion, but it was *her* ambition that secured him the spot, not his own.

As for Orpheus, no doubt she wanted him to follow in her footsteps. To use his art as an entrance to even higher levels of politics, to pave the way for an advantageous marriage that would ensure their family remained among the legacy families and create a possibility that his children could be future members of the Thirteen.

His relationship with me was never going to serve that purpose. My mother may be Demeter, and now my oldest sister may be Hera, but so much of Olympus still sees us as countryfolk, as outsiders. Calliope likes me well enough, but I'm not the partner she would choose for her son.

With all that said… "I thought you were happy. You seemed like it when we were dating before."

"I was happy." He shrugs. "It feels good to have the spotlight of Olympus's attention shining on you. It made me feel like a god.

It wasn't until you were gone, and I stopped performing for them, that I realized how fickle that light is."

It's a hard lesson to learn, and I sympathize. Not that the golden light of Olympus ever shined on me. I have been tolerated even more than my sisters because I never made waves, but that's a long way from actual approval. My family's presence is a bone in the throat of all the legacy families, a reminder that they rely so heavily on those of us who come from the countryside around the city. My mother won her title by popular vote of all of Olympus's citizens, both those in the city and those in the country. And that, the legacy families cannot stand.

"But the truth is," he continues, "that as bad as things were for the last year, there was also relief mixed into the whole mess. I didn't have to perform anymore. Losing my art hurt, but the rest of it was all unnecessary window dressing."

I almost point out that he had an arrangement with the gallery set up before everything that happened with us, but I bite the words back at the last moment. I don't need to tell him that. He knows. He stopped painting for the last year, so he had nothing to sell. But he's painting now.

I take a breath and relax back into my pose. "Okay."

"Okay?" He leans around the canvas to frown at me. "That's all you have to say?"

"Yes." A perverse part of me wants to leave him hanging, but that isn't fair. "You answered my question. You want to paint. I understand."

"Just like that?"

"Just like that." I watch him hesitate, and then finally go back to painting. His expression isn't exactly peaceful, but his movements

are slow and methodical. It continues to soothe me as we sit in relatively comfortable silence. I don't know exactly how long it goes
on for, only that the light through the window has shifted, darkness
creeping in as night falls.

Finally, Orpheus sits back and shakes out his hands. "It's going
to take me a while to get back up to speed. I'm out of shape." He goes
about cleaning his brushes, a line of concentration appearing as his
brows draw together. "I hear what you're saying, Eurydice. It's going
to take me some time to wrap my mind around it, but I *am* listening."

"That's all I ask." I sit up and do some stretching of my own.
No matter how comfortable the position, sitting in place for an hour
and change leaves a person stiff. "I know you've said I'm your muse
in the past, but I can't be your everything. I don't want to be. I want
to have my own life, and I want you to have your own life—and I
want us to choose each other."

"And Charon."

I study him carefully, but there's no unhappiness in his expression. He states it as fact. Still, I don't want there to be any misunder-
standings between us. "I care very deeply about Charon too. Just as
much as I care about you, though it's a little different. He's not an
addition to the two of us, just like you're not an addition to me and
Charon. Maybe I could work in a pair, but I don't think any of us
could deny that it feels good to be a trio."

"Yeah." Orpheus grins suddenly. "It really does feel good to
be a trio."

As if on cue, the door opens and shuts down on the first floor. I
lift my voice enough to carry. "We're up here."

A few seconds later, Charon walks into the room. He looks

utterly exhausted, and he nods at Orpheus before he comes over to the couch and drops down next to me. I open my mouth to ask him what's going on, but he slips an arm behind my back and tugs me firmly against his side. "Just let me hold you for a few minutes." He holds an arm out to Orpheus. "Both of you."

Orpheus only hesitates for a few seconds before he walks over and takes up the empty position on Charon's other side. I swallow down my questions until Charon relaxes fully against me. It takes long enough to worry me. "That bad?"

"Worse. It's going to be war. We don't know the full scope of it yet, but it's bad." He brushes a kiss to my temple, more like he needs comfort than like he's trying to give it. "Circe was the second Hera. Her information on Olympus is only slightly outdated, but if Hermes is on her side, then we're well and truly fucked."

Because Hermes would've been feeding her information. With her help, Circe would know our moves before we even had a chance to make them. Hermes is known for having secrets she shouldn't, and if she's passing those on to the enemy…if that's the case, we never stood a chance of stopping this.

I try to reconcile the idea of Hermes as a traitor. It doesn't feel right. But then, what do I know? Up until a year ago, I only interacted with her in passing. Once I came to live in the lower city, I spent more time with her though. She's a trickster and clever enough that half the time I have no idea what she's talking about, but to help instigate a war on the city that she is supposed to protect? "I'm not ready to believe Hermes is on her side."

"I don't want to believe it either. We'd be fools not to look at this from all angles though." Charon takes a long slow breath. "But not tonight. The whole mess will be waiting for us in the morning. Tonight, I'd like to focus on the three of us."

Orpheus carefully, almost tentatively rests his hand on Charon's chest. "Yeah, I think it's time we talked."

It's funny how, despite everything else I've dealt with in the last couple days, this is the thing that makes me most nervous. "So let's talk."

ORPHEUS

EURYDICE HAS ALREADY GIVEN ME A LOT TO CHEW ON, and now we're driving right off the deep end again. I'm trying to take what she said to heart, but it's hard to reconcile with the feelings I've been carrying around for the last year. Nothing has been what I expected. I'm still having a hard time believing that she really wants a future with me...that they *both* want a future with me.

"Have either of you eaten?"

Eurydice and I exchange a look over Charon's chest. She doesn't seem in a hurry to answer, so I answer for both of us. "We might have missed lunch."

"Thought so. Come on, we can talk while I cook."

We make our way down to the kitchen, and Charon herds us into the chairs at the counter. I start to get up to help, but Eurydice shakes her head at me. If feels wrong to sit here and watch Charon cook for us, but I understand why after only a few minutes.

He moves about the kitchen with a growing relaxation, chopping vegetables and heating up two pans to cook them and the meat.

Cooking unwinds him, removing some of the stress of the day. Once all the ingredients are sizzling happily away, he turns to us. "You seem more at ease with each other. I take it you talked this afternoon?"

"We talked."

I wait for Eurydice to continue, but she's got a stubborn set to her jaw that I recognize all too well. It's the same expression she wore earlier when she backed me into a corner about what I want to do with my life. I'm still feeling raw after that. It felt like ripping open my rib cage and exposing my still-beating heart to her. Everyone knows I love to paint, but I've never admitted that I hate all the other bullshit. I don't even know that I understood my feelings on it until my life fell apart and I realized how little I value the same things my so-called friends hold so highly.

I still don't see a way forward entirely. Networking is a necessary part of the art world, which means I'll have to engage in it to some extent. But I don't have to do it right now. More than that, if Charon's right that war is coming, there's going to be little need for art in a city under siege. I don't know if that thought stresses me out or brings a little relief. For better or worse, I have time to figure my shit out.

Still, there's one thing left to address. I clear my throat. "You didn't have to buy the painting supplies for me. It's too extravagant. I don't deserve…" I shoot Eurydice a guilty look. "It's too much," I finally say.

"It's a gift, Orpheus," Charon says mildly. "I did it because I wanted to."

"But—"

"Did it feel good to paint again?"

I don't want to admit exactly how good it felt, but doing anything else amounts to a lie. I drum my fingers on the countertop, glaring at them instead of at Charon and Eurydice. The words try to stick in my throat, but I push through. "Yes. It felt like waking up after a long sleep. It will take me some time to get into the rhythm of it again, but it felt very, very good."

Charon nods as if I answered a question beyond the apparent one. "Then it was well worth the cost." He crosses his arms over his chest. "And the rest?"

I lift my gaze to him, questioning. What *rest*? What's he talking about?

It's Eurydice who answers for us this time. "I told Orpheus that although I enjoy him on his knees, I don't want him there every hour of every day. He needs something for himself, just like both of us have something for ourselves. I had to back him into a corner to get an answer, but he wants to paint."

"And you want to work for Hades." He pins her with a long look. "Hades is a fair boss, but you've moved yourself from sheltered sister-in-law to employee. He won't coddle you anymore. He'll treat you like the rest of us, and I expect that will mean training as soon as there's space for it."

She lifts her chin. "I'm aware."

"I know. There's no shame in changing your mind though. Remember that as things get even messier in the coming months."

This conversation is all well and good, but it's not what I thought we were going to talk about. With Eurydice and Charon staring each other down, I should probably stay silent, but I can't quite help myself. "What about us?"

"Elaborate." Charon speaks so softly that for a moment I wonder if I've made a misstep. It takes me a few seconds to realize he's being just as careful with us as Eurydice and I have been with each other. We're all doing this delicate dance where no one is quite saying what they want. I could maintain that, but I can't stand the thought of not knowing. No matter how uncomfortable this conversation gets.

"Us. You, me, and Eurydice. Is there a future with the three of us?"

He looks at me for a long moment, and then turns his attention to Eurydice. "Well?"

She clenches her fists, and then seems to make an effort to unclench them. The silence gains weight until it presses unbearably against my skin. Earlier, she said that she cares about me—about both of us—but it's a long way from caring to wanting to build a life together. I've been such a little prick, and even though I'm trying my best, I'm going to continue to fuck up. It won't be on the same level as a year ago, but that doesn't mean that I'm entitled to them assuming good faith.

She finally exhales in a slow, steady stream that can't quite be called a sigh. "Look, I love Orpheus. Even with all of the bullshit and baggage, I don't think I ever stopped loving him." She holds Charon's gaze. "I love you too. You've been my best friend for a year, and you've given me the space and safety to learn things about myself I didn't think were possible. I know it's greedy, but I don't care. I want both of you."

Charon stares at her for a long time. I search his expression, but I don't know him well enough to guess what he's thinking. I get the feeling that it could take me years, and that knowledge will still elude me. He finally turns to me. "What are your feelings on the matter?"

Fuck, this is hard. The temptation to make a joke or divert the conversation is nearly overwhelming, but I respect both of them too much to shy away from the possibility of *us*. If I take the cowardly way out now, I don't know if I'll get another chance. "I love Eurydice. I haven't always loved her well, and I sure as fuck don't deserve her, but I love her." I take a shaking breath. "I don't know you well enough for love, not yet. But I respect the fuck out of you. You're strong, you're capable, and you don't use either of those things to overpower those weaker than you. When you came to me, you could have told me to stay the fuck away from Eurydice, and I would've listened. The fact that you were fair, that you put her needs before yours, speaks volumes." I clear my throat with a self-conscious smile. "And I'll be honest—I really like fucking you."

Charon's lips curve. I can't help staring; the desire to paint that barest hint of a smile is nearly overwhelming. After so long without any inspiration at all, I am glutted on it. Now isn't the time for that though.

Eurydice leans forward and props her elbows on the counter. "We've shown you ours; now show us yours. You don't get to play the restricted, quiet one when we're putting our hearts on the table."

"I love you," he says simply. "I have for long time. I meant what I said when I told you we're endgame, no matter what that looks like. At the time, I thought that meant making my peace with Orpheus's presence in our lives." He looks at me. "It hasn't been that long. I won't lie to you and say it's already love, but there's a lot about you I like—and I'm not just talking about fucking you. You're different than I expected, and your willingness to put aside your pride to make things right when you fuck up is incredibly sexy. The foundation for love is there. I like how the three of us fit together. It feels seamless in a way that I never could've anticipated."

"That's exactly the word I was looking for. *Seamless*. It feels as natural as breathing to be with the two of you." Eurydice tucks her hair behind her ears. "So where does that leave us?"

Charon stirs the vegetables and flips the chicken. "Orpheus, when you came to the lower city, your intention was to bring Eurydice back across the river. No, don't deny it. You might not have admitted to yourself that it's what you wanted, but it *is* the truth, isn't it?"

I clear my throat. "Yeah, that's what I wanted."

"And now?"

Now things are infinitely more complicated, and yet they've never been simpler. I look at him, and then at her. "You're happy here. You've made a life here you're proud of, and you found a place that's yours and yours alone. I would never take that from you."

"Even if that means you stay in the lower city too?" Charon presses.

"Yes. I follow where she leads."

I still don't quite know how to reconcile my family in the upper city with Eurydice in the lower city. Choosing this path will break my mother's heart, but I've been breaking her heart for nine very long months. At least this way I'll be happy, and even if my mother may have preferred my life to look a certain way, I think happiness is a strong silver medal. Or at least I hope so.

My father will follow my mother's lead, but I genuinely think that Apollo will be happy for me. I'm doing what he always wanted me to, stepping out on my own to succeed or fail without access to the family purse. Besides, it's not like I'll never see them again.

Charon busies himself with grabbing three plates out of the cabinet and filling them with our dinner. He sets them in front of us with the ease of long practice, and then goes about filling three cups with some kind of juice he had in the fridge. He catches Eurydice watching him and shrugs. "With everything going on right now, I don't think it's wise for any of us to drink. There's a good chance that I, at least, might get a call in the middle of the night."

"I didn't say anything."

"I know." He smiles a little. "You weren't saying anything rather loudly."

Dinner is...comfortable. We sit and eat and engage in a little small talk, and it's like looking through a window into a possible future. One where we truly have built a life together, where dinners like this are the norm instead of a brand-new experience. It surprises me how much I crave that. Oh, I knew I wanted these two people. But I want the *life* too.

I've only been in the lower city for a few days, but the differences between it and the upper city are still startling. In the upper city, the sensation of being watched permeates everything. The only place I feel like I can really breathe is my own apartment, and then only if I'm alone. Everywhere else, I'm all too aware that anyone I come across is one photograph or video away from selling a story to MuseWatch. In the before times, I told myself that that little feeling of being prey was something I liked, even craved. At least they wanted to talk about me.

In the lower city, people watch me, but it's only because of the company I keep. As soon as they realize I'm a welcome guest, not someone bothering Eurydice, they move on with their day. For the first time in my life, I'm being treated like a civilian. I fucking love it.

That realization, more than anything else, has me speaking. "I know there's shit going on right now, but I would love for the two of you to show me the lower city."

Eurydice smiles at me, and it's like the sun peeking out from behind a cloud. It warms me right through. "Of course. I think there's a lot down here that you'll find inspiring."

"Of that, I have no doubt."

CHARON

IT SURPRISES ME HOW MUCH I LIKE HAVING ORPHEUS IN my house. So much about this man goes against my assumptions and expectations of him. Even something as small as him taking the initiative to do the dishes after we eat is a bit of a revelation.

He catches me watching him and gives a surprisingly sweet grin even as he blushes. "Why are you looking at me like that?"

"Why are you asking questions you already know the answer to?"

If anything, he blushes harder. Orpheus is one of the most beautiful men I've ever encountered, let alone had in my bed. Add in the fact that he enjoys playing the same games that Eurydice and I do... Well, I already decided to keep him, didn't I?

"Don't tease poor Orpheus." Eurydice moves around the table and slips onto my lap as if that's the most natural thing in the world. There might come a day when I take her closeness for granted, but somehow I don't think so. I've wanted this for so long, I wanted her trust and her intimacy and, yeah, her body. The shape of this might look different than I expected, but it's better.

I tug her back against my chest and arrange her how I want her, guiding her to lean against me and spread her legs on the outside of mine. "Would you rather I tease you instead?"

"It's only right." I can hear the smile in her voice. "You wouldn't want to distract him from his task."

Orpheus stares at us for several long seconds, and then turns back to the sink. It's hard to tell from this angle, but I think he might be washing even faster than ever. It pleases me. It obviously pleases Eurydice too, because she wiggles on my lap, grinding her ass against my hardening cock.

"*You're* an unforgivable tease," I murmur in her ear. "At this rate, he's going to break a plate."

"If he does, we'll just have to punish him." She doesn't pitch her voice low, and the way Orpheus's shoulders twitch, it's clear he heard her. Eurydice turns her face to brush a kiss against my lips. "Hey."

"Hey." I nip her bottom lip. "Take off your pants, baby."

Eurydice really is a little tease, because she doesn't stand up to take the most efficient route to follow my commands. No, she leans back harder against me and lifts her hips to work her jeans down to her thighs. Then she grinds that tight little ass against my cock while she lifts her legs and slides the jeans down them. It's the sweetest agony, and I'm going to make her pay for it.

I tug her shirt over her head and toss it to the side. She arches her back, giving me a good look at her lacy bra. It's definitely meant for seduction, the faint floral pattern seeming to frame her brown nipples. It's hard to see exactly from my angle, but I think her matching panties are doing the same thing to her pussy.

"Tease."

"It's only a tease if I don't plan to do something about it." She takes my hands and guides them to the inside of her knees. Even as I tell myself to take charge of this, I'm curious to see where she'll guide us. I sit there submissively and let her run my hands up her smooth thighs until my knuckles brush against her panties.

I glance at Orpheus as I drag my knuckles up and down slowly. Eurydice wiggles, but I hold her tight to me with a grip on either thigh. She's not the only one who knows how to tease. "If I pull your panties to the side, what am I going to find?"

She shivers. "Why don't you do it and see for yourself?"

"Not yet." I keep idly stroking her as Orpheus continues with his task. It's hard to tell for certain, but I think he slows down once he realizes my game. He all but confirms it when he glances over his shoulder for the sixth time, and his gaze sweeps from my hands up to our faces. He catches my eye and winks.

"Orpheus!" Eurydice's voice is a little breathy. "You're going slow on purpose."

"Just doing a thorough job." The smugness in his tone gives lie to his intentions. It's so satisfying, I have to hide an answering grin against Eurydice's hair. Her little huff of indignation is so pleasing that I can't help palming her pussy.

"*Oh!*" She tries to lift her hips, but I keep her pinned. The new position frees up one of my hands though. I waste no time skating my fingers up her stomach to pull down the lace of her bra. It puts her tits on full display, and the next time Orpheus looks over his shoulder, he drops the glass in his hand. It clatters into the sink with a worrisome sound.

I lift my brows. "Am I going to have any undamaged dishes left by the time you're done?"

He stares at her breasts and licks his lips. "I'm going to be honest. I can't promise anything."

"If you think it would be more beneficial for us to leave the room..."

"That won't be necessary." He turns back to the sink. Where before he had been focused on going slow to tease out Eurydice's pleasure, now he's back to moving with impressive speed.

I watch the lines of his back as I absently pluck at Eurydice's nipples. She shifts and moans and tries to rub herself against my palm, but I don't give her a chance to. "Take off your clothes, Orpheus."

He doesn't hesitate to obey. He pulls his shirt over his head and tosses it into the growing pile of discarded clothing. His pants and underwear quickly follow. I like that. He's not trying to play coy with us. Not when his cock, hard and long, is on full display. It makes my cock give an answering pulse of need.

We sit in silence and growing tension as Orpheus finishes up his task. He even takes the time to dry and put the dishes away. Then he turns to us, color high on his cheeks. "Now what?"

"Now we go to bed." I catch Eurydice by her hips and lift her onto her feet. Her outraged expression is almost enough to make me come in my pants right then and there. I love it when she gets riled. Before she can start in on me, I lean forward and cover her pussy with my mouth, licking her through the lace. It's a quick kiss, but effective. Her gasp of outrage turns quickly to a breathy moan.

Then Orpheus sweeps her into his arms and starts for the stairs.

It's a good move. It's almost like we coordinated it. I stand, take a moment to adjust my pants, and follow them.

No one speaks as they pull my clothes off and then we divest Eurydice of her panties and bra. It's almost as if we stepped out of time and space, as if no one exists in this world but us. It's the most natural thing in the world for Eurydice to run her hands up my chest and press her body to mine as she kisses me. For me to grab Orpheus's hand and pull him to us, guiding him into our embrace.

He kisses me as Eurydice sinks to her knees and takes my cock in her mouth. A little moan slips free despite myself, and then his hands are in my hair, tugging almost painfully as he nips my bottom lip and twines his tongue with mine. It's a consuming kiss.

One that feels like mutual ownership.

I know what Eurydice is up to the moment her mouth leaves my cock and Orpheus tenses against me. *Wicked little thing.* I break the kiss long enough to look down to find her with a fist around each of our cocks. She's teasing, taking him deep enough to make him moan, and then moving onto my cock to do the same.

I lace my fingers through Orpheus's hair at the nape of his neck and urge him to look down. "One day. One day I want you to paint this."

"Yeah." He swallows hard. "Yeah, I can do that. We might have to, um, do it a few more times so I can get my references right."

Eurydice flicks the tip of his cock with her tongue, her expression mischievous. "How are you going to paint while I'm sucking your cock, Orpheus?" She strokes him a few times and then runs her lips down his length. "Maybe next time we take a picture. It'll last longer."

I'm not normally one to fuck with dirty pictures, but I can't deny the power of her statement and the visual she suggests. "Yeah, let's do that. Next time." For tonight, I'm tired of waiting. "Orpheus, get the lube." I catch Eurydice under her arms, lifting her easily and tossing her onto the bed. I'm on her before her body finishes bouncing, covering her and pouring all my need and frustration into a kiss.

The bed dips as Orpheus crawls to us, the lube in one hand. I roll onto my back with Eurydice on top of me. She plants one hand on my chest and sits up a little bit to look between us. "Before you ask me, the answer is yes. I want you both. At the same time."

I chuckle. "So greedy, baby. You don't know what I was going to offer."

She pricks my chest with her nails, but her eyes are alight with mischief. "Oh? You weren't going to tell Orpheus to take my ass while you work your big cock into my pussy? Silly me."

I tighten my grip on her thighs. "Playing with fire."

"Neither of you will let it burn me." She leans down until her breasts press against my chest and looks over her shoulder Orpheus. "Take my ass, Orpheus. Please."

She relaxes against me. I don't have to see to know what he's doing behind her. The evidence is there in the way she writhes and kisses me harder as he works his cock into her ass. In his hitched breathing and the slow shift of her body against mine. He's being careful with her, as he should.

I kiss my way along her jaw to her shoulder, and she buries her face in my neck. Only then can I see him, see evidence of his strain, the muscle standing out on his body and his face a mask of concentration. "That's right, Orpheus. Be a good boy and go slow. Make sure she's taken care of."

"I am," he grinds out. Seconds tick by as he moves in small increments until he's fully seated inside her. "There."

Now it's my turn. I have to help him shift her back so he can band one arm over her ribs and keep her in place. The picture they present is one I want tattooed on my brain. Both of them are so turned on that they're panting, her pussy swollen and wet and needy...and empty.

I drag a single finger through her folds. "You like anal, baby?" I circle her clit with my finger.

She jerks a little and moans. "Sometimes. Definitely yes right now. Please, Charon. I need your cock too. We both do."

I already knew that I could deny my woman nothing, but the compound need of the two of them is overwhelming in the best way possible. I stroke my cock once and then shift down so I can press to her entrance. It was a tight fit before, but with Orpheus taking up so much space, I can barely get inside her.

Somehow, that's even hotter.

I drag them down my cock slowly, gritting my teeth to maintain control. It feels too fucking good. I see my struggle reflected in Orpheus's face. Neither of us are going to last too long like this. Which means we need to get her there first. "Her clit, Orpheus."

He reaches around to stroke her clit as I finally seat myself fully inside her. In our current position, full strokes would be a bit of a challenge, but I don't need that range of motion to get her there. To get any of us there.

Instead, I rock her on my cock, grinding her onto both of us. It's the tiniest of motions, but her pussy clamps around me like a vice. Eurydice leans back against Orpheus's shoulder. The trust she gives us, letting us play with her body, knowing we'll make her come harder than she's ever come before…

It goes straight to my head.

Eurydice cries out and then it's too late. In her current position she can't move so we have to do it for her. We pulse her on our cocks and Orpheus never stops stroking her clit, working her up to the pinnacle and then taking her over the edge again and again and again. It's only when she goes boneless that I lose control and give in to the pleasure gathering deep inside me. I pound up into her as much as I'm able to and come so hard that I see stars.

Eurydice slumps onto my chest, and I hold her close as I watch Orpheus carefully fuck her ass. He pulls out at the last second and comes all over her back. And then he meets my gaze, looking just as shell-shocked as I feel. I move on instinct. I reach up, hook the back of his neck, and pull him down for a devastating kiss.

He sinks into it but draws away after only a few seconds with a breathless laugh. "You better stop kissing me like that unless you want to go again."

It's on the tip of my tongue to say that's exactly what I want. Because it is. I've barely scratched the surface of my desire for these two. We could spend days—weeks, months, fucking *years*—in bed together, and it wouldn't be enough.

Unfortunately, that's not an option right now. With all the danger circling, I need to be at the top of my game, which means sleep. For all of us. I kiss Orpheus one last time and then press a kiss to Eurydice's temple. "We need a shower and then sleep." I hold

Orpheus's gaze. "All of us in my room tonight, unless you have an objection to that."

His smile goes soft and sweet. "No objection. No objection at all."

EURYDICE

IT'S STRANGE THAT WITH SO MUCH BAD GOING ON, THIS is the happiest I've ever been. Waking up in bed with Charon and Orpheus is something I'm not sure I'll ever get used to. I don't think I *want* to get used to it, not if the alternative is to lose this feeling of wonder and peace.

But reality always intrudes, and we have a lot to worry about today outside the confines of this bedroom. I roll over to face Charon where he's wedged between me and Orpheus, only to find him already awake.

He smiles a little, though his eyes are worried. "Morning, baby."

"Morning. You're up early."

"Been up for a while. There were no emergencies through the night, but I want to get back to the house early so we can start planning on contingencies. We need to figure out who is fucking with us. Knowing their boss's name ultimately doesn't change much. We have to get them out of the lower city."

I don't tell him to be careful. His very job description is the opposite of that. He needs to be able to be decisive, and it's impossible to be decisive if you're second-guessing every decision. It's also impossible to stay safe.

The thought of something happening to him reaches its cold dead hands into my chest and sinks its claws into my heart. I wiggle my way closer, wrap my arms around him, and bury my face in his chest. "Come back to us tonight. Every night. Promise me."

"Baby, you know I can't do that. I'm not going to take any unnecessary risks, but there's no guarantees in life." I feel him smile against the top of my head. "Just like I'm not going to ask you to stay in this town house until the situation is resolved. We both know you won't do it, so I won't ask for that promise."

Something akin to guilt rises, but I swallow it down. "This isn't going to be easy, is it?"

"Nothing worth having ever is." He gives me one last hug, and then carefully extracts himself from the bed. I watch him walk away, the claws in my heart pulsing with each step he takes. With all the conversations yesterday and last night, I let myself forget the sheer amount of danger we're in right now.

If Olympus falls, the first thing Circe will do is eliminate all the leaders and those loyal to them. If she's managed to come this far, she's too smart to do anything else. Whether she decides to extend that order to the legacy families is up in the air.

My mother, my sisters, Orpheus's family. Hades, Hermes, and all the rest. It will be a bloodbath.

"Charon…"

"I know, baby. We'll get through this. Try to get some more sleep if you can." He slips into the bathroom and quietly slides the door shut. A few seconds later, the shower starts.

I flop back onto the bed with a sigh. As lovely as it sounds to go to sleep again, it's not going to happen. My mind is too alight with all the possibilities of what could go wrong. Orpheus stirs and tosses an arm over my waist. "We have to trust him. We have to trust everybody in power right now. There's not a whole lot that you and I can do by ourselves."

I blink up at the ceiling, feeling sick to my stomach. "You heard all that?"

"Yeah." Sleep still lingers in his voice. He tugs me closer, arranging me against his body. It's familiar and comforting. I will myself to sink into him, to let his warmth soothe me. His breath ruffles the hair of my temple. "Since we both know you're not going to sit around twiddling your thumbs, why don't you tell me what our agenda is for the day?"

"Our agenda?"

"Eurydice, if you think I'm letting you out of my sight with all this shit going on, you're out of your damned mind. I'm not trained the same way Charon is, but he and I will both feel better if one of us is with you. Between me and Minthe, we'll keep you safe."

But who's going to keep *him* safe?

It would be so easy to pretend we have nothing to worry about, but the truth is that he's in danger because of his proximity to me. His family and brother might be the cause in the upper city, but in the lower city, I'm the one to blame if something happens to him. Panic flutters in the back of my throat.

I just started to get settled into the idea of a future with the three of us, and now it's actively in danger. I can't tell them to stay here and stay safe any more than they can tell me to do the same.

We are who we are. That doesn't make it easier to watch Charon come out of the bathroom, fully dressed with an empty shoulder holster in place. He moves to the safe in the nightstand and retrieves a handgun.

He catches me watching. "I wear this every day."

It's true, but that doesn't change how I feel. "I know."

"Where are you headed today?" I can tell how much it costs him to ask, instead of telling me. It's there in the slight tension in his shoulders and the way he clenches his jaw. Poor Charon. All he wants to do is keep the people in his life safe, and we keep making it difficult for him.

Well, I can give him this at least. "I had planned on going to see Ariadne. I know she's given us all the information she has, but I'd feel shitty discarding her like yesterday's trash after we've gotten what we wanted from her." Yesterday, the only thing she seemed to feel about the abortion was relief, and we're not exactly friends, but nobody should be alone after they've made such big decisions. And she's made more than a few.

He hesitates like he wants to tell me that it's not a good idea, but finally gives a short nod. "You will wait for Minthe."

"I will. I promise. I won't go anywhere without her today."

He doesn't exactly look relieved. "Good. If you run into any trouble, call me. I'll let you know if something happens and I'm going to be late tonight."

"Okay." This feels almost awkward, but I don't know how to ease it. Maybe there is no fixing the fact that we're both going to spend the day worried about each other. I watch him walk out of the room with my heart in my throat. Really, nothing's changed from yesterday. We knew there was danger; we just didn't know the exact source. Now we do.

My phone rings before I have a chance to get moving. I don't know whether to be relieved or nervous that it's my sister's name scrolling across the screen. "Hello?"

"You're going to see Ariadne today. I'm coming with."

I blink. "Good morning to you too, Persephone."

"You weren't asleep, and I haven't had a good night's sleep in weeks, so stop with the snarky little sister remarks. I'm leaving here in fifteen minutes, so if you want to meet me there, you'd better get moving." She hangs up without saying goodbye.

I drop my phone on the bed with a sigh. "Hades is not going to be happy about *that*."

Orpheus turns on his side and reaches over to link his fingers with mine. "I know your sister has no reason to like me, and normally I would make myself scarce to avoid making anyone uncomfortable, but I meant what I said about not letting you out of my sight today."

I give his hand a squeeze. "I love you. My family is going to have some issues with that, and we'll have to navigate their disapproval, but eventually they'll realize you're not the same person you were before, just like I'm not the same person I was before. It'll be fine." I really hope I'm not lying right now.

My family does love me to distraction. They're also fiercely protective and borderline murderous when it comes to the people who've harmed one of us. Possibly more than borderline, though those rumors about my mother are unsubstantiated.

"Let's get moving before we get left behind." I give his hand one last squeeze and slip out of the bed. It's quick work to get my hair under control, put on just enough makeup so I don't look exhausted, and dress myself in a pair of my favorite faded jeans and the knit sweater Persephone bought me last holiday.

"I just need a few minutes to get dressed." Orpheus stands and heads through the door into the bathroom. I take a moment to appreciate his truly outstanding body, but only a moment. I can't afford to get distracted when we need to meet my sister. Instead, I head downstairs to find Charon has already started the coffeepot and set out two travel mugs. One is the sparkly purple thing I bought mostly as a joke from the summer market earlier this year. The other still has the stickers on it. "Always taking care of the people around you," I murmur.

Fifteen minutes later, Orpheus and I are climbing into the back of yet another from Hades's fleet of black sedans. Minthe adjusts the driver's mirror, waits for us to buckle our seat belts, and then we're off. Really, we could've walked.

Or rather, *we* could've walked. These days Persephone doesn't walk anywhere. She's almost through her first trimester, but because it's twins, everyone is on edge. I know it frustrates her to the point where she wants to have a full-on toddler meltdown, but she's been mostly gracious about letting us be overprotective.

We pull up next to a car identical to ours. My sister leans against the side, her head tilted back and her eyes closed in the morning light. I know she's been grappling with the changes to her body, the stress of being the coruler of the lower city, and the general worry that comes from living in Olympus during current times, but she's never looked better. I thought the whole pregnant-women-glowing thing was a myth, but no one can look at my sister and say she's doing anything but glowing.

"Do you want me to wait in here until it's time to go inside?"

I shake my head. "No, she has to make her peace with this whole thing eventually. We might as well start now."

Sure enough, the moment Orpheus follows me out of the car, Persephone narrows her eyes. "We haven't really had a chance to talk about this, but just know that I don't approve."

"Then it's a really good thing that what I want is your love, not your approval." It's not, strictly speaking, true. I intensely dislike that I'm disappointing my sisters and mother right now, but they're not thinking clearly. I can't say for certain that I am, but at least I know my own mind better than anyone else. More than that, I know Orpheus.

Her attention flicks to him and stays there. "If you hurt my sister—again—then you won't survive long enough to cross the River Styx back to the upper city."

"Persephone!"

Orpheus isn't exactly unbothered by my sister threatening him again, but he doesn't flinch. "I'll be paying penance for the wrongs I did Eurydice until my dying day. But respectfully, that's between her and me...and Charon."

My sister studies him for several long moments. "My threat stands." She turns to face the apartment building. "Shall we?"

EURYDICE

MINTHE CLIMBS OUT OF THE DRIVER'S SEAT AND SURVEYS us. "Where's your security detail, Persephone?"

"It's Medusa. I'm here to pick her up."

Minthe props her hands on her hips. "You know the kind of danger we're facing right now, and you went out without a security detail? Are you out of your damn mind?"

"It was a two-minute drive, and I knew that you, Medusa, and Calypso would be here when I arrived," she says mildly.

I raise my brows, but Orpheus leans close to say, "In case you're wondering, you won't be able to successfully use that line of reasoning on us. I bet it doesn't work on Hades either." He's not exactly speaking quietly though.

I laugh a little. "I'm simply taking notes from my big sister."

"Don't start that." Persephone points at us. "And don't start calling me a hypocrite either. Let's get inside and meet up with my security detail."

The apartment is roomy, but not nearly roomy enough to

comfortably fit seven grown adults in the main living space. Medusa isn't any happier with Persephone showing up on her doorstep than Minthe was. "You were supposed to wait at the house for me to come get you."

"I decided to skip a step." She inhales deeply and closes her eyes. "Is that…pie?"

"Cookies, actually." Ariadne speaks from her place in the kitchen. "I bake when I'm stressed."

I move around my sister and make my way to Ariadne. She looks better than she did yesterday, the color back in her cheeks. There are still circles beneath her eyes, but I don't think any of us are sleeping particularly well these days. "How are you doing?"

"Oh, you know, absolutely stunning. It's not every day that I betray my father and country, and—" She shakes her head. "I made the right choice, but my emotions are all over the place. I don't expect that's going to resolve itself anytime soon."

"Did you say cookies?" Persephone nudges me aside to peer at the wire racks in front of Ariadne. "They smell like a pie." Truth be told, the cookies look more like pies than cookies. They are little triangles, puffed up, and appear to be filled with apples.

"I guess they're kind of like apple pie cookies." Ariadne stares at my sister's stomach for a beat too long. "Would you like one?"

"Yes, thank you." Persephone carefully picks one up and inhales deeply. "You can't stay here indefinitely."

"Excuse me?" Ariadne says at the same time that I snarl, "For fuck's sake, Persephone."

My sister takes a bite and moans in a way that's uncomfortably sexual. But when she speaks, she's all business. "In the lower city, I mean. My husband offered you sanctuary because he's a good man and the thought of someone suffering when he could save them is unbearable. I, however, am a mean bitch with a vast amount of experience in politics."

"Hades gave his word," I say.

"Yes, he did. Which is why I need you to release him from it." She holds Ariadne's gaze. "My husband will do everything in his power to protect you if you want to stay here, but I think we both know that he will fail. Not because of your father, and not because of Circe."

Ariadne's shoulders slump, and she looks so defeated that I want to hug her. "There's no reason to think *he'll* come for me."

"On the contrary, you wouldn't have made this bargain if you thought anything else." She takes another bite and makes another godsawful sound. "I'm sorry, these are just so good, and I can't stop eating them."

"Thanks, I guess."

"I have no intention of turning you out without a plan. I'm not a monster." She pops the last bite of cookie in her mouth and chews slowly. "There's one way to ensure you will be folded gently into Olympus, though I think we can all agree it would be best you don't stay in the city proper."

I am battling the urge to throttle my pregnant sister. I know she can be ambitious and occasionally ruthless, but I've never seen her turn it on someone who didn't deserve it. I'm sure in her mind Ariadne is fair game since she is Minos's daughter, and Minos is the source of so much pain and suffering in our city right now. But Ariadne *helped* us. Hades gave his word.

"You have an offer. I would like to hear it." Ariadne's mouth twists. "Especially since it sounds like I don't have much choice."

"I've taken the liberty of speaking with our current Aphrodite, and they have agreed to find you a nice, kind match. There are a lot of lesser houses who reside in the countryside. Aphrodite will provide you with a small list of suitable candidates, and I will personally vouch for each one. We have no desire to marry you off to someone who would mistreat you after the service you've done for Olympus. But you can't stay here."

I really *am* going to throttle my sister. "That's not fair."

But Ariadne shakes her head and lifts a hand to stop me. "On the contrary, it's a better deal than I anticipated. I fully expected to suffer some sort of unfortunate accident in the next couple weeks. At least this way, I get to live."

Maybe I really am naive, because her words shock me to my core. "You made this deal thinking you wouldn't survive it?"

"I made this deal because I had no other choice." She turns to my sister. "I accept your terms."

Persephone nods. She doesn't look particularly happy, and that's the only thing that keeps me from losing my shit. I know my sister doesn't see things that way, but it's hypocritical in the extreme. I'm essentially in the same boat as Ariadne, but she would go to great lengths to make sure I was never hurt because of the family that I was born into.

Persephone motions to Medusa. "There's a safe house set up for Ariadne. I need you to arrange transportation for her there."

Medusa pulls out her phone. "Consider it done."

I cross my arms over my chest. "In the upper city or the lower city?"

"If I told you that, it wouldn't be much of a safe house, would it?" She shakes her head. "We can fight about this later if you'd like. Right now, there's business to attend to. You wanted to be on Hades's payroll. This is what that looks like. Making hard decisions to protect the lower city."

To protect the lower city...or to protect Hades?

I don't ask the question. It's not fair, and I'm certain I won't like the answer. Instead, I turn to Ariadne and take her hands. "If you have any reservations about this at all, tell me now and I'll fight this. I promised you safety, and you're in this mess because you believed me."

She gives my hands a single squeeze and slips free. "Like I said, I had a good idea of what I was getting myself into when I called you. It was only a matter of time before my father bargained me away in marriage. At least this way, I'm making a choice for myself instead of having him make it for me." She won't quite meet my gaze. "And there was the other thing."

Right. I'm not in danger of forgetting that. Still... "Are you sure?"

"I'm sure."

I glance at where Orpheus stands just outside the kitchen, leaning against the wall. I'm not sure what he thinks of the situation. The few times he's met my sister before coming to the lower city, she was firmly wearing her sunshine mask. Bright and happy with not a single harsh thought to her name. That's not the woman who stands before him now. He catches me watching him and offers a small smile of solidarity.

"Eurydice, I would like a word. Privately." Persephone motions to Minthe. "Come along." When Orpheus takes a step forward, she pins him with a glare. "What do you think you're doing?"

To his credit, he doesn't wilt. He also doesn't puff out his chest and lean too hard into bravado. He just meets her gaze steadily. "I gave Charon my word I wouldn't let her out of my sight."

My sister raises her chin, hazel eyes flaring. "I outrank Charon and I'm telling you to wait inside."

"With all due respect, Persephone, *I'm* not on Hades's payroll. I don't answer to him, and I don't answer to you."

For a moment, I think my sister might be provoked into actual violence. It never would've been a fear of mine three months ago, but three months ago she wasn't pregnant with twins and riding the waves of emotions and hormones that I find terrifying.

She gets herself under control though. "So be it." She turns and leads the way through the apartment and out the door. Our strange little group ends up clustered around one of the trees that line the street in front of Medusa and Calypso's apartment. My sister draws herself up and gives me her full attention. "You have something to say. Say it."

"This is shady and underhanded. Hades gave his word that Ariadne would be protected, and the first thing you two do is marry her off to some asshole?"

She lifts a brow. It's an expression I've witnessed her husband make a hundred times, and it's incredibly disconcerting to see on my sister's face. "We grew up with those so-called assholes. They were our playmates and friends and companions until ten years ago when we came to the city proper. If things had fallen out differently with Mother, *we* would've married them. I'm not going to allow anyone who is a monster on that list. They'll treat her well, and it will remove her from the firing line."

She has a point, but it doesn't mean I'm going to let her have it. "It's still not her choice. It's not right."

"Surely you can't be that naive, even with how thoroughly we've protected you. Minos has been shopping her around since he arrived in Olympus. You know the kind of people who populate the legacy families in the upper city. Can you honestly say that they are better options than the one I'm giving her?"

I open my mouth to say exactly that, but I can't quite manage it. Because she's right. Almost to a person, the scions of the legacy families are predators. There's a reason my sisters worked so hard to avoid a marriage match. Ironic, that. All three of them are married to three of the most dangerous men in this entire city. Eros and Hades treat Psyche and Persephone like spun glass, but that doesn't change the fact that they're still predators.

It just turns out that my sisters are too.

I don't know where that leaves me. I might be stronger and more capable than they give me credit for, but that doesn't mean I'm fully comfortable swimming in the depths alongside them.

"I hear what you're saying, and I don't necessarily disagree, but that doesn't mean I like it."

My sister's smile is knife-sharp. She's never looked more like Callisto in this moment...or more like our mother. "Now you're getting the idea." She glances at Orpheus and leans close. "Now, I think we need to talk about—"

A strange sound cuts her off. For a moment, I think a car might be backfiring, and I actually turn to look for the source. That's when I see the van. It's completely nondescript. I notice too late that the plates have duct tape over them. Even as I watch, the back door slides open, and two people appear, dressed in black with masks over their faces marring their features.

Too late, I notice the guns in their hands.

My body locks up. A distant part of me screams to move, to hit the ground, because that's what you do when people are about to shoot you. The rest of me can't believe this is happening. My instincts are all fucked up. Time seems to slow down and speed up, all at once.

One of the muzzles flares as they fire. I feel silly, because no one could mistake this for a car backfiring.

I hear a scream, and then a hard body hits me in the side, taking me roughly to the ground. A hand catches my head right as it's about to bounce off the concrete, but that doesn't stop my body from flaring in pain in half a dozen locations. There are a few more gunshots. Then tires squeal as the van takes the corner on two wheels and flies away.

Reality comes crashing down on me in waves. The dozen cuts and scrapes from my fall. The weight of a body on top of me. The scent of...Orpheus.

Just like that, time slams back into motion.

"Orpheus!" I run my hands up his chest and cup his face, lifting it so I can look him in the eyes. "Are you okay? Are you hurt?"

He blinks down at me and gives himself a little shake. "I should be asking you that. I don't think I've ever tackled someone before.

If there's an art to it, I don't know it." He gently feels around the back of my head. "Did I catch you in time?"

I'm about to answer when a low curse reminds me that we weren't the only two people standing on the sidewalk. Panic flares. "Oh my gods. Persephone!"

ORPHEUS

EURYDICE TRIES TO SCRAMBLE OUT FROM BENEATH ME, but I press her more firmly to the ground. "Wait. We don't know if it's safe yet."

"That's my fucking sister." I expect her to sound as panicky as I feel, but there's a terrifying resolve in her voice. "Let me up, and call Charon. Now, Orpheus."

My adrenaline is surging so hard, it's a challenge to think clearly. I'm not certain I *am* thinking clearly at all. But she's right. We can't stay out here on the sidewalk. There's nothing to stop the attackers from making another pass. That, more than anything, gets me moving. "Stay low."

"I will." She slides out from beneath me and crawls to where her sister and Minthe lie. That's when I see the blood. It's a bright crimson against the light gray of the sidewalk. I haven't had cause to be around severe injuries up to this point, so I have no idea if it's a little or a lot. The fact that it's outside someone's body is problem enough.

I rise to a cautious crouch and pull my phone out of my pocket.

Thankfully, it's intact even after I tackled Eurydice. Charon just put his number into my contacts yesterday, and a part of me mourns the fact that this is the first time I have cause to use it. In crisis.

He answers on the first ring. "Orpheus?"

"There was an attack." My voice is shaking. That's not helpful. I take a deep breath and make an effort to firm it. "A drive-by. Eurydice is okay, but someone else was hurt... I don't know yet if it's Persephone or Minthe."

There's the barest pause as he processes my words. "Hold on." I hear him barking orders with an urgency that makes my stomach drop. Obviously, I knew there was danger in Olympus right now. But apparently I still had plenty of naivete, because I honestly didn't believe it would touch us.

I move closer to where Eurydice is carefully guiding Minthe onto her back. Minthe is a little pale, but her color is otherwise good. Persephone clutches her stomach, but I don't see any wounds aside from a scrape on her cheek. *Where is the blood coming from?*

On the phone, Charon is back. "Is everyone alive?"

"Yes."

"Okay." He exhales slowly. "A doctor's on the way, along with one of the security teams. If everyone is okay to move, go inside, but otherwise hold the location."

I don't tell him that I'm not a soldier, that I don't know how to hold any fucking location. I've never even held a gun. My brother has tried for years to convince me to take some kind of self-defense class, whether it's hand-to-hand or range shooting, and I've always had a reason to put him off. I've never had cause to regret it until now.

If we get through this, I'm going to have Charon set me up

with something, so I never feel this helpless again. So I can protect Eurydice if she ever needs it. "Okay. I can do that."

"You've got this, Orpheus." There's still plenty of tension in his voice, but it takes on a reassuring edge that unknots the spot between my shoulder blades, just a little. "Tell me what happened."

I swallow hard. "Persephone wanted to talk to Eurydice outside. They were already planning on taking Minthe, but I insisted on going outside too. There was a gray van. I can't tell you make and model off the top of my head, but it was old and beat to shit. The engine actually backfired as they came around the corner and onto our street."

"Which way did they come around the corner?" There's sound in the background as he starts moving.

"They turned left onto the street, and then they turned right after they shot at us."

"Did you get that?" It takes me a moment to realize he's not speaking to me. There's a light voice in the background that answers him, and a few seconds later he curses. "Got you, motherfuckers."

I'm about to ask for clarification when Minthe snarls, "It's just a fucking scratch. A graze. We have to get inside. Now." She shakes off Eurydice and turns to Persephone. "Can you stand, or do I need to carry you?"

"I'm fine. Just got the wind knocked out of me." But Persephone does reach out a hand so Minthe and Eurydice can gently pull her to her feet. She turns to me. "Is that Charon on the phone?"

"Yes."

She motions for me to hand her the phone, and I don't hesitate to do so. The scratch on her cheek is deeper than I thought, and a trail of blood oozes down her jawline. The sight leaves me cold. Everyone knows how much Hades values his wife. He's going to go on a rampage for this.

I can't blame him.

When she speaks on the phone, she's all business. "They went down Maple. There are cameras and half a dozen businesses there. Find them, Charon. I want them on their knees before us by end of day. Don't bother sending a team here. We're on our way home." She hangs up and hands my phone back to me.

Behind us, the door flies open and Medusa charges out onto the sidewalk, a gun in each hand. She takes in the scene with a single sweeping glance. "What the fuck?"

Persephone wipes her face, smearing the blood. "Get Calypso and Ariadne. We're leaving."

To her credit, Medusa doesn't question the order. She just leans back into the doorway and starts yelling. I cross to Eurydice and take her shoulders gently. "Are you okay?"

"I think so. Just some bumps and bruises." Her smile is a little fragile. "That was fast thinking on your part. I barely processed what was happening, and you already had me on the ground."

It was panic, pure and simple. The realization, in between heartbeats, that I might lose her. All it would take is a single bullet, and the fragile future we've barely begun to promise to each other would be gone forever. I didn't have time to think. My body took over for me. "I've never tackled anyone before," I say again.

"You did a great job." She wraps her hands around my wrists and gives me a gentle squeeze, even as she guides my hands from her shoulders. "We need to get back to the house. It's fortified, so it's the safest place in the lower city. If we're there, Charon and Hades aren't going to be worried about us. They need to focus on the hunt."

"Words after my own heart." Persephone looks at us, and there's something different in her hazel eyes this time. Something almost like respect. She gives me the tiniest nod. "You did well, Orpheus."

Things happen quickly after that. It only takes a few minutes for Medusa and the others to arrive at the car and shuffle us all into it. Fitting seven people into a five-seat car is ridiculous, but I take one look at Persephone's face and bite down the suggestion of taking two vehicles.

Riding together is the only way to ensure we don't get separated, even if the drive itself isn't comfortable. I hold Eurydice in my lap and try to let her presence comfort me. If feels like the firm ground beneath my feet has turned to quicksand. I don't know what happens next.

All I can think is that I've gone from Eurydice being in danger to Charon being in danger. The people who attacked us are the same people who have been giving him such grief. They're obviously professionals, which means there's a chance he won't come home.

Less than ten minutes later, we sweep through the front doors of the house behind Persephone. I've never seen her like she's acted today, and it's frankly terrifying. This is not a woman I would want to cross.

"Hades?"

It's not her husband who answers her. A handsome man with medium-brown skin hurries down the hall toward us. "Persephone, I have a doctor here. Please come with me."

I take a step toward him, but Persephone plants her feet. "Where is my husband, Thanatos?"

He flinches. "Hades, Charon, and a small team went off in pursuit of the shooters. He gave clear command that you were to stay in the house until he returns. The moment you arrived, we went on lockdown." He says the words carefully, as if feeling his way.

Persephone gets a terrible look on her face. Eurydice opens her mouth, no doubt to try to comfort her sister, but I press my hand to her back and shake my head. Persephone is a bomb waiting to go off, and I don't want Eurydice to take the brunt of the reaction I can feel simmering beneath the surface.

When Persephone speaks, it's in carefully clipped tones. "Have the doctor see to Minthe first. I will be in the study." She walks off without another word, her spine straight and her step steady.

The moment she turns the corner in the hallway, we all wilt a little bit. Thanatos shakes his head and runs his fingers through his thick black hair. "For the longest time, I didn't understand what they saw in each other, but I get it now. She's just as scary as he is when she's riled." He turns to Eurydice, and his smile takes on a new level of warmth. "Hey, there."

"Hey, Thanatos." She smiles too. "Wild day."

"You can say that again." He turns to Minthe, and then he's all business. "How bad is it, really?"

"I keep telling them," she says through gritted teeth, "it's barely more than a scratch. I might need a stitch or two, but that's the worst of it."

Thanatos shakes his head. "Yeah, well, we'll see when the doctor checks you out. Come with me."

Calypso turns to Medusa and Ariadne. "Let's head to the kitchen while we wait. I bet Georgie is cooking up a storm right now. If she won't let us help her out, then maybe she'll let us taste test." It's very clearly an effort to remove the lost expression from Ariadne's face. It's an effective one. They head off in the opposite direction, leaving me and Eurydice alone.

Her smile falls away in an instant. "Those people were clearly professionals. They've managed to avoid Charon for weeks, which is no small feat. He's in danger."

I don't know what to say to comfort her, because I'm not comforted right now at all. "Charon is one of the most capable and dangerous people we know. He'll come home to us."

"If you hadn't reacted so quickly, I might not be coming home to us tonight. Anything can happen." She worries her bottom lip. "Maybe we should—"

"Who's Thanatos?" I ask the question in a rush, determined to get ahead of whatever suggestion she's about to make. Because if she wants us to sneak out and go after him, I'll be helpless to do anything but exactly that. And, damn it, I *know* that's not the right answer.

Instead, I pick a fight, following the thread of jealousy that curled through me at the familiarity between Eurydice and Thanatos. I'm honestly surprised to feel it; I don't mind our duo becoming a trio with Charon. If I felt jealousy there, it's a dual thing—jealousy in that he gets to touch her and she gets to touch him, where before I was only able to watch.

That's not the same sensation I'm getting with Thanatos.

The way Eurydice takes a step back and won't quite meet

my gaze only makes the feeling more pronounced. "Oh, uh, he works for Hades, but I met him for the first time a little while ago at the club."

"The club," I repeat. "You mean Hades's kink club."

"In the lower city, when people refer to the club, they're only speaking of one place." She actually shuffles her feet. "Look, we had a tiny kiss, it doesn't mean anything, and I already got read the riot act by Charon. It was before you came across the river."

I don't ask the other question bubbling up behind my teeth. Ultimately, it's none of my business. I only meant to ask about it to distract her from climbing out a window and going after Charon. Still, it does bring up one question I hadn't even realized I had. "We're a trio, right? Which means we're polyamorous."

"Yes," she says slowly.

I feel silly and I haven't even asked a question yet, but I lick my lips and force the words out. "Does that mean we're open?"

"Do you *want* to be open?"

No. Absolutely not. But I'm afraid to draw that firm a line when things between us still feel so new. "I asked you first." It's a dodge, and not even a good one at that.

Eurydice studies me for several beats. "Ultimately, that's something to discuss with the three of us. We'll figure out our boundaries together, just as soon as Charon comes back to us." She goes back to worrying her bottom lip. "Would you like to see the library? It's almost big enough to get lost in; it's a really nice room. We can wait for him there."

It seems almost childlike, the way we avoid speaking our fears, as if to say them aloud will make them real. I'm not going to be the one to burst that bubble. I nod and hold out my hand. "Show me the library."

CHARON

"YOU SHOULD'VE WAITED BACK AT THE HOUSE." IT'S THE same thing I've said several dozen times in the last fifteen minutes. And just like every other time, Hades ignores me. He taps the screen of the tablet in his hand, his expression intense. Thanks to Orpheus's quick thinking in calling me, we were able to catch the van on cameras and use that network to track them to where they're headed.

To a boat waiting for them in the warehouse district.

We'd suspected they might have come from the upper city. It's the only thing that makes sense. Our network of cameras and intelligence on this side of the river is hardly exhaustive, but it's thorough enough that they shouldn't have been able to evade us for this long.

Unless they weren't staying here at all. It takes a particular ruthlessness for Circe to require her people to cross the river—and the boundary—every time they want to attack us, but it's the only way they had a chance of escaping cleanly each time.

Until now.

"Hades."

"I heard you." He sits back with a sigh. "I am the fucking lord of the lower city, and they came into my territory and fucked with my people, destroyed my property, and shot at my wife and unborn children. They wanted my attention. They have it."

Yeah, that's what I'm afraid of. Hades hasn't lost his shit like this since he discovered my uncle kept the truth about his family—or, more accurately, his father—from him. I thought he'd kill the old man, but in some ways his punishment was even worse. Exile without actually being exiled. He sent Andreas to a retirement home in the country. Every need is catered to, the best care money can buy, but Andreas is miserable.

I don't blame Hades for making that call, just like I don't blame him for making this call today, but when his family is involved, sometimes he behaves irrationally. It makes it hard to protect him.

He won't agree to stay in the car, just like he didn't agree to stay back at the house. I'm sticking to his side like glue. I readjust my grip on my own tablet and lean over. "In that case, let's go over this again. Our people in the area were able to take care of the boat before they could cross back to the upper city. They retreated to this warehouse here, and they know we're coming. Here's how I would like to proceed."

By the time we park one block over from our target, we have a solid plan in place. We have eyes on the streets around the building, but not inside. Since we don't know what we're walking into, we can't just blow the place up. Civilian casualties are not acceptable. Beyond that, explosions mean fire, and the last thing we need to do is set fire to our own damn warehouse district.

No, we go in quiet. We know there's at least five of them, but it's entirely possible there are more. We take out all but two. The survivors, we'll transfer back to the house and lock up for questioning. Minos keeps acting like he doesn't know anything, but these soldiers definitely do. I don't look forward to the possibility of torture, but I've done worse in the name of protecting the lower city.

I check my vest as I come out of the car. Next to me, Hades does the same. We exchange a look, and it's clear he's not going to let me take the lead. This is the same man plagued with guilt from when he shot Eurydice's attacker...except he's not the same at all.

That Hades was sure that his actions, his so-called monstrousness would lose him the one person he cared about more than any other.

But *this* Hades? This Hades has taken full ownership of the lower city in the last year, guarding it possessively and making the hard calls to ensure his people stay safe. *This* Hades has a pregnant wife who he will commit untold acts to protect. He's not going to balk at pulling the trigger this time.

There's a part of me that mourns the man he used to be, but I can't deny that he's a much more effective ruler this way. He's become the boogeyman that they always accused him of being. Ironically, it's not hate that made him this way. It's love.

That, I understand intimately.

I check my gun, ensuring there's a bullet in the chamber. "Let's go."

There are ten on our team, including me and Hades. We split and wait for several precarious minutes while the other team reaches the second exit. I motion at Arai. "Take care of the doors."

They nod and scurry off. They're a lean white person, with close-cropped red hair and a penchant for getting into places they shouldn't. I'm nearly one hundred percent sure they're a cat burglar in their time off, but they are loyal to a fault, so I don't question how they spend their evenings as long as it doesn't bring any heat from the upper city. They're also a genius when it comes to explosives.

The next few minutes are tense and seem to last forever. Arai works best alone, and when they don't want to be seen, they're practically invisible. That doesn't stop the worry worming its way through my stomach until I hear the faint, "Got it. Doors out of commission in three...two...one." Faint pops sound in the afternoon air, almost like fireworks going off.

"Move." Hades doesn't raise his voice, but he doesn't have to. No one would dare disobey him when he speaks in that tone.

We move.

We hurry down this side of the warehouse in single file. Hades pauses so that I can move ahead of him and kick down the door. It's reinforced, but I have a lot of strength behind that kick. I duck out of the way immediately, just as gunfire erupts.

Hades takes a slow breath that I can barely hear, and leans around the edge of the door and jerks back before a hail of gunfire erupts. "Just the one."

"Let me." He looks at me. Just looks, not saying a single word. It's enough for me to lift my hands in surrender. "Fine. Be careful."

He shifts into a crouch and angles his hand around the doorframe. He pulls the trigger once. There's a pained cry and the gunfire stops. Hades peers around the corner again. "There. Let's go."

We rush inside.

Most of our time is spent on security and ensuring the people of the lower city are protected. But Hades is a paranoid motherfucker, so we've practiced drills like this ever since Persephone came to the lower city. First, it was because he worried Zeus might come for her. Then, it was because he had something particularly special to protect.

We move like clockwork. We have already pulled the blueprints, so we know the floor plan. It's a large open space with a rickety-looking staircase leading up to offices. In the warehouse proper, there are half a dozen vehicles and several large pallets of boxes. *Those* weren't in the blueprints.

I catch Hades's gaze and motion at the pallets. We don't know what's inside them, so we can't risk them catching a stray bullet and blowing us the fuck up. He nods and relays the information through my comm. "Don't shoot unless you know you'll hit your target."

We circle the perimeter, and I'm doing my damnedest to see everything all at once. It's too quiet. They left one person at each door, apparently to guard their retreat, but there's nowhere to retreat *to*. They're trapped in the warehouse itself. There are at least three enemies left. Why hide when they must know we'll find them?

Hades must be thinking the same thing. He straightens slowly and looks around. "This doesn't feel right."

"They should be here, fighting for their lives." My attention shifts up to the door at the top of the stairs. "Do you think they're holed up in there?" That doesn't make sense either. In fact, it's sloppy as fuck that they let us track them back here...

Oh, fuck.

"It's a trap," says Hades, echoing my train of thought. "They drew us here on purpose." He speaks so calmly, almost resigned. "And fools that we are, we blocked off the most readily available exit."

I grab his arm and start dragging him toward the door, barking orders. "Everybody out. It's a trap."

We're the first ones to reach the door we entered through...only to find it barricaded. "Fuck!" I kick it and kick it again, but it's no fucking use. "We're trapped." I thought not promising to come home to Eurydice and Orpheus tonight would make the possibility of failing easier. It isn't. I want that future more than I want anything. And I made a vow to keep Hades safe. My carelessness is making a gods-damned mess of this. I made a vow that I'd keep Hades safe. Two promises I'm going to break with my carelessness. "Fuck, fuck, *fuck*."

Hades seems to snap out of the strange mood that took him when he realized that we misjudged the situation so thoroughly. He shakes his head sharply. "The hinges. Now."

My frustration boils over, but it's a relief to have something to *do*. We have to get out of here. I have to get *him* out of here. I pull a knife from each of my boots and hand one over. Then we get to work hammering the hinges with the hilts. Too long. It's taking too fucking long. "No guarantee this will work." I move faster, putting more strength behind each strike.

"Probably won't." One last slam and the top hinges pop off.

I finish on the lower hinges just as two of our people rush up. And that's when I hear it. It's almost like a sharp inhale that pulls every bit of oxygen out of the room. I have the space of two seconds to throw my body over Hades, pinning him to the door, before the explosion roars through the warehouse, and heat sears my back.

It blows the door right through whatever barricade had been set up on the outside. We're airborne for one breathless moment, and then hit the ground with bone-crushing force. My whole world is pain and fire and heat. I command my limbs to move, and for a moment I think I'm okay, but I'm not the one moving my body. It's Hades beneath me, rolling me carefully onto my side. He's bleeding from a cut along his hairline but seems otherwise okay. "Charon! Charon, talk to me."

I tried to speak up. Really, I do. But all that emerges is a pained sound.

Hades looks up and tenses. "Stay down," he says softly. Then he's moving. Gunshots sound, too close. I have to fucking *move*. If something happens to him because I was too fucked up to protect him... No, it doesn't bear thinking about.

I flop back onto my stomach and force myself onto my hands and knees through sheer determination. There's something seriously wrong with my back. It's one long line of agony, and all I really want to do is lie down and close my eyes. Spend a little time in blissed out unconsciousness.

That's not a fucking option.

Miraculously, my gun is still in my holster. I pull it out and thumb the safety off. More gunshots sound as I fight to my feet. I catch sight of Hades hunkered down against the side of a car and stagger over to lean against the cool metal next to him.

He glares at me. "I told you to stay down."

"Need someone...to watch...your back." Even my voice sounds fucked up, too raspy. I don't ask about our people. There are two bodies on the pavement near where we landed. They're not moving, and I hope like fuck that it's because they're unconscious. Not dead.

I catch movement out of the corner of my eye and twist in a move that makes my head spin. But my body knows the motions, even if it hurts. I manage to squeeze off two shots, sending the masked person to the street in a puddle of their own blood. Everything is spinning even though my feet are planted... At least I think they're planted. "We're in trouble."

"Yeah, no shit." Hades surges up and squeezes off another two shots. "There's more of them than we thought."

"They've been ahead of us since the beginning."

In the distance, an engine roars to life. Hades and I exchange a look of dawning horror. I know that engine. Arai had me working on it for the majority of the summer a few years back. It's attached to a monster of a beast, a giant truck that might've started out as something familiar but now has so many things attached to it that it looks more like a tank. "They wouldn't."

My comm crackles in my ear, and then Arai's voice is there. "I assure you, they *would*. I'm coming for you and anyone left alive. I already picked up the team on the other side of the warehouse. They fared better than you. Let's run these fuckers over."

They barely finish speaking when the tank—because really, what else am I supposed to call the damn thing?—hurtles around the corner and skids to a stop between our two fallen team members and the gunmen. Bullets bang into its side as our enemies try to shoot it, but nothing's getting through those reinforced doors.

I take one step toward the tank, and the world tilts sideways. *Shit, this is bad.* It's going to hurt when I make contact with the ground. Except I don't. Hades is there, sliding under my arm and hauling me up. It hurts like a motherfucker, possibly more than if he just let me drop. He practically drags me to the tank and shoves me up in the back seat, following quickly behind. It takes mere seconds for the other team to get the two of us off the ground and into the back.

"Finish them, Arai." There's no forgiveness in Hades's voice. Just judgment.

They grin, but it's a shadow of their normal joyful expression. "Sure thing, boss." They gun the engine and the tank shoots forward far faster than it has any right to. Obviously they've made some upgrades since I helped them get this thing running. There's a faint scream, and the vehicle jostles if we've hit some particularly nasty speed bumps.

"Stop." Hades has his hands on either side of the seat. "We collect them and take them back to the house. If any of them are still alive, I want them to stay that way."

This isn't over yet.

EURYDICE

ALL THE FEARS I'VE BEEN TRYING VERY HARD TO KEEP control of come rushing to the fore when Persephone walks into the library, looking pale and shaky. I surge to my feet and rush to her side. "What's wrong? Is it the babies?"

"They're fine." She pulls me into her arms and hugs me tight. "It didn't go well. They're on their way back now, but Charon and several others need medical attention. I don't know how badly they were hurt."

Terror takes hold and nearly steals my voice. This is my worst fear. Charon, hurt. *Dead.* I knew this would be dangerous today, but a part of me hoped that I was overreacting. I feel strong hands on my shoulders and allow Orpheus to pull me back into his embrace. It's only then, with him supporting me, that I see the look on my sister's face. It's sympathetic, yes, but that's not all it is. I frown. "You're asking me if I can handle it."

"It's okay if you can't. The first couple times, I had issues with it too." She takes a breath and her hand falls to her gently rounded stomach. "But if you can't, then you'll be a distraction, and we can't afford that right now. If you want, you can wait here, and I'll—"

"I can handle it." I squeeze Orpheus's arm and step out of his embrace. There's absolutely no way I'm going to allow them to shuffle me off to the side. I've fought too hard to be taken seriously. But that's not even the driving force right now. I need to see Charon, to know he's going to be okay. My sister looks doubtful, so I repeat, "Persephone. I can handle it."

To her credit, she doesn't question me again. She nods. "Then let's go." She turns and strides out of the room.

I go to follow but stop and turn to Orpheus. He looks just as worried as I feel. I open my mouth, but he gets there before I'm able to speak. "If you're about to offer me an out, I don't want it. I'm worried about him too."

"I know you don't like blood." Gods, I hope Persephone overstated things. The truth is that I don't like blood much either. I learned to deal with it. You can't live on a farm—even a very rich one—without bumping up against the messiness of life, but it never got easier. And this is *people*. My stomach twists in knots.

Orpheus steps around me and offers me his arm. The gentlemanly gesture should look ridiculous, especially considering our current circumstances, but on him it's as natural as breathing. "We're wasting time." He says it gently, as if I can't see the tension in his jaw or the worry in his dark eyes. "Are you ready?"

"No." But I place my hand in the crook of his arm, and we walk out the door together.

Persephone leads us to a part of the house that I've never been in before. Based on my mental map, it's on the opposite side of the garage than I usually enter from. I understand why it's new to me the moment we walk through the doors and find an arsenal. There are gun racks filled with weapons on three of the walls. There's also what appears to be tactical gear and a number of other things I have no names for. That's not where my sister heads though.

Her destination is a door I missed on my first glance. It leads into a hallway studded with more doors. She glances over her shoulder at me. "This is where most of our staff sleeps, or at least the ones who don't want bedrooms on the second floor."

Considering *I'm* the only one I know who sleeps on the second floor, it seems like everyone who works for Hades and Persephone prefers to be housed down here. "I see."

We turn a corner and push through double set of doors into a room identical to one we would find in a hospital. The only difference is that it's quite a bit bigger than I expected, but if I don't miss my guess, they have everything they need here in order to conduct a surgery. The room isn't empty either. There's a trio of people in scrubs at the sinks on the far side of the room, washing their hands. Hades stands a few feet back from them with his arms crossed over his chest and a forbidding expression on his face. It only lightens a little bit when he catches sight of my sister as she hurries to him and throws herself into his arms.

I'm happy my brother-in-law is safe. Really, I am. But he's not what catches and holds my attention. No, that's the five gurneys with bodies on them.

My legs are shaking, but I muscle past that instinctive response as I carefully cross the room to look down at the people. Two of them are burned so badly I'm not even sure who they are. I recognize the other two, but I don't pause until I get to the final one. To Charon.

At the sight of him on his side, my knees really do buckle. Only Orpheus's arm around my waist keeps me off the floor. I suspected it would be bad when Persephone tried to warn me away, but I had no idea. Charon isn't as badly injured as the first two, at least on the front. But his back? The burned skin has my stomach attempting to rebel. "Oh, Charon."

"The burns are nasty, but he'll be fine as long as they don't get infected." This is from the nurse who I hadn't even realized had approached. He's a tall white man with an easygoing smile and a comforting energy. "We gave him something for the pain, which is why he's unconscious right now."

I want to believe him, but I don't think I'll take a full breath until Charon opens his eyes and tells me with his own words that he'll be fine. It's not going to happen right now.

The nurse motions toward the door. "The others, however, need our help immediately. It would be best if you waited in the hallway while we work to save them."

"Of course." Orpheus tightens his hold on my waist and steers us toward the door. "We'll wait outside, but please come get us when he wakes up."

"I will."

Part of me wants to argue that I don't want to leave the room, that I want to ensure Charon doesn't leave my sight. I can't shake the feeling that if he does, I'll never see him again. The only thing that keeps my lips pressed together is the fact that Hades and Persephone have also been exiled to the hallway.

Now, without the distraction of those gurneys, I actually take in my brother-in-law and realize that he looks like shit. He's limping, and half his face is caked in blood. It doesn't slow him down even a little. He leads the way to the next door over, which reveals a comfortably appointed waiting room.

Persephone sinks down onto one of the overstuffed chairs. "What happened?"

In answer, Hades curses longer and harder than I've ever heard him before. "They played us. They set a trap and we walked right into it, and we couldn't even salvage it by taking one of them captive, because they fought to the death."

My sister goes pale. "It was all for nothing?"

"Not for nothing." He shakes his head slowly. "But at this juncture, I have to make a hard call, little siren. One you're not going to like."

Orpheus and I exchange a look, and I feel the same worry I see reflected in his expression. Somehow, I know that the next words out of Hades's mouth will change everything.

My suspicions are confirmed when he takes my sister's hands and says, "I can't allow this to happen again. There's not a damn thing I can do about the upper city right now, but I can protect the lower city."

"What do you mean?"

"I'm closing passage between the upper city and the lower city. After today, no one crosses the River Styx."

Shock makes me forget myself. "Can you *do* that?"

"Yes." He looks at me, and then past me at Orpheus. "It wasn't an option under the last Zeus because he would've starved us out. It also served my purpose to allow his spies over the river. That ends now. No one comes into the lower city that I have not personally welcomed through the barrier."

My sister's mouth works, but no sound comes out. Finally, she clears her throat. "But the barrier is failing."

"The external barrier." He holds up two fingers. "That one is keyed to Poseidon and his descendants. The one around the lower city is keyed to me and mine. Right now, that includes me and you... by virtue of the children you carry."

My sister's still visibly struggling with what he's suggesting. "But my family." She glances at me. "Our family."

"It's not forever, little siren. I wouldn't make this move if we weren't in desperate times. Our enemies crossed the river to attack us—to attack *you*. If I don't do this, there's nothing to stop them from doing it again. I will not allow it. Even if it causes a rift between me and the rest of the Thirteen, it's a small price to pay. They will stand against Circe—or fail—on their own."

"Hades—"

"Until they can come to me as a unified front, I'm done endangering our people for their petty politics." He turns to me. "I need you to deliver Ariadne to one of the bridges as soon as possible. The barrier goes down at sunset. As for you." His gaze flicks to Orpheus. "Both Eurydice and Charon value you, and for the sake of my love for them, I will grant you permission to stay here. But you *will* stay here, Orpheus, until—if—I lower the barrier again. If that's not what you want, then you need to cross the bridge into the upper city before sunset as well."

It's all happening too quickly. I'm afraid to look at Orpheus.

It was one thing for him to decide to stay with us when he still had access to his family, but Hades is taking that away. I know Orpheus loves me, and that he can see himself falling for Charon, but what is that compared to his family that he all but worships?

"I understand." He slips his hand into mine and squeezes. "Let's go get Ariadne."

The second we stop in the hallway, I dig my phone out of my pocket. Persephone made promises to Ariadne, but she's not going to be thinking about those right now. And Hades obviously isn't thinking clearly either, or he wouldn't tell me to just drop her at one of the bridges. She won't be safe. I understand she's not his priority right now, but it still frustrates me.

Easier to focus on that frustration than on the worry about what comes next. I cling to the nurse's assurance the Charon will be okay. He *has* to be okay.

I stare at my phone as we walk down the hallway. Who do I trust enough to hand off Ariadne to? Eris is the one who got me into this in the first place, but she's not Aphrodite any longer, and I don't know the person who currently holds the Aphrodite title very well. Not enough to trust.

I certainly don't trust my mother enough.

Really, in the end, there's only one answer. One person powerful enough to keep Ariadne safe from the rest of the Thirteen. I take a deep breath and I call Callisto. It's almost as if she's waiting to hear from me, because she answers on the first ring. "Hello, Eurydice."

"I need your help." I quickly detail the situation—including the promises Persephone made. The promises *I* made. "Can you do it?"

She laughs in a way that is not at all reassuring. "Of course I can.

Anything for my little sisters. Though, if this proves anything, it's that you're both too soft. That girl is a weapon in the right hands."

True fear sparks through me. I don't know if anyone else has noticed the moves Callisto has been making since she married Zeus and became Hera. *I've* noticed. MuseWatch did a single article on my sister renovating the orphanage the comes with her title, but no one paid much attention to it. Or if they did, they think it's a cute little hobby. They don't see it as her rebuilding the base that the last Zeus spent most of his reign undermining. With him, Hera became an empty title for his doomed spouses and nothing more.

My sister would never be satisfied with an empty title, for her whole identity to be someone's wife. She also doesn't hold much in the way of love for the city itself. The only people she cares about are me, our sisters, and our mother. That's it.

"I want you to promise me that you won't hurt her, and you'll keep our promises to her. I want your word."

Orpheus and I reach the stairs and start up them. It takes two flights before my sister answers me. "Did either of you give her a choice? Or did you just decide what would be best for her?"

"*Callisto.*"

She laughs again, the sound no more comforting this time than it was the last. "Fine, fine. I'll play nice with your little war prize. Bring her to the Cypress Bridge. I'll be waiting on the other side."

ORPHEUS

I CAN BARELY THINK AS I FOLLOW EURYDICE DOWN THE hall toward the kitchen. Hades really means to do it. He means to close the boundary between the upper city and the lower city. I suppose I should be grateful that he's even give me a choice to stay. But the cost is so damn high.

What happens if Olympus falls?

I don't realize I've spoken aloud until Eurydice pauses and looks over her shoulder at me. "If the upper city falls, then I suspect we'll have a civil war on our hands. You heard Hades. He won't raise the barrier until the Thirteen present a united front. He's not bluffing. Considering their history, even with the threat of war on the horizon, it might be years before his terms are met." Her hazel eyes are kind and filled with understanding. "I know. That's so long to be separated from our families. I was just on the other side of the river a few days ago. I'll have Persephone, but..."

It's on the tip of my tongue to tell her we should both go back to the upper city. The words die before I even have to decide whether I'm going to speak them or not. Leave Charon behind? Unacceptable. And even if I was willing to do it, Eurydice isn't.

It turns out I'm not either.

"It's a long time. I won't pretend I'm excited about it, but the alternative is unthinkable. I want to be by your side, Eurydice. I want to be here with you when he comes out of the hospital. I want to be with you...both of you." It's such a relief to say it. To make the decision.

She searches my face for a beat, the knowledge slowly settling for her. "Yeah, you're right. Besides, if things get bad enough, I don't doubt Hades will allow us to bring our families to the lower city and claim sanctuary."

We start walking again, and her words dog my steps. *Sanctuary.* I think there used to be some kind of law about that, a long time ago, but the details slip through my fingers like smoke. More important are the implications. "It would have to be really bad for our families to leave the upper city."

"Yeah." Eurydice stops in front of the door. On the other side, we can hear Ariadne and Calypso speaking. Laughing. Her brows draw together. "It would have to be really, really bad. I want to say it'll never happen, but a lot of things that I thought would never happen turned out not to be as impossible as I assumed." She smiles a little. "Kind of like me and you."

"I guess we are pretty impossible, aren't we?" I find myself smiling in response. "Let's get this errand done and come back to our man."

"Okay. Let's."

Ariadne is remarkably resigned as we explain the situation to her. She doesn't argue; she just follows us down to the garage and climbs into yet another identical sedan. Medusa and Calypso come as well. Even though this first wave of enemies is supposedly dead, there are no guarantees, and Eurydice knows better than to argue with either of them about taking a security detail.

Medusa drives us to the Cypress Bridge and parks against the curb half a block over. "We walk from here."

I am achingly aware of the sun sinking toward the horizon as we approach the bridge on foot. It is as empty as it was the other night when I walked across it. That, more than anything, makes me shiver. Medusa leads the way, her hand on the grip of her gun and her eyes seeming to take in everything at once. Calypso brings up the rear, and while I can't see any weapons on her, the way she moves makes me think she has several hidden away. She might look softer than her girlfriend, but I have no doubt she's equally as dangerous.

We stop at the entrance to the bridge. Eurydice looks like she wants to reach out and take Ariadne's hands, but she manages to resist the urge. There's something empty in the other woman's eyes that worries me. As much as we've gone through in the last week, she's been going through more for longer. I'm not in charge. Even if I was, I don't have a solution that's better than what Hades, Persephone, and Hera have come up with. Whatever it is that the latter has in mind, anyway. I'm just assuming she'll keep her word to her sister.

I sure as fuck hope I'm not wrong.

"I'm sorry." Eurydice seems to make herself meet Ariadne's eyes. "I know my apology isn't worth the air it took me to speak it, but I am sorry. My sister will—"

"With all due respect, I don't believe you. Hera will use me for her purposes. It's fine. I just have to ensure I'm valuable enough for her to want to keep me alive." She turns without another word and walks onto the bridge.

There's no fog in the early evening to obscure our vision. We stand there in silence and watch her cross the bridge to where a lone lean figure awaits her on the other side. They speak for a few seconds, and then Ariadne follows Hera to an SUV and climbs into the back.

"Did we make the right decision?"

Medusa shakes her head. "If you think that was your decision, you're delusional. Hades and your sister made that call. We're just the ones implementing it. It's the life of a soldier, Eurydice. Welcome."

"For fuck's sake, Medusa." Calypso smacks her lightly with the back of her hand. "You know damn well that you reject any order that doesn't align with our values. This one just happened to. We're not mindless worker ants to dance to the tune our leaders have set."

"How do you know?" Eurydice wraps her arms around herself. It's the most natural thing in the world to slip my arm around her shoulders and tuck her against my side. She's shivering, but I don't think it has anything to do with her temperature. "Which orders, I mean. How do you know what the right ones to push back on are?"

Medusa shrugs. "You feel it." She taps her upper chest, right over her heart. "But if you're going to challenge Hades, do it privately, and make sure you have a damn good reason for it. He'll listen. It doesn't mean you'll win the argument, but he'll hear you out. That's more than most people give."

Eurydice seems to chew on this for a little while. Finally, she nods. "Okay. I'll try to remember that." She glances to where Ariadne disappeared. "And you're right; this wasn't an easy decision, but it was the right call."

Gently, I turn her back toward our car. "There's nothing to do for her now. Let's go home to Charon."

My skin chooses that moment to tighten almost painfully. I actually flinch. "What the—"

The answer is readily apparent as I look up into the sky and see a gold shimmering curtain descending. I only visited the boundary that separates Olympus from the rest of the world once, on a field trip back in high school. It had impressed even teenage me, the faint metallic shimmer in the air something beautiful and strange. I spent weeks after that trying to replicate the effect in my artwork, but I never quite pulled it off.

I knew there was a barrier between the upper city and the lower city, but like everyone else in Olympus, I assumed it was a lesser barrier. Less powerful because it was less visual. I was wrong. The curtain of shimmering…whatever it is…descending from the sky to the ground is identical to the barrier around the entire city. Except that's not quite right, is it? Ten years ago, the external barrier was patchy and inconsistent. This one isn't. It's seamless and appears strong enough to bounce off. "Wow."

"It's so beautiful." Eurydice's hand finds mine as we stare up at it together.

"More like terrifying," Calypso murmurs. She shifts closer to Medusa. "No going back after this."

"That's for sure." Eurydice looks worried. "This is going to cause a lot of problems. I'm not exactly sad that I'm not the one who has to deal with them. Let's get going."

We have an entirely uneventful ride back to the house. It's almost anticlimactic. But after the day we've had, I'm not about to complain. Especially when we take the stairs down to the room where we left Charon. He's awake this time.

"Charon!" Eurydice releases me and rushes to his bed. He still looks like shit, and he's propped on his side instead of sitting up, which seems to suggest the burns on his back are just as bad as I feared.

But he's awake. That, in and of itself, is miracle enough.

Eurydice carefully holds one of his hands, but she doesn't hesitate to slip to the side a little bit to make room for me. Charon looks up at me with a question in his eyes. "Heard Hades lowered the full barrier between the upper city and lower city."

"He did. It went down just a little while ago."

"You're still here." Is that relief in his voice? I'm not entirely sure. And then I am, when he keeps speaking. "I'm glad."

I slowly, almost tentatively slip my hand into his free one. Then it's the most natural thing in the world to wrap my arm around Eurydice's waist. A closed triangle. It feels so fucking right, I can barely stand it. "I know I just said last night that I don't love you yet, but I'm sure as fuck falling. Really, really hard."

"Yeah." Charon's eyes drift close. "Me too."

"How bad is it?" Eurydice asks softly.

Charon opens his eyes and gives a faint smile. "Not as bad as it looks. Burns hurt like a bitch, but they should heal up just fine without too much scarring. I'm not the one who got the worst of it."

She strokes his knuckles. "In that case, I suppose Orpheus and I get to play nursemaid." Her smile goes impish, though her eyes remain worried. "He'd look stunning in a sexy nurse outfit, don't you think?"

Charon rasps out a chuckle. "Don't make me laugh, baby. It hurts." He smiles at me. "But she's right. We should look into about getting you one of those costumes. Make sure there are thigh highs involved."

I stroke my hand down Eurydice's back. "I can't decide if you're joking or not."

"You should know better. I never joke about sexy nurses." His lips quirk. I can tell he's in a lot of pain and trying to put on a brave face. Charon exhales slowly. "Things are going to get uncomfortable for a while. Maybe it's selfish to be grateful that you're both here on this side of the river, but fuck it, I'll be selfish. I'm glad you're here with me."

"Of course we are. There's no place we'd rather be." Eurydice lifts his hand to her lips to press a kiss to his knuckles, and then she guides his hand to my face so I can do the same. "I love you, and Orpheus is falling for you. You're stuck with us, Charon."

"By stuck with you, you mean I'm the luckiest son of a bitch in Olympus." His eyes start to drift closed. "Will you stay with me for a while?"

Eurydice and I exchange a look. I smile. "Yeah, Charon. But not just a little while—we'll stay with you forever."

ARIADNE

TEN WEEKS AGO

MY FATHER GAVE ME STRICT INSTRUCTIONS TO STAY IN
the house on this afternoon of blood and death. It's the smart thing
to do. No matter what else is true, I want to live. I've shared what
information I could in the only way I knew how, and it's up to
Apollo and Cassandra to figure out the rest. Strange how knowing
that doesn't make me feel better.

But then I've always been a coward.

Tension seems to bleed into the hot and sticky afternoon air,
pressing against my skin as I slip through the back door and out onto
the grounds. If I was braver, I would try to warn my father's guests
of what's coming. I would put myself between them and danger.

Instead, I head for the maze. It's a monstrous creation, predat-
ing my father's ownership of this house. The previous owner was
incredibly eccentric—or *is*, I suppose, since Hermes is here at the
party right now. This house and its grounds feel like something out

of a novel, a fantasy world where turning down the wrong corner can land you in a portal to another realm. I'm far too old to believe in that kind of nonsense, but that doesn't stop me from entering the maze and winding my way through the tall walls of green.

Since my father brought us to the countryside in the outskirts of Olympus, I find myself coming to the maze more and more often. Today, I don't even have to count the turns. My feet know the path by heart. Within minutes, I enter the center.

No one else in my family bothers to come here. My father didn't even notice that I've absconded with several of the lawn chairs and gone so far as to plant flowers. I doubt I'll be around next year to see them bloom, but gardening calms me all the same. This space is as close to privacy as someone like me can manage. Well, except for...

I hear him well before he finds me. He makes no effort to hide the weight of his footsteps. Even though there's a part of me that awakens in his presence, I can't help the shiver of dread. Everything's changed. It was always going to, but knowing that doesn't bring me any peace. My father has had a decade to put the foundations in place for this plan. To train two unstoppable killers to do his dirty work.

One of them is hunting me right now, tracing my path through the maze as if he can see evidence of it. The truth is far less magical. Asterion comes to the maze nearly as often as I do so that even in this refuge, I can't escape him.

Not that I try very hard.

Today of all days, I don't want to see him. Not when he's finally fulfilled the violent purpose my father intended. Taking the life of one of the Thirteen so that he can claim the title for himself.

Somewhere on the grounds, Theseus is doing the same. All in service to the destabilization of Olympus. With two of my father's household sitting among the most powerful positions in the city, the real reign of terror can begin.

I can't make myself look up as *his* shadow falls over me, blocking out the sun. The Minotaur. The man so fearsome that my father doesn't refer to him by name. No one does. According to most people, he's more monster than man.

He's always been Asterion to me. At least until today.

I might be a coward, but I can't sit here and ignore the truth indefinitely. I drag in a breath that feels hot and sticky on my tongue and look at him. I understand why everyone fears him. With his massive body, his scars, and the blank look in his dark eyes, he *is* terrifying. He's also beautiful in his own way: long, dark red hair and medium-brown skin, strong hands that are just as capable of building things as they are holding a weapon, and his mouth... sensual and decadent.

His eyes aren't blank right now. They're so hot I'm surprised I don't burn up on the spot. I may have been studying his form the way I always do when it's just us, but he's doing exactly the same thing, drinking me in as if he might never get another chance. There's a level of desperation to the chemistry that snaps between us. It can never be. He's my father's perfect weapon, and I'm the perfect daughter destined to be married for the family's political gain. In no world would my father give my hand to a murderous orphan, part of his household or not.

I lick my lips without meaning to. "Is it done?"

"Ariadne." His voice is just as scarred as his body, rough and jagged. He takes one slow, stalking step toward me and then another, eating up the distance between us with long strides until he can lean down and plant his hands on the arms of the chair on either side of me. I'm not a small woman; what my body lacks in height, it makes up in plentiful curves. I'll never be the delicate little doll my father wishes for, but I've never felt lacking in Asterion's eyes.

He's so close. I can see the sweat dampening his skin and making his dark shirt press more firmly against his carved torso. *Gods help me.* I inhale deeply, chasing the scent that is him and him alone.

"Answer my question," I whisper.

"I let her get away." He releases the chair with one hand to clasp it loosely around my throat. "For you. I will weather your father's rage. For you."

I can't catch my breath and it has nothing to do with him restricting my airflow. He's not. But in all the years we've known each other, he's been incredibly careful to never touch me. Not like this. Not with intent and...possession. "You can't talk like that."

"Can't I?" He leans closer yet, until he blocks out the very sky. Until his cheek brushes mine as he speaks directly into my ear. "Now we've both betrayed him."

He knows.

But that's impossible. There's no way he could know that I left information for Apollo to find. Now is the time to push him away, to demand he remember his place. To retreat to a safe distance with the truth that I will never be his.

I don't move. I don't speak. I can barely seem to breathe at all.

"Tell me no, Ariadne."

"What?"

"Tell. Me. No." I don't realize he's released the chair until he grips the front of my dress with his other hand. His rough knuckles press against the delicate skin of my breasts, sending a jolt of pure need through me.

Understanding dawns, bringing with it conflicting emotions of fear and desire. "We can't." My father may look the other way when it comes to how Asterion watches me, to the strange almost-friendship that has cropped up between us over the years, to the way we seem to gravitate to each other again and again. But he won't forgive this trespass. If we cross *this* line, he will slit Asterion's throat. I'm afraid to think of what he might do to punish me. "We *can't*," I repeat.

"Tell me no." The rumble of his voice makes me press my thighs together. "Or I'm going to rip this dress off you."

Now's the time to do exactly that. If I speak now, he'll stop. Asterion may be a monster in so many ways, but not with me. Not like this.

I don't tell him no.

He pauses for one beat, and then another. I expect him to rip my dress down the center, to send the line of vintage buttons flying. Instead, he thumbs open the top one. And then the next. And then the next. Exposing me, inch by agonizing inch. All without moving away or putting any distance between us. It's just as well; if either of us had a chance to think this through, surely common sense would reassert itself. We would remember who we owe everything to. Me by blood, him by circumstance.

By the time he bares me to the waist, I'm shaking so hard that I rattle the metal chair against the gravel. Asterion drags his knuckles up the center of my body to catch my chin. He still has a hold of my throat, and he's still not doing more with his grip than claiming me. Now, finally, he moves back so that he can capture my gaze. "You've been mine from the moment I saw you."

My stomach flips and I want to hate what he's saying, to reject yet another man choosing to own me. I've never belonged to myself, not from the moment I was born. I never had a chance. No matter what else is true, being claimed by Asterion will change everything. "You're wrong."

He drags his thumb roughly over my bottom lip. "I'm not." He reaches down without breaking my gaze and shoves up the bottom half my dress, baring me from the waist down. "But if I am, then tell me no, Ariadne." He slips his fingers beneath the band of my panties and wraps his fist around the fabric. "Because if you don't tell me no right now, I'm going to take what we both know is mine."

No one has ever touched me like this. Other people my age who are interested in sex have done plenty of exploring, whether it's out in the open or in secret. My brother certainly has, leaving a trail of broken hearts in his wake. Not me. Not Minos's precious, innocent daughter. According to him and people like him, my value hangs on the hymenal thread. I think it's bullshit, but when it comes to my life, I'm not the one who holds the power.

Except…it feels like I'm holding the power right now.

I may be shaking and overwhelmed, but there's a fine tremor in Asterion's hand where his knuckles press to my pussy. All it will take is one word, two little letters, and this all stops. *What is power if not that?*

I reach up with a tentative hand and fist the front of his shirt.

Agreeing to this will damn us both, but I'm not sure I care. We were damned from the moment my father decided to bring us to this place. Any deaths that happened today are only the beginning. That blood is on my hands by proxy. "You didn't kill anyone today?"

"I didn't."

Maybe I'm a fool for believing he did it for me. So be it. I drag in a breath. "Do it. Don't stop."

He doesn't ask me again. He rips my panties from my body with a violence that makes me jerk. And then his mouth is on mine, his fingers tightening around my throat ever so slightly as he marks me with his tongue and teeth.

I may have been a passive passenger for most of my life, but I'm choosing this. I'm choosing *him*, even if it's only right here, right now. It can't be forever. But I don't say that as he breaks our kiss long enough to pull off his shirt and shove down his pants. His cock is big enough to make a thread of fear dampen my desire, but Asterion drops to his knees and buries his face in my pussy before I can decide if I really *do* want to say no.

The first drag of his tongue through my folds makes my brain short out. I've read about this. I've bought toys that are supposed to mimic this. What a joke. There's nothing like the feeling of his tongue on the most intimate part of me. His fingers dig into my hips, pulling me several inches off the edge of the chair so that I can spread my legs wider for him. I don't make a conscious decision to shove my hands into his hair, to lift my hips and seek more, but my body has overridden my brain. His broad shoulders make a perfect perch for my thighs and he licks me as if he'll never get enough.

What we're doing is strictly forbidden, and we're not even

having the decency to do it under the cover of night. The sun bears witness to my orgasm cresting, to Asterion pressing his palm to my lips to stifle my cries as I come all over his face. He gives me one long lick, and then another. There's a pause as if he might keep going, might not stop until I'm coming yet again. As if he might *never* stop.

But then he turns his face to my thigh and bites me. Hard. I shriek against his palm, the pain getting mixed up in pleasure. It confuses me. That feeling only gets more complex when I look down to see blood. He bit me hard enough to break the skin.

He rises and wraps a giant fist around his cock. "After this, you might have been tempted to forget. Now you won't."

He angles his cock to my entrance and looks at me, tracking the tears that leak from the corner of my eyes. Asterion shifts his hand away from my mouth long enough to say, "Tell me no. Tell me no right fucking now or I'm going to take this virgin pussy and claim it as mine. Forever."

"That's not how virginity works." I don't know why I say it. My thigh is one throbbing massive pain and no matter if I'm already feeling empty and achy for more pleasure, I can't pretend my orgasm has washed away all the reasons we shouldn't do this. His bite made sure of that.

"It is with us."

Some instinct overtakes me and I dart forward to set my teeth into the space between his thumb and forefinger. He watches me as I bite down. Not hard. Testing him. Daring him to continue. Instead of pulling away, he presses his hand more firmly into my mouth, against my teeth. At the same time, his cock breaches my entrance.

He doesn't go fast, but there's no time to adjust to the sheer size of him. It hurts. Oh fuck, it hurts.

"You can take it." He slips one arm behind my hips and pulls me closer, allowing himself deeper. "Leave a mark, baby."

I bite down in sheer desperation. The coppery taste of his blood hits my tongue just as his cock sinks fully inside me. Pain and pleasure dance together, confusing my senses. It's only as pleasure takes the lead that I realize he's not moving. That he hasn't moved from the moment he sealed us together.

My tension turns into pure need. I shift restlessly against him. Only then does he begin to move. Long, harsh thrusts that hit something inside me that makes everything go hazy. I've orgasmed before plenty on my own. I've used toys and techniques and explored my body to find out what works for me.

Nothing has ever felt like this.

This time, when my orgasm rises, it feels world-ending. There's no taking this back. I don't want to. I couldn't stop for anything. I bite harder on his hand even as I grab his hips and pull him deeper into me. He growls, the fierce rumble vibrating through his body and into mine. That's what makes me come. My orgasm goes on and on, driven to new heights I didn't think were possible. And then he grinds into me, starting the whole process all over again. It's only as he stills that I realize he's following me over the edge.

He tugs his hand out of my teeth and replaces it with his mouth. Our kiss tastes of blood and sex and a promise that I'm not certain I can follow through with. Yet in this moment nothing matters. Nothing but us.

He thrusts into me one last time and then withdraws. We both look down to where his seed leaks out of my pussy. Distantly, part of me is screaming that I'm going to regret this. We didn't use a condom. It didn't even occur to me to ask for one. All of that feels very distant right now.

Asterion grips my thigh over his bite and squeezes hard. "You're mine, Ariadne. *This* is a promise. When you start questioning that, look here. Remember." He takes the time to button up my dress as I stare at him. Then he pulls on his clothes in quick, efficient moves. One last claiming kiss and he's gone, striding out of the maze the way he came in.

He...took my panties with him. And I'm left there, absolutely wrecked and reeling. My world has shifted on its axis and I don't know how to right it.

What the fuck have I done?

ACKNOWLEDGMENTS

I will never stop appreciating the support y'all have shown this series. We were never supposed to get this far, and yet Dark Olympus has made waves that will continue long past the last book. I am continually humbled and amazed at how you show up, book after book, to see just how wild these stories will get. THANK YOU!

Speaking of support, my endless gratitude for my editor, Mary Altman, for championing this series, and for always being willing to let me swing hard with these books and characters. I wouldn't be nearly as fearless with anyone else as an editor in this wild ride!

Thank you to Pam Jaffree and Katie Stutz for being the best publicists an author could ask for! I know I'm chaos personified sometimes, and you do a hell of a job of wrangling me, listening when I need you to, and going to bat for me!

Big appreciation to the production team at Sourcebooks! Dawn Adams, Aimee Alker, Laura Boren, Antoaneta Georgieva, Rachel Gilmer, India Hunter, Cameron Kirk, and Deve McLemore. Your continued support of this series from beginning of the process to the end and beyond is everything!

Endless thanks to Jenny Nordbak for encouraging my increasingly unhinged texts while I was drafting this. You didn't immediately block me when I said, "Jenny, am I writing puppy play? I think I'm writing puppy play." I enjoy sharing an id list with you!

Big thanks to Nisha Sharma, and Asa Maria Bradley for always being there when I'm having bad days, good days, and the ones in between!

As always, all my love and appreciation to Tim. I wouldn't dare go half as hard without you cheering right there at my side. It's so easy to be fearless with you as my partner. I love you for always!

ABOUT THE AUTHOR

Katee Robert (she/they) is a *New York Times* and *USA Today* bestselling author of spicy romance. *Entertainment Weekly* calls their writing "unspeakably hot." Their books have sold over two million copies. They live in the Pacific Northwest with their husband, children, a cat who thinks he's a dog, and two Great Danes who think they're lap dogs. You can visit them at:

Website: kateerobert.com
Facebook: AuthorKateeRobert
Instagram: @katee_robert
Twitter: @katee_robert
TikTok: @authorkateerobert